CASSIE
OF T

Winner o
Achievement

"Cassie Edwards writes action-packed, sexy reads!
Romance fans will be more than satisfied!"
—*Romantic Times BOOKreviews*

A CHIEF'S GREAT SECRET

"I feel such a connection with you and your people
and we have only recently become aware of each other's
existence," Lavinia murmured. "That first time, when
I saw you in the tree, I was not afraid, but instantly
drawn to you."

"You have also seen the white panther," he said,
searching her eyes for her reaction. He could see that
she was surprised he would speak of it, confirming the
existence of the mystical creature.

"The white panther is something that everyone has
learned to avoid," he went on, now wanting to change
the subject.

This was not the time to share the magic that he held
within his heart. It was something that might frighten
her away from him.

And he could not chance that.

He needed and wanted her too much!

CASSIE EDWARDS

SAVAGE FLAMES

LEISURE BOOKS   NEW YORK CITY

A LEISURE BOOK®

March 2008

Published by

Dorchester Publishing Co., Inc.
200 Madison Avenue
New York, NY 10016

ISBN 10: 0-8439-5877-4
ISBN 13: 978-0-8439-5877-5

Printed in the United States of America.

10 9 8 7 6 5 4 3 2 1

Visit us on the web at www.dorchesterpub.com.

I recently received the very sad news of the passing of Beverly Stevenson, a special person, friend, and very proud bookstore owner.

It was at Bev's bookstore at the Village Square Mall in Effingham, Illinois, that I did one of my very first autographings as a new author. Bev made me feel welcomed and relaxed on a day that became very special to me as I autographed books for so many of my readers who were as new to reading my first books as I was to writing them.

It is with much thanks, warmth, and love, that I dedicate my book Savage Flames in Bev's memory.

Always,
Cassie Edwards

Animal spirit
What are you to me?
Are you that powerful being within me?
Are you there where even my eyes cannot see?
Show yourself to me, I plead,
Come to me when you know that I am in need.
Are your eyes so like mine
That I have seen you in my lifetime?
Animal spirit,
To you I am bound,
As the sky to the ground.
I call to you, yet I hear not a sound.
Is it me that you surround?
Animal spirit,
Forever, together, are we truly bound?
Animal spirit,
What part of me have you truly found?

—Mordestia M. York,
Poet and friend

SAVAGE FLAMES

Chapter One

Let men tremble to win the hand of woman,
Unless they win along with it the utmost
Passion of her heart.
                    —*Nathaniel Hawthorne*

Florida . . . 1851

The magnolia trees were abloom.

White herons and pelicans shadowed the bright blue sky as they soared from one tree to another.

Spanish moss, resembling fancy lace, festooned the cypress forest and nearby swamp, cloaking the trees.

Lavinia Price stood outside her huge, pillared white mansion in her flower garden. She was delicately formed, with golden hair and violet eyes, her white skin slightly freckled from the sun.

Although her flower garden was already vast and colorful, Lavinia was on her knees, planting new seeds, which would one day grow into more beautiful flowers.

Tired, her face flushed from the late-morning heat, she rose slowly to her feet.

She removed her straw hat and fanned her face with it. She groaned when she looked down and saw the dirt smudges on the skirt of her dress. The morning had been so beautiful, without a cloud in the sky, and she had been so anxious to get outside to work in her garden, she hadn't changed from her pretty dress into one of those she usually wore to garden.

Now dirt was smeared across the front of the full-skirted pink dress with the delicate white flowers embroidered on it.

She swatted at the worst smudges with her hand but only succeeded in spraying dust up into her nose, making her sneeze fitfully.

When the sneezing finally subsided, she caught sight of her eight-year-old daughter, Dorey, who was romping and playing with her best friend Twila, an eight-year-old African girl, the daughter of slaves at the Price Plantation.

Twenty-four years of age, Lavinia had been blessed with only one child, her sweet Dorey, but she still hoped for more children. Her daughter gave her so much joy and peace.

Lavinia smiled when Dorey squealed happily as she ran across the green yard. She and Twila were playing tag.

Lavinia always enjoyed seeing the girls together. She hated slavery with a passion and regretted that her husband kept slaves on the plantation he had recently purchased with his brother Hiram. Virgil was willing to free their slaves, but Hiram refused to allow it, saying they would never find anyone to work their tobacco fields.

Lavinia sighed heavily as she thought about how her husband and Hiram, his older brother by one year, didn't approve of Dorey's association with Twila and the other slave children.

But when both men were away, Lavinia gave her daughter permission to play with whomever she pleased. Lavinia had even bought the same dolls for Dorey and Twila last Christmas.

It had warmed her heart to see them playing with their toys together when her husband and his brother were away on business, as they were today.

She turned and looked at the Bone River, which ran alongside the vast plantation. Sunlight poured over the green and brown expanse of saw grass and water, shining and slow-moving.

Not far downriver the Everglades began. There, huge swamps were connected by a maze of narrow waterways, and the few small islands of dark trees were inhabited by poisonous snakes.

It was certain that when Lavinia went canoeing, eager to explore her new home, she avoided those more dangerous places deep in the swamp.

Instead, she went downriver only a short distance, enjoying the exotic sight of blossoming flowers, as well as forests with an endless variety of green foliage and cool shadows, where the trees were hung beautifully with Spanish moss.

Lavinia had taught Dorey to be alert to danger when in the swamps, and she now trusted her daughter to know which places to avoid. Recently she had begun allowing Dorey to make short trips in the canoe by herself.

But Lavinia would feel much better if her daughter didn't have such a love of adventure and exploring.

She was afraid that one day she might regret having given her daughter such freedom.

But Lavinia had always been the adventurous sort herself, and had vowed long ago that she would not stifle that part of her daughter's character. Lavinia believed she would not have grown up to be as strong an individual as she was had her parents not allowed her such freedom.

Having rested enough, Lavinia started to put her hat back on, but as she turned, she was startled by something in a massive live oak tree that stood near the house with lovely Spanish moss hanging from its limbs.

She paled and clutched her throat, dropping her hat as she found herself gazing directly into the green eyes of a snow-white panther. It was resting on a thick limb, halfway up the tree.

It didn't seem at all threatened by her presence nearby. On the contrary, it continued to sit there calmly, its beautiful white coat contrasting dramatically with the dark green leaves of the tree.

Lavinia had heard about a lone white panther that stalked the Everglades, but never had she seen the creature.

Then she blinked her eyes and saw something equally startling in that same tree, on that exact spot where she had seen the panther only seconds ago.

Was it true?

Was it real?

Was she now seeing a magnificently handsome Indian resting there instead of the panther, his green eyes gazing back at Lavinia with the same interest as she felt seeing him?

He had long, flowing black hair, and his muscles bulged under his deerskin breeches and a tunic which looked as though it were made from Spanish moss.

His face was strong, with a dignified aquiline nose, and if he were standing on the ground, she knew he would be tall.

Her wonder at what she had just experienced was cast aside when she heard Hiram, her brother-in-law, frantically shouting her name.

She turned quickly and everything within her went cold when she saw Hiram running toward her. Her husband Virgil lay limp in his brother's arms, with an arrow protruding from his chest.

When Hiram shouted that Virgil was dead, it was too much for Lavinia. Her knees buckled and she fell to the ground in a dead faint.

As small, round-faced Twila stood quietly by, Dorey ran to her father and stopped, staring at his lifeless form.

Tears quickly flooding her eyes, she looked up at her Uncle Hiram. "Is . . . Papa . . . truly . . . dead?" she asked weakly.

"Yes, Dorey, he's dead," Hiram said thickly. "An Indian did it. I didn't actually see the attack, but the arrow in your daddy's chest is proof enough."

Sobbing frantically, Dorey looked away from both her papa and Uncle Hiram.

Twila ran to Dorey and put her tiny arms around her in a comforting hug, although she knew that such personal contact was forbidden by Massa Hiram.

Still holding Dorey in her tiny arms, Twila dared to look up directly at Hiram.

She had always been afraid of the one-eyed man with his flaming red hair and mean temper. "What 'bout my own pappy?" she gulped out. But she always smiled inwardly every time she recalled how he had lost his eye. She had seen it happen one day while he was whipping another slave. Hiram had momentarily lost control of the whip, and the end of the lash had coiled clumsily around and slapped him in the left eye, instantly blinding it.

"How dare you speak to me!" Hiram spat out. "Don't you know your place yet?"

Then he shrugged. "Yep, your pappy died, too," he said, enjoying seeing the misery his words brought to the child's eyes.

"But . . . where is my pappy?" she managed to ask between heart-wrenching sobs. "I don't see him nowhere."

"And you never will," Hiram said. He smiled wickedly. "The river took his body away, deep into the Everglades. More'n likely he's already been eaten by an alligator."

Twila gasped.

Her eyes widened with fear.

Then she turned and ran toward her mother, who was working in the fields.

Chapter Two

We may affirm absolutely that nothing
Great in the world has been accomplished
Without passion.

—*Georg Hegel*

As the sun spiraled down through the leaves of the beautiful cypress trees that stood on both sides of the narrow channel of Bone River, Chief Wolf Dancer made his way through the water in his canoe.

He was on his way back to the home he had established amid the swamps, in a place he had named Mystic Island.

The muscles of his arms flexed with each pull of the paddle through the hazy green water, his mind on the vision he had just seen.

The beautiful white woman with golden hair.

He would still be gazing upon her except for the interruption of a white man carrying another white man in his arms. He had seen an arrow lodged in one man's chest, yet knew that none of his warriors were responsible.

He had taught his people not to do anything that would annoy whites and bring the white man's soldiers to the Everglade waters.

His Seminole people had learned long ago to

beware of white men, especially those who carried white flags with them, which the whites called "flags of truce."

All Seminole now knew to call them "flags of deceit," for most of the Seminole people had been forced off their homeland and sent to what were known as "reservations," where his people's pride was stolen from them, as well as their freedom.

His Wind Clan of Seminole had successfully eluded capture and the reservation.

Some white soldiers had tried to reach his island, but none had ever succeeded. As long as he was chief, they would not come and interfere in his people's lives.

He would think no further about the downed white man, or who he might be.

That was only one more white man who could never do his clan an injustice like so many whites had done to other clans.

He was proud that he had established his clan in a remote, inaccessible portion of the Everglades, where there were fields of corn and other foods that his people had planted for their cook pots. The land of the Everglades also provided much game, as well as food taken from the water that surrounded their island.

Turtle meat was one of the best-loved foods, as well as alligator meat; the tails of the smaller, younger alligators were the most valued and tender.

He smiled as he remembered the many times he had wrestled a large alligator to get to the smaller ones. After killing the big one, he would proudly take home its skin, which was used for making clothes and household products, while the meat from the smaller one would go to the cook pots.

No, neither he nor his clan would ever give up their home or their freedom to whites.

It made him angry all over again when he recalled how some of the Seminole had been enticed to give up their homeland for eight hundred dollars to each warrior and four hundred to each woman and child.

He was proud to say that his forefathers had not been among those who were tricked by the Spaniards, or by the Americans.

The only white person he would like to know was the woman with the long and flowing golden hair and eyes the color of violets.

Only recently had he dared to travel this close to the tall white house that was called a mansion. On three sides of it were fields of tobacco, and on the fourth, the river that he was now traveling on to return to his home and his duties as chief.

Although he had vowed to himself only moments ago not to think about the murdered white man, he could not help wondering what he was to the golden-haired woman. For when she had discovered that he was dead, she had collapsed into a faint.

Could that man have been her husband?

Wolf Dancer had seen her loving manner toward the white child and wondered if this child was her daughter.

He chided himself for his curiosity about the golden-haired woman, yet she had captured his heart in the brief moments he'd observed her. He could not erase her from his mind any more than he could deny his own identity as a Seminole!

But he knew that she was forbidden to him; to care for a white woman might bring trouble into his people's lives, and he had protected them from the moment he had become chief upon the death of his father seven moons ago.

Suddenly his thoughts were interrupted by the sight of something unexpected a short distance away in the river.

It was a canoe floating aimlessly about, and from his vantage point, he could only conclude that it was empty, for he saw no one in it.

He was curious as to whom the canoe might belong to; it had been made in the same way his people made their canoes, from a hollowed cypress tree; such boats were called pirogues by his people.

He went onward, then stopped when he had his own pirogue alongside the other one. As he looked down, he saw how wrong he had been to think no one occupied the canoe.

A black man lay there on his back, unconscious, an arrow in his upper right shoulder, with blood dripping onto the floor of the pirogue.

Wolf Dancer knew about the slaves that worked the fields for whites and could only assume that this man was an escaped slave.

Yet who had shot him?

He studied the design of the arrow. It was of his own Seminole people's design.

But as he had concluded when he'd seen that

other arrow lodged in the white man's chest, none of his people were responsible.

No one in his clan was foolish enough to do anything to bring harm to the women and children of their village.

So who could be responsible?

Who was trying to cast blame on his people?

This was not the time to reason the mystery out in his mind.

The black man had suffered the loss of much blood.

He might even be near death.

Determined to do what he could to save the wounded man, Wolf Dancer climbed from his canoe into the other, gently lifted the man into his arms, and transferred him to his own pirogue.

Allowing the other pirogue to float away, Wolf Dancer arranged the man on bottom of his canoe. As carefully as he could, he broke off the portion of the arrow that protruded from the man's shoulder.

He had no choice but to leave the other half embedded in the man's flesh until he could get him back to Mystic Island, where his people's shaman could then take over.

Suddenly the black man's eyes slowly opened and looked directly into Wolf Dancer's. He grabbed Wolf Dancer by the arm, his hand trembling.

"Mah name's Joshua," he managed to say between gasping breaths. "You should know . . . no Indian did this to me. It . . . it . . . was done by one of my massas. It . . . was . . . supposed to look like an Indian kill, when and if my body wuz . . . wuz . . . ever found."

"You do not need to explain," Wolf Dancer said gently. "You must save your energy. I will take you to my shaman. He will do what he can for you."

Joshua's hand tightened on Wolf Dancer's arm. "Hiram . . . Price . . . is de one," he said, his voice now almost a whisper, yet strong enough for Wolf Dancer to hear. "He's de man that done left me fo' dead in the river. I . . . was . . . lucky that I found a canoe. That canoe saved me from the clutches of death. Thank de Lord that you came along . . . and . . . cared enough to try and save me."

Since he saw that Joshua was determined to continue talking, Wolf Dancer saw no wrong in questioning him.

"Why did the man you know as Hiram Price do this to you?" he asked. He watched the man's eyes drift closed, and then suddenly open again.

" 'Cause I witnessed my one massa kill de otha," Joshua said. He swallowed hard. "Dey were brothas. One brotha killed the other brotha."

"Why would a brother hate his brother enough to kill him?" Wolf Dancer asked, feeling the man's hand weakening in his grip.

" 'Cause de massa who killed de other wants not only all the Price Plantation, but also de woman . . . his brotha's wife," Joshua said, his voice now a shallow whisper. "Dat's why. Hiram is a sinner in many ways. De Bible says to covet another man's wife is very . . . very . . . sinful, but when Hiram killed fo' her, he took one more step into hell today."

Hearing the name of the plantation made Wolf Dancer know exactly which woman Joshua was making reference to.

He knew the name of the plantation where he had been watching the golden-haired beauty.

His scout had discovered the name of the place not long ago and had brought it to his chief's attention.

He had been curious to observe the plantation today because it had only recently changed hands. He had wanted to see the new owners, to judge whether or not they were just people, and whether they represented a threat to his small band. Until today, he had not known enough about the new owners to make a judgment. But now that he knew one owner had used an arrow to kill his brother, Wolf Dancer realized that he was going to be dealing with people who would be working against the Seminole.

But the woman!

He envisioned even now the woman that Joshua was talking about . . . her long, golden hair, her violet eyes, her tininess, and her innocence.

"Sweet Lavinia no longer has a husband," Joshua said, his eyes closing. "He was killed by his very own brotha."

This news confirmed to Wolf Dancer that the woman was now alone. She no longer had a husband to protect her. And she was living in the same house as the man who had killed her husband.

Wolf Dancer was determined to find a way to know her and to protect her.

Yes, she must be saved from such a man as would kill his very own brother to have her!

"My name is Chief Wolf Dancer," he said quickly, for Joshua looked as though he was ready to drift off again. "You are with a friend."

Joshua's eyes remained open long enough to meet the dark gaze of Wolf Dancer. Joshua knew now that he was in the company of the most elusive Seminole chief of all.

He also sensed that Wolf Dancer was a man of peace . . . a good and honorable man of integrity. He spoke gently and his words tugged at Joshua's heart and inspired his spirit. He had heard that Wolf Dancer was very smart and could match wits with any white man.

Joshua believed that Wolf Dancer would find a way to make wrongs right for Lavinia, as well as for Joshua's own family . . . his wife Lorna . . . his daughter Twila.

Joshua could not help believing that he would have been dead if this kind Indian had not come upon him floating in the river in the canoe, and was doing what he could to save his life.

Also he would not believe that the good Lord would allow him to die, not when he had a wife and daughter to look after.

Yes, Joshua did believe the good Lord above would keep him alive so that he could be with his wife and child again.

They needed him.

He . . . needed . . . them.

Just the thought of his Twila and Lorna brought him a feeling of gentle peace. He carried them with him always, in his heart.

When Wolf Dancer saw a look of peace come into Joshua's eyes just before he closed them and drifted off into an unconscious state, the chief felt that that peaceful feeling alone might help save the wounded man.

But Wolf Dancer also knew that precious time had elapsed in talk and discoveries, and that the delay might have dangerously weakened Joshua.

He lifted the paddle and worked his way toward Mystic Island.

And there was someone else to consider. Wolf Dancer's mind wandered again to the woman who intrigued him so much.

He must . . . he would . . . help her!

Lavinia.

Yes, the name of the white woman was Lavinia.

The name was as lovely as the woman to whom it belonged!

Chapter Three

Love bade me welcome;
Yet my soul drew back,
Guilty of dust and sin.

—*George Herbert*

A cool breeze fluttered the sheer curtains at Lavinia's bedroom windows.

The sweet smell of magnolia flowers wafted into the room along with the breeze.

All the shutters had been thrown open in order to help cool the bedroom.

Lavinia's four-poster canopy bed was positioned between two windows so that there would be a cross breeze blowing over her for her comfort.

A wide stone fireplace took up the center of the far wall opposite the bed. On another wall stood a chest of drawers with a round, gilt-framed mirror above it. A blanket chest sat at the foot of the bed. A handsome braided rug covered most of the polished oak floor.

An attentive, worried Dorey sat on a rocking chair beside her mother's bed, her eyes filled with tears as she watched and waited for her mother to wake up.

Hiram had carried her mother up to her bedroom after she'd awakened from her faint.

The realization that an Indian had killed Virgil with an arrow, and the hideous sight of that arrow still protruding from her husband's chest, had been too much for Lavinia to bear.

She had since escaped the horror of it all by sleeping.

As Lavinia slowly awakened now, the instant recollection of what had happened to her husband was like an arrow to her own heart.

Their marriage had been one of convenience instead of true love, arranged by their parents, but she had cared about him nonetheless.

She had been good to him, had done her wifely duties at night, even though his touch never stirred pleasure within her.

That she had given him pleasure had been enough, for he was the kindest man she had ever known besides her father, who was now gone from this earth, as was her mother.

Her parents had been caught in the crossfire of two gunmen on the streets of Atlanta, Georgia, and killed instantly.

And now her husband was dead, too?

She now had only her daughter to live for. She vowed to make certain Dorey was happy and well cared for. That would be enough for Lavinia, along with her memories of Virgil.

"Mama, I'm so glad you are finally awake," Dorey said, quickly standing. She gazed down at her mother with love shining in her eyes. "You've been asleep for such a long time. Are you going to be alright?"

Even with her daughter at her bedside, sweet and caring, Lavinia could not banish the awful picture of Hiram walking toward her with Virgil in his arms. The memory of the arrow in her husband's chest made her feel sick to her stomach even now, but she forced herself to face the way life was now changed for both herself and her daughter.

"I will be alright," Lavinia finally said. She sat up and positioned her pillow behind her back to make herself more comfortable.

She noticed that she still had on the dress she had worn since morning, but her shoes had been removed.

Her feet felt the comfort of the blanket that her daughter must have drawn over her after removing the lovely silk and lace-trimmed bedspread that Lavinia herself had made.

She was so glad that she had never shared a bed with her husband, or it would be impossible to stay there now, to continue resting while trying to accept the reality of Virgil's death.

Although they had been loving toward one another, once he had come to her bed each night to take his pleasure, he had been in the habit of returning to his own bed in a room down the corridor.

They both had preferred it that way.

They each had enjoyed having a bed to themselves, especially Lavinia. Virgil snored so loudly that when she had at first tried to sleep with him as a newlywed, she had not gotten a wink of sleep.

It was his suggestion that he sleep elsewhere if

she would not feel neglected by his doing so. She had quickly told him that she never felt neglected while he was with her beneath the same roof. It wasn't necessary for them to share the same bed for a full night.

"Uncle Hiram . . . removed . . . the nasty arrow from papa," Dorey said, visibly trembling.

"Thank goodness," Lavinia said. She shuddered as she again envisioned her husband with the arrow lodged in his chest. It was a sight she might never be able to forget. "I'll go soon and start preparing him for burial."

She gazed at Dorey, whose eyes were swollen from crying. "The funeral will be a quiet and quick one," she murmured. "It will only include our family."

"I'm glad," Dorey said. She wiped tears from her eyes with the back of her hand. "It would be horrible to wait for distant relatives and friends to arrive."

"That is exactly why I am doing it this way," Lavinia said.

She gazed at her daughter, marveling as always at her loveliness. Her hair was the same golden color as Lavinia's, and she had a pretty face, delicate in every respect. Dorey had seen too often how cruel the world could be. She had not only lost her father, but both sets of grandparents as well.

Lavinia was all that was left of her daughter's world, for neither of them included Hiram when they spoke of family.

He was a deplorable, disgusting man. He reeked of sweat. His hands were always dripping with it.

And his one eye never stopped watching Lavinia. It was as though he were always mentally undressing her.

"Do you think the Indian that killed Papa will come and kill us, too?" Dorey suddenly asked, jarring Lavinia back to the moment.

"Please don't worry about that," Lavinia said, trying to reassure her daughter. She took one of Dorey's tiny hands in hers.

"But, Mama, the Seminole Indians live so close," Dorey said. She swallowed hard. "Do you think they are responsible for Papa's death?"

"I can see why you would think that, but, Dorey, they haven't given us any problems, or anyone else as far as I know," Lavinia said softly. "And your father didn't interfere in their lives, either. He left them alone, for he felt safer that way. He certainly didn't want to make an enemy of any Indians."

"Then . . . what Indian did this?" Dorey persisted.

"I don't know of any other Indians in the area who would have cause to attack your father," Lavinia said thickly. "But someone did. Who hated him enough to kill him? I just don't know, Dorey," Lavinia said, sighing. "Please, dear. I just don't want to talk or think about it any more. I am so tired. This has taken everything out of me."

Dorey leaned down and hugged Lavinia. "Mama, I'll leave you alone if that is what you want," she murmured. "Is it?"

"Dear, you stay if you wish, or leave if you would rather do that," Lavinia said as Dorey stepped slowly away from her. "I know this isn't any easier on you than on me."

"Mama, Hiram told me not to be afraid about what happened to Papa," Dorey said. "He said that he is here for us and that he will care for us in Papa's absence. He . . . he . . . even said that he would marry you to make it proper for us all to live together under one roof. He said that would keep people from . . . talking."

"Lord," Lavinia said. She shivered with disgust at the very thought of Hiram touching her with his sweaty palms. "I would never let that man touch me, much less . . . marry me. There is nothing about him that I like. Even Virgil was becoming wary of him and his antics, and he was Hiram's brother. Sometimes Virgil hated claiming Hiram as a relation."

She paused, then again shuddered. "Marry Hiram?" she said softly. "I think not. Oh, how horrible a thought!"

"But, Mama, I truly believe he is planning to marry you," Dorey said. She took a quick step backward when Lavinia swept the blanket away from herself and left the bed.

In her bare feet Lavinia began pacing the floor. "I have a plan that, for a while at least, might keep Hiram at arm's length," she said tightly. "I will see to your father's burial; then I will find safety and solace here in my room. After your father's burial, I will let Hiram think that I am too distraught to leave my bed. For as long as I must, until he forgets this lunacy of thinking I will marry him, I will hide away in my room. He will think I am in my bed, day and night."

"Mama, I'll help you," Dorey said. "I'll spend my time here with you, reading books and embroidering. When Uncle Hiram inquires about why I am spending so much time with you, and why you won't leave the room, I'll tell him I am reading to you to comfort you because you are still so distraught over the loss of Papa."

Suddenly Dorey covered her eyes and broke down in hard sobs. "Twila now has no mama or papa," she cried. "While you were asleep, Hiram killed Twila's mama in a fit of rage, and her papa's body will surely never be found."

"Joshua . . . and . . . Lorna are both dead?" Lavinia gasped. "Joshua was killed by an arrow, too? And Lorna? Why did Hiram kill Lorna? She . . . was . . . such a gentle soul, and so sweet."

"She didn't do what he ordered as quickly as he wanted," Dorey said, her voice breaking. "It happened right after Uncle Hiram carried you to your bed. He . . . he . . . went out to yell at the slaves for not working hard enough. It was then that he told Lorna about her husband's death. When she broke into tears and just kept on sobbing instead of returning to work in the fields he . . . he . . . pulled his pistol on her. He . . . killed . . . her."

"The maniac," Lavinia said, pale at hearing the horrible news.

Lavinia placed her hands on Dorey's shoulders as she gazed down into her daughter's eyes. "Dorey, I will leave my room long enough to instruct Hiram to assign Twila house duties so that you can keep an eye on her while I am hiding away in my room," she said. "I don't trust him any farther than I can throw him. Since Twila no longer has parents to watch out for her, Hiram might take liberties with her. I will not allow that to happen."

"Mama, I don't trust Uncle Hiram at all," Dorey said, her voice drawn. "The way he looks at me with his one eye sometimes makes me want to vomit."

"Daughter," Lavinia said, bending to her knees so that she could be at eye level with Dorey. She framed Dorey's face between her hands. "While I have breath left in my lungs, I assure you that Hiram won't touch either you or Twila. Go now. Tell Twila to come to the house. I'll make things right for her with Hiram. When I get done with him, he'll know to keep his hands to himself as far as you and Twila . . . and myself . . . are concerned."

"Oh, thank you, Mama," Dorey cried as she flung herself into her mother's arms. "Thank you for both me and Twila. I'll go now and get her."

Lavinia rose slowly to her feet as Dorey ran from the room.

But before leaving her room, Lavinia went to one of the windows and swept the curtain aside so that she could look at the huge old oak tree where she had first seen the green-eyed white panther, and then . . . moments later . . . a green-eyed Indian!

Had she truly seen them?

Had she truly seen one and then the other, or neither?

She was known to have a very vivid imagination. Had her imagination played tricks on her when she had gazed at that old oak tree?

Surely she would never, ever know!

Chapter Four

Ah, love! Could you and I with him conspire
To grasp this sorry scheme of things entire?
                                        —Edward Fitzgerald

When Wolf Dancer arrived at Mystic Island, he quickly beached his canoe and lifted Joshua from it.

He made his way through the thick vegetation that protected the village from the view of outsiders. This island in the midst of the Everglades was his people's sanctuary, a place of safety and serenity, where the undergrowth had been cleared away to make room for a hundred huts.

Each home was built of flexible poles that were bent over and tied together at the center to form the round shape.

Once the basic structure was in place, the owner would cover the poles with rushes, bark or animal skins.

Also hidden from view from the river stood the Wind Clan's garden where corn, squash, green beans, and melons of all sorts had been planted.

His people depended on these crops to supplement the meat and fish they hunted. Fortunately the vegetables and fruit were growing well this year and there was plenty to eat for all.

Now the growing season was at its end, and most of the crops had been picked and prepared for storage.

As Wolf Dancer hurried onward with Joshua, he heard a rustling of the thick vegetation at his right side and soon saw the sentry who was posted there step quickly into view. The sentry, Blue Sky, stopped abruptly when he saw Wolf Dancer coming toward him with a black man hanging limply in his muscular arms.

"This man has half an arrow embedded deep in his left shoulder," Wolf Dancer said, his voice drawn and tight. "I found him in a canoe, unconscious, floating in the river. I must get him to Shining Soul. Our shaman should be able to save his life."

"Who do you think is responsible?" Blue Sky asked, keeping up with Wolf Dancer as he made his way to their village. "Do you think he was trying to escape from the plantation where he was a slave and was shot?"

Wolf Dancer gave Blue Sky a quick glance. "This man was not shot while trying to escape," he said. "And the white men I have seen carry firearms, not bows and quivers of arrows."

"Then who?" Blue Sky persisted as the huts came into view through the thick foliage.

"It was an arrow of Seminole design, but there is no one among our Seminole people who would have cause to shoot this man," Wolf Dancer said. "And, anyhow, I know who did it. It was a white man trying to make it look as though a Seminole were responsible."

"A slave owner?" Blue Sky prodded. "Was it a slave owner who attempted to kill his own slave?"

"Yes, and we must make certain that the wounded man defies the one who attempted to kill him, by living," Wolf Dancer said. "Run on ahead, Blue Sky. Alert Shining Soul that I am bringing a wounded man to him. He must have his medicines ready."

Blue Sky nodded, then ran quickly ahead of Wolf Dancer and was soon out of sight.

Wolf Dancer only hoped that he had found Joshua in time, and that he would live. He was also worried that the beautiful, golden-haired woman might be in as much danger as this black man and her husband had obviously been!

Although she, a white woman, should be nothing to Wolf Dancer, he could not help caring about her welfare. She was so petite and vulnerable, he couldn't keep himself from being concerned about her.

When he finally reached the village, Wolf Dancer rushed into his shaman's personal lodge without even announcing himself. It was the custom of his people to announce themselves outside someone's personal lodge, never entering without permission. Privacy was cherished and honored by all who lived in his village.

But today things were different.

There was a need for haste. The injured man had already lost a lot of blood.

Shining Soul, a wrinkled, shrunken old man with

kindly eyes, was dressed in a long robe with designs of the sky people on it, such as the rainbow, moon, sun, and stars. He had already prepared a pallet of furs for his patient.

Shining Soul even now gestured with a bony, long-fingered hand toward it.

"Place him there," he said, closely studying Joshua's face. He had never before been so close to a black man.

After Joshua was stretched out on the furs, Shining Soul knelt beside him. "Blue Sky did not tell me where you found this man, nor why he was shot with an arrow," Shining Soul said. He tore Joshua's shirt away from the wound, giving him a clear view of the injury.

Wolf Dancer went and knelt on the opposite side of the pelts from Shining Soul as the shaman gently pressed his fingers all around the puckered skin where the rest of the arrow was still lodged.

Wolf Dancer quickly told Shining Soul what he knew as the shaman skillfully opened the wound. With delicate fingers he removed the other half of the arrow from Joshua's body, then quickly put a compress on the wound, which was again bleeding.

"I believe that poison was placed on the tip of the arrowhead before it was shot into the man," Shining Soul said as he stopped the bleeding and began applying various herbs to the wound. "That is why the black man sleeps so soundly. But I have applied medicine that will keep the poison from killing him. Under my care, he will be well soon."

"Thank you," Wolf Dancer said, sighing with

relief. "This is a kind man. He did not deserve the treatment he was given by the white man. We will make certain he never hurts this man again. I am going to ask Joshua, which is the wounded man's name, to stay among us in our sanctuary. It will become his, too, if he agrees."

"What of his family?" Shining Soul asked as he softly applied a white doeskin cloth to the wound.

"I know not of his family," Wolf Dancer said, standing to leave. "When Joshua is ready, he will tell us."

Wolf Dancer patted Shining Soul softly on his shoulder, then left the shaman's lodge.

Wolf Dancer found most of his people outside, waiting to hear about the black man that had been brought among them.

Never holding anything back from his people, Wolf Dancer took his time explaining to them about what had happened, and that Joshua would possibly be staying to make his home among them.

Wolf Dancer trusted in his shaman so much that he was certain the man with black skin would not die. As he had so many times before, Shining Soul had worked his magic on the black man's wound.

When everyone's concerns had been alleviated, and his people had dispersed, Wolf Dancer went to his own home.

His personal lodge was different from all others of his village. Although it was built of many of the same materials, like palmetto thatch and cypress logs, his house was two stories high. On the upper floor was a kind of porch that was open to the air and looked out over the village.

The balcony was a breezy, cool spot where he could watch the activity of his people.

It was one of his favorite places to spend time.

After getting an orange and peeling it, Wolf Dancer sat down on a thick pelt on the second-story balcony that overlooked his village. As he enjoyed the orange, he watched his people: The adults went about doing their daily chores, while the children were happily romping and playing amongst themselves.

His mind returned to the white woman who was now widowed. He would go and watch her some more as he planned how to get her away from the evil white man who had widowed her.

From what little he had observed today, he'd noticed that she had two children with her. One was black, surely a child of a slave, and the other was white-skinned, an exact replica of the woman, with her same golden hair and pretty face.

Surely this white child was the woman's daughter. The child, too, must be in despair over the loss of her father.

In time, Wolf Dancer would save her as well from the clutches of the evil man, providing her mother would let him come into their lives to help them.

It had been many moons since he had allowed himself to be infatuated by a woman. His wife, Pretty Butterfly, had died after being together as man and wife for just one night.

An alligator had killed her the next day. It had found its way onto the island while his wife was away from the village, searching for turtles for her cook pot.

It had taken him years to begin getting over his loss, but now that much time had elapsed, he knew his heart was healed enough for him to love a woman again.

Yes, he did hunger now, not only for a woman, but also for a family of his own.

Driven to know whether the white woman was alright, Wolf Dancer left his home and went to check on Joshua. After discovering him sleeping peacefully, he continued on to his canoe and slid it back into the river.

His heart beat with an anticipation that he had not felt for years. Each stroke of the paddle taking him closer to the white woman made him realize just how empty his life had been without a woman in it to share laughter and conversation with him.

Yes, he would observe what was happening at the huge plantation house. He would make certain that the widow and her daughter were safe enough for the time being, until he decided how he could claim them both as his own!

And he would.

Somehow . . . he . . . would!

Chapter Five

Dost thou love life?
Then do not squander time, for that's the
stuff life is made of.
                              —*Benjamin Franklin*

Unable to stop thinking about what had happened on this fateful day—the murder and burial of her poor husband—Lavinia scooted lower in her bed and covered her head with her blanket.

Sobs racked her body as she relived the moment when she had seen her husband lying dead in Hiram's arms, an arrow in his chest.

She still couldn't believe that the peaceful Seminole Indians who made their home in the nearby swamp could be responsible.

In fact, she was certain that they weren't.

Did that mean another band of Indians also lived somewhere near?

If so, no one had ever mentioned their causing problems before.

The slaves worked safely in the fields, and Lavinia came and went in her horse and buggy when she pleased.

Some inner sense told her that whoever had killed

her husband had used an arrow to make it look as though Indians were responsible.

But who would have wanted to kill Virgil?

Her husband, being the kind man that he was, had no known enemies.

He had never had problems with anyone.

He was even kind to his slaves. The slaves had grown to admire him for his gentleness, though they hated the very sight of Hiram, who used his whip too casually on them even after Virgil had warned him against such a practice.

Only one man came to mind when she thought of evil and meanness . . . and that was Hiram!

But surely . . .

No.

She wouldn't allow herself to believe that Hiram could kill his own brother. Yet Hiram had much to gain if Virgil were out of the picture.

He would be able to run the plantation by himself, the way he wanted.

He was even planning on marrying his brother's wife!

That thought made Lavinia stop crying and angrily push the blanket away from herself.

She slid out of bed, and barefoot went to the shutters at one window and threw them open.

She inhaled deeply, enjoying the fresh air as it wafted into her room.

She knew she had to get hold of herself.

She had much to plan and do.

Besides burying her husband, she had accomplished one other thing today.

Twila was no longer living among the slaves in the quarters.

She was now at the house, with a little room of her own, and with housekeeping duties that were much easier than the chores she'd done before. Hiram was furious that Lavinia had given Twila so much freedom.

"And that's only the beginning," Lavinia whispered to herself.

She went to her dresser and took up her hairbrush.

As she pulled it through her long, golden hair, she went back to the window and found herself gazing at the massive live oak where she had seen the mystical panther earlier in the day.

The sunset was casting an orange glow on the moss, which hung from the limbs like the lace at the neckline of her delicate white gown.

Then she dropped her brush, gasped, and grabbed at the bedpost as she found herself gazing at the white panther, which was leisurely resting on the same limb as before.

Seeing it again convinced her it was real.

It wasn't a figment of her imagination, unless . . .

"Mama?"

Dorey's sweet voice drew Lavinia's attention as she came into the room. The smell of tomato soup wafted toward Lavinia, who turned abruptly to look at her daughter.

"Mama, I've brought you your soup," Dorey

said, taking the bowl over to the bedside table. She placed it there and set a spoon beside it.

Dorey went to Lavinia. "Mama, you've been crying again," she murmured. "Yet I'm glad that you are at least out of bed and brushing your hair. But, Mama . . . there is something I see in your expression that puzzles me. What is it, Mama? What's wrong?"

Lavinia smiled weakly. She laid her brush on the bed, then turned slowly to look out the window again.

She had to see if the beautiful white panther was really in the oak, or just a figment of her imagination. If she still saw it there, she would point the creature out to Dorey. If Dorey saw it, too, then Lavinia would know without a doubt that it was real!

When she gazed at the exact spot where she had seen the panther, the limb was empty. A strange feeling of panic clutched her insides; she needed to know for certain that it had been there.

She didn't want to believe that she was on the verge of losing her mind!

She stepped closer to the window.

She grabbed hold of the sill, and her heart pounded as she looked almost desperately from tree to tree, to see if the panther had gone to rest elsewhere.

But no!

It wasn't anywhere to be seen!

And then she gasped. Down on the Bone River she caught a glimpse of an Indian paddling away.

He turned his head as if he knew that she was there, watching him. As he looked up directly at her, Lavinia grabbed the sill even harder, for her knees had gone strangely rubbery, as though they might not hold her up any longer.

Oh, Lord, had she been wrong not to believe an Indian had killed her husband? Could this very Indian be the one responsible?

But no!

She had seen his face well enough today when he was resting in the tree earlier. This Indian she was now gazing upon at was one and the same.

So, no. He could not be responsible for her husband's death. She had seen this same Indian only moments before Hiram had appeared, carrying Virgil in his arms.

This Indian could not have been in two places at once!

And he had not carried a quiver of arrows on his back, nor had he been clutching a bow in his hand earlier today as he rested in the tree.

But then again, there had been that white panther in the tree, and she had seen it at almost the same time she had seen this Indian!

Oh, she was so confused.

Or . . . she might truly be losing her mind.

The sound of Dorey speaking brought Lavinia out of her puzzled state. "Mama, you are behaving so peculiarly," Dorey said. She stepped up to Lavinia and took one of her hands. "What are you looking for outside the window?"

Lavinia smiled weakly at Dorey.

"Mother, you look as though you have just seen a ghost," Dorey said, her eyes wide as she saw how pale her mother's face was. "What on earth is wrong? Please tell me."

Lavinia saw that she was worrying her daughter. Not wanting to address her questions at this time, since she truly had no answers, she bent over and brushed a soft kiss across Dorey's brow.

"It's been a very tiring and troubling day, that's all," she murmured. She went to her chifforobe, took a robe from it and slipped into it, then pulled on some slippers.

She went to a soft, upholstered chair that stood beside the bedside table and sat down.

She picked up the bowl of soup and scooped a spoonful from it. She softly blew on it first, then sipped the rich tomato soup into her mouth.

The first taste warmed her stomach, yet she truly wanted nothing to eat. Her stomach was still unsettled by the day's sadness, and from seeing the Indian again.

She set the bowl aside on the table and forced a smile as she looked at Dorey. "How is Twila doing?" she asked. She knew she must try to calm herself by talking about ordinary things. "Does Twila like her room?"

"She adores it," Dorey said. She plopped down on the rocking chair that was positioned near the chair upon which her mother sat. She giggled. "But I must confess, she spends more time in my room than her own. I've been showing her all my things. She loves my doll collection and my storybooks. Mama, I'm going to teach her so much. And she is so eager to learn."

"That's wonderful, Dorey, wonderful," Lavinia said, though she had not actually heard much of what Dorey had said.

Lavinia kept gazing over at the window, her eyes lingering there as she thought about what she had seen.

First the panther, and then the Indian!

It was all so mysterious; so unbelievable!

Chapter Six

I saw and loved.

—Edward Gibbon

It's been two weeks now," Lavinia said as she sat on her bed, resting her back against the headboard.

She was in a robe, for she never knew when Hiram might decide to come and check on her, to see if she felt strong enough today to leave her room and join him at the dining table for dinner.

"Do you think it's been long enough, Mama?" Dorey asked as she worked on her embroidery. "Aren't you tired of being in this room? Surely Uncle Hiram has lost interest in his idea of making you his wife."

"In just two weeks?" Lavinia said, laughing. "He won't forget it until he has one foot in hell. I would gladly go there so that I could push him in the rest of the way."

"Mama, he asks me too often about you," Dorey said, resting her embroidery work on her lap. "It's making me nervous. I have to tell him one lie after another. I'm getting quite uncomfortable making up so many stories."

"I'm sorry to be the one to make you lie," Lavinia said. She sighed heavily. "But there is no other way. I despise the very ground Hiram walks on. I would die if he so much as touched me. And if I were his wife, I would be . . . duty bound . . . to allow him to do more than that."

"I will tell him the necessary lies until the day I die if it keeps you from having to endure something as horrible as that," Dorey said. She shuddered. "So don't worry, Mama. I'm sure God understands why these lies are necessary."

"It's only a game, and it shouldn't have to be necessary for much longer," Lavinia said. She slid from the bed. She ran her fingers through her long, golden hair, slipped her feet into soft slippers, then went to a window and threw open the shutters so that the morning sunlight could filter in and brighten the room.

As usual, she gazed at the old oak tree where she often saw the Indian sitting and looking, it seemed, directly up at her window. She hadn't seen the panther for a few days and wondered why.

"Mama, Twila seems happy being here in the house with us," Dorey said.

Her daughter's voice drew Lavinia's eyes from the tree, but she never seemed now to be able to put the handsome Indian from her mind. Lavinia turned just as Dorey got up from her chair and came to join her by the window.

"I'm so glad that Twila is doing alright even though her parents are no longer there for her to love and spend the evenings with. The evenings were the only time they had together, you know," Lavinia said. She took Dorey by the hand and led her to the bed, where they both sat on the edge as they continued to talk.

"Hiram pushed them so hard even after Virgil begged him not to be so cruel to the slaves," she murmured. "Your father was too soft-spoken. He allowed Hiram to walk all over him, and it was Hiram who got his way for the most part. Now? With Virgil not here to keep an eye on what's going on, I would hate to see how Hiram is treating the slaves."

"At least Twila doesn't have to take such abuse," Dorey said. "Uncle Hiram hasn't so much as laid a hand on her since she moved into our house. He knows how much you and I love her. And surely he must feel some guilt over how he treated her parents . . . killing her mother in cold blood. Mama, we should have gone to the authorities and turned him in, but even they have no pity for slaves or how they are abused by their owners. It would have been time wasted."

"Dorey, I've been wanting to talk to you about something very private," Lavinia suddenly said. She looked intently into her daughter's smoky-violet eyes. "It seems only right that you should know, especially now, since your Uncle Hiram is causing us both such distress, wanting me to marry him. One day you will meet a man and want to marry him. I want you to know that there is more than one reason to marry a man."

"What do you mean?" Dorey asked. She looked in wonder into her mother's eyes. "What other reason can there be besides loving the man you marry?"

"There are such things as arranged marriages," Lavinia said, her voice tense.

"Arranged . . . ?" Dorey said. She arched an eyebrow. "What do you mean . . . arranged?"

"Dorey, that is why your father and I were married, not out of love," Lavinia murmured. "You see, my parents and his were best friends. Both families were wealthy in their own right. They wanted to combine this wealth. They saw a marriage between myself and your father as the best way, because they knew how much we cared for one another already. But what we felt wasn't true love. We just cared for one another as friends who admired each other."

"So it was because of money that you and Papa married?" Dorey asked, her eyes widening in surprise. "But you seemed so devoted . . . so loving. Surely you were in love."

"There are many ways to love a man," Lavinia said. She suddenly felt awkward, and somewhat trapped, for she had never discussed anything like this with her daughter before.

Yet she knew this had to be done. One day her daughter would meet a man and fall head over heels in love with him. Lavinia wanted Dorey to feel comfortable with such a love as that.

"And you just didn't love Papa in a way that made you feel passionate about him?" Dorey asked, causing Lavinia to gasp. She had never dreamed that her daughter even knew the word "passionate."

"And how do you know about such things as . . . passion?" Lavinia asked guardedly, taking both of her daughter's hands.

"Mama, you know how much I love books and that I am an avid reader," Dorey said, blushing slightly. "I love going through the books in our library. That word 'passion' appears often when relationships are written about in books."

"My word, have you been reading romantic novels?" Lavinia asked, pulling her hands away from Dorey's and placing them on her daughter's cheeks.

"I wasn't certain they were called that, but yes, I have read books that describe the love between men and women," Dorey said, blushing. "But this love never goes beyond kissing in the books I read, Mama, and holding hands."

"I should go to our library and check the books more carefully," Lavinia said, laughing absently.

"Mama, I am no longer a child," Dorey said. She gently took her mother's hands from her face. "I am going on nine, you know."

"And that is so old," Lavinia replied, laughing softly. "But back to what we were discussing: my marriage to your father. I respected him and he was good to me, as I was to him. I still find his death devastating. But I just felt that you needed to know about my reason for marrying your father. Our marriage had worked for both of us until he died. We were content together, and a precious, sweet daughter was born of our comfortable marriage."

"Oh, Mama, I miss Papa so much," Dorey said, suddenly flinging herself into her mother's arms and hugging her fiercely. She sobbed. "Why, oh, why did he have to die?"

"I'm beginning to think we will never know," Lavinia said, smoothing her fingers through Dorey's soft, golden hair.

Dorey leaned away from Lavinia and gazed into her eyes. "Thank you for telling me about your feelings for Papa and why you married," she murmured. "I hope one day to find a man . . . a true love for myself."

"Darling, you will," Lavinia said. "In time, you will. You are too young now, though, to think about it. But you aren't too young to understand what I've told you about marriage and love."

Dorey suddenly left the bed. She turned and gazed into Lavinia's eyes. "Mama, I would love to do something today that you might not approve of," she said, her eyes no longer filled with tears, but instead with a quiet excitement.

"And that is?" Lavinia said, moving off the bed, too.

She went to the window and gazed at the old oak tree again, trying to fight back her curiosity about the handsome Indian.

"I want to go canoeing," Dorey blurted out, bringing Lavinia's eyes quickly to her again. "I haven't gone since before Papa's . . . death. I . . . I . . . need this, Mama. Canoeing gives me such peace. And I miss my time alone in the canoe, exploring."

Lavinia tried not to show her uneasiness about her daughter leaving the plantation grounds.

But she understood Dorey's restlessness.

Lavinia had been the same sort of child; she could never stay in one place for long.

She had always loved exploring.

She . . . still . . . did!

And surely always would.

She didn't want the loss of her husband to take away her love of adventure.

"Alright, go and do your exploring," Lavinia agreed. "But do not venture farther than where I have instructed you is safe. Stay within shouting distance of the slaves in case you get into trouble. They will alert either me or Hiram if necessary."

"Oh, thank you, Mama," Dorey cried, again hugging her.

Then she stepped away from Lavinia and asked, "Do you think Twila can go with me this time? I believe Uncle Hiram has gone to Fort James. Usually when he goes to play poker with his friends at the fort, he is gone for some time. He will never know that I have taken Twila canoeing with me."

"Dorey, don't you know . . . your Uncle Hiram seems to have eyes in the back of his head. Truly, you'd best not invite Twila to go with you," she said regretfully. "It could cause trouble should Hiram ever find out. It is not wise to tempt fate. It is good that we have Twila staying in the house where we can keep an eye on her. Let's leave it at that."

"Can she at least go with me to the river and see me off in the canoe?" Dorey asked, begging with her eyes.

"I see nothing wrong with her doing that," Lavinia said. "Go. Scat. Have fun."

"I shall," Dorey said, hurrying to the closed door. She turned and smiled at Lavinia. "Oh, Mama, I shall! Thank you."

Lavinia nodded and watched her daughter leave the room, then went to the window again and peered out at the old oak tree.

She knew it was strange that she wasn't concerned about Dorey going canoeing today. Somehow she sensed that the Indian was close and would keep her safe.

It seemed that the handsome Indian came often now, as though he were keeping an eye on the plantation, making sure Lavinia was safe. He seemed to have appointed himself her protector, even though they had never actually met or spoken.

She just saw him in the tree, watching.

Sometimes she still saw the panther, too, but not as much as she had at first.

Lavinia's eyes were drawn elsewhere as she watched Dorey and Twila running toward the river, hand in hand, giggling.

Several large canoes rested on the banks of the river, along with one small one, which was Dorey's. Dorey dragged her canoe into the water as Twila watched.

Twila's voice wafted up to Lavinia as she asked Dorey to keep an eye out for her pappy. The girl added hopefully that maybe he was not dead at all, but hiding somewhere in the Everglades.

Lavinia was glad when she heard Dorey tell Twila that she was not going to travel as far as the swamp, but only a little way downriver to smell the tropical flowers that grew not far from the plantation grounds.

Lavinia saw Twila wipe tears from her eyes as she watched Dorey paddle away. Then she turned and walked with lowered eyes back toward the house.

Lavinia wanted to go outside and comfort Twila, but although she knew that Hiram should be gone for some time, she did not want to take the chance of his suddenly appearing and finding her well enough to have left her bed.

For now, it was best that she still play this game, but she knew that it couldn't go on much longer.

She must never allow herself to forget that Hiram was not as stupid as he seemed!

Chapter Seven

I love those who yearn for
The impossible.
          —Johann Wolfgang Von Goethe

$\mathcal{T}$he morning sun streamed through the open door of the lodge where Joshua lay on a thick pallet of blankets and furs. He was healing quickly from the wound made by the poisoned arrow.

Chief Wolf Dancer had just brought him some warm soup made from turtle meat and was sitting beside him.

Warmed by the soup, and feeling thankful that he was alive, Joshua gave Chief Wolf Dancer a wide, toothy smile. "Thank you for saving my life," he said, although he had already thanked the young chief many times. "I wish my wife and daughter were here with me. They are not safe while they are at the plantation with dat evil man. If he would shoot his very own brotha', who is to say what he might do to mere females who are helpless to protect themselves. With me no longer there to work in the tobacco fields, he might decide that both my wife and daughter are too worthless to keep around. He often gripes about how much food he has to feed the slaves. Now he might choose to stop feeding my family altogether."

"I will find a way to bring them to you," Wolf Dancer said, pausing when two young braves came to the door and peered inside. He went outside to them.

"What is on your minds this morning?" he asked, looking from one to the other.

"Can we go exploring today in our canoe?" Running Bear asked, speaking for himself and his ten-year-old brother, Deer Shadow, who stood beside him. "When we asked our mother, she said to ask you. As our chief, you say who can and who cannot leave our island."

"I see no harm in your going a short distance," Wolf Dancer said. He placed a gentle hand on Running Bear's shoulder, which was already showing muscles even though he had only eleven winters. "But remember not to venture too far from the safety of our island."

"We promise," they said in almost the same breath. "We understand the danger."

Running Bear looked past Wolf Dancer. "How is the black man faring?" he asked, gazing up into Wolf Dancer's eyes. "We heard he was shot with a poisoned arrow. Is that true?"

"It is true," Wolf Dancer said, frowning. "And so you see why I warn you not to travel far. Although I know who shot him and do not expect the madman anywhere near our village, I still warn you to be careful. Take your bows and quivers of arrows. Do not hesitate to use them if you find yourself in danger."

"We can even shoot a white man?" Deer Shadow asked, his eyes wide with wonder.

"Only if he threatens you with a weapon of his own," Wolf Dancer said solemnly. "But I do not expect such a thing will happen or I would not give you permission to leave our village."

He patted both boys on the shoulder, one at a time, smiled, then gestured with a hand toward the river, where the young braves' canoe was moored with the others. "Go," he said, smiling. "And if you find more turtles, bring them home for your mother's cook pot."

Deer Shadow frowned. "I have never enjoyed taking turtles to eat," he said. "They seem so defenseless."

"If you want to grow up and be strong like the warriors of our village, you must not think that way, for food is what sustains our people," Wolf Dancer replied. "Turtle meat is one of our people's favorites. It is necessary for you to gather turtles for their meat. Do you understand?"

Deer Shadow humbly lowered his eyes. "Yes, I understand," he said meekly. He looked quickly up at Wolf Dancer again. "I want to be a skilled hunter and to make you, my chief, proud. If that means bringing home turtle meat, I shall do it."

"That is good," Wolf Dancer said. He gently patted the boy on his shoulder. "Go. Tell your mother that I have given permission for you to leave the village, but do not stay away from your home long. Your mother will worry."

"We will be gone only long enough to enjoy our

time on the river and then return," Running Bear
said, sliding an arm around his younger brother's
shoulders. He gazed into Deer Shadow's dark eyes.
"Come, brother. We must tell our mother, and then
we can do as we planned."

As the young braves looked into each other's
eyes, Wolf Dancer thought he saw some silent com-
munication between them, as though they had a
plan that they were not sharing with him.

It was the mischievous, anxious look in their expressions that told him this, yet he did not speak of
his feelings and suspicions. He did not want them
to think he did not fully trust them.

He watched them turn and run off, go into their
mother's hut, then soon leave again, giggling and
running hard toward the thick brush alongside the
river.

Wolf Dancer continued to feel uneasy as he saw
them disappear into the thicket, their giggles still
audible as they spoke anxiously to each other about
their adventure.

Wolf Dancer tried to hear the details of the adventure they were discussing, but it was impossible.

When he couldn't hear their voices any longer, he
shrugged and told himself the young braves were
just happy to be allowed to leave the village for a
while. All children their age needed some adventure.

Having talked long enough with Joshua, and
knowing that the injured man still needed rest in order to regain his full strength, Wolf Dancer walked
toward his home.

He only stopped occasionally to stare in the

direction from which he had last seen and heard the young braves.

He wondered again why they had seemed more anxious than usual to go canoeing today. Again he shrugged and went on his own way.

Meanwhile, the young braves had reached the canoe, pushed it out into the water, and climbed aboard.

"Big brother, I have never been so excited as I am now," Deer Shadow said. He drew his paddle through the water in unison with his brother. "Do you think the plan will work?"

"It should, for we have been careful to make our preparations whenever we were allowed to leave the village," Running Bear said. He looked over at his brother and smiled broadly. "I am so excited. Today might be the day we see and abduct her."

Both wore only breechclouts and moccasins, as well as a necklace around each of their necks, with the fangs of a snake hanging from it.

They were proud of their necklaces. Deer Shadow had stood by and watched his brother kill the two snakes from which he had taken the fangs.

Deer Shadow smiled even now as he remembered how his brother had done it.

Running Bear had cut a pine knot from a tree and used it as a club to kill each snake. After cutting off the heads, he'd taken out the fangs and hung them on the necklaces.

Both their father and their chief had applauded their bravery, so they wore their necklaces with much pride every day.

Their long, black hair fluttered in the wind as they paddled down the river away from their village.

"I'm so excited," Deer Shadow said, his thoughts about their matching necklaces already far from his mind. "We have the tree house ready, but what if she doesn't come today? She hasn't for several days now. What if she never goes canoeing again?"

"I have watched her many times, and I can tell that she has the same adventurous nature as we do, little brother," Running Bear said, smiling. "It is that adventurous nature that attracted us to her. So, if she does not come today, perhaps she will tomorrow, or the day after that. All I know is that we are ready for her. We just have to be patient."

"I know," Deer Shadow said, sighing. "But I do not like having to be patient. And I am not certain how many more times our chief will allow us to leave the village. He might already be suspicious of what we are doing."

"What if our plan brings whites searching for the white girl and causes trouble for our people?" Deer Shadow asked anxiously.

"Stop whining, and stop thinking such things," Running Bear said, his tone impatient. "We have this planned out carefully. We will not cause trouble for our people."

"I am not so certain of that," Deer Shadow said, flinching when his older brother cast him a heavy frown.

"Little brother, we are going to steal away the white girl that we have seen traveling alone in her canoe," Running Bear said. "We have carefully prepared a place for her to be taken to. In time she will realize that we do not mean to harm her, but only to enjoy being with her for a while, so that she can tell us of her customs. Will that not be exciting, little brother?"

"I do not believe she will be excited, but instead very, very afraid," Deer Shadow whined. "And then . . . angry."

"Little brother, we will show her that there is nothing to be afraid of," Running Bear said. "And, yes, she will be angry, but surely she will find the experience an adventure. We will tell her that we only want to talk with her for a while and then we will set her free."

"When we set her free she will go and tell her parents what we did to her. They will want to punish our people," Deer Shadow still argued.

"You are spoiling this," Running Bear spat. "Be quiet if all you can do is cast doubt upon our plan. You were just as excited about it as I . . . until now, when we are so close to succeeding."

Deer Shadow cast down his eyes, then went quiet and resumed paddling through the marshy water, his eyes now fixed straight ahead, watching for the girl.

He silently prayed to the Great Spirit, the Seminole's Master of Breath, that she would understand why they were doing this to her!

Chapter Eight

I am the Love that dare not
Speak its name.

— Lord Alfred Douglas

The room was filled with smoke from the cigars being puffed around a gaming table at Fort James. Hiram was gambling with his friend Colonel Fred Cox and several other men of the colonel's regiment.

Playing cards was a way for Hiram to work off the frustrations that had been building due to Lavinia's strange behavior.

He was certain that she was lying about not feeling up to eating at the dining table with Hiram. He knew she had no love for him and had always kept her distance from him even when Virgil was alive.

Well, he would show her a thing or two about avoiding Hiram Price, he thought angrily to himself.

He planned to go to his sister-in-law's room as soon as he returned home from visiting his old pal Fred. After getting a few drinks in him, he would have the courage to face Lavinia. He would have his way with her by one means or another.

He had waited long enough.

And Virgil was no longer there to protect her.

Just thinking about having Lavinia in bed with him brought a sly, mocking grin to his lips.

"Well? You got more'n I have showin' on the table, Hiram?" asked one of the soldiers named Jake, his pale blue eyes squinting as cigar smoke rolled into them. He blinked his eyes. "You got a full house, Hiram?"

A sheen of sweat lay across Hiram's brow. He wiped it clean with the back of his hand, which was already just as sweaty. "Wouldn't you like to know?" he growled out. He cast his one eye at Jake, who was anxiously waiting to show his cards.

"That's what we're here for, ain't it?" Jake said, laughing. "Show us what you've got, Hiram, or give up and go on home. Ain'tcha got a pretty thing waitin' on you since your brother's death? You are beddin' up with her, ain'tcha?"

Colonel Cox intervened. "We'll not have any more talk such as that, Jake," he said tightly. "Now just play cards. Nothing else. Do you hear?"

"That's what I'm trying to do if One-Eye'd just play his hand," Jake said, still glaring at Hiram, who sat across the table from him.

"One-Eye?" Hiram said, trying to keep his anger at bay. He wiped his sweaty palm on his pants' leg. "Call me that one more time and I'll show you more than my cards."

"Both of you, play cards or the game ends here," Fred barked out, glaring from Hiram to Jake.

"Yep, I have a full house alright," Hiram boasted.

Hiram slammed the cards down on the table,

faceup. He ran his hand across his brow and wiped it again, as he had so often during the card game.

"Well, I'll be damned," Jake grumbled. "You do, after all."

"Well? What do you have, big-mouth?" Hiram asked, chuckling beneath his breath. "Show us what you got, Jake."

Jake's face turned as red as his hair as he slammed the cards on the table, face side down, then shoved his chair back. He rose so quickly, it tumbled over backward on the floor.

He glared at Hiram, then hurriedly left the room.

"Got no spine, that one," Hiram said. He watched as the other players, five in all, threw down their cards.

"Seems I'm taking home quite a few coins," Hiram said, snickering as he slid the coins over to himself, then swept them from the table and eased them into his pockets.

He was dressed in his usual black suit with a slim, black tie contrasting against his white shirt. His collar-length black hair was swept back from his face, making his one eye more pronounced. Sweat clung to his hair in translucent, pearly beads.

"Time to call it quits," Fred said, gathering the cards as the men passed them to him. "Later, gents. Later."

All of the men but Hiram and Fred left the table.

Fred handed Hiram a fresh cigar and leaned over the table to light it after Hiram shoved it between his lips.

Then Fred, dressed immaculately in his blue uniform, with the gold buttons shining beneath the light of the lantern, lit his own cigar. He slid his chair back from the table and stretched his long, lean legs out, crossing them at the ankles.

"Hiram, I can tell that you've come today for more than playing cards," Fred said, eyeing Hiram speculatively. He winced with distaste at how heavily Hiram was sweating. "What is it? Things aren't going so good for you since your brother's untimely death, eh? Hiram, did you ever figure out who was the shooter? Or . . . do you even care?"

"And what do you mean by that?" Hiram demanded. He smiled mischievously as smoke spiraled from his mouth, the cigar now resting on the edge of an ashtray. "What might you be implying, Fred? Huh?"

"It took no genius to see how jealous you were of your brother, Hiram," Fred said, resting his own cigar in the same ashtray. "I knew long ago how much you hated Virgil and coveted his wife. Everyone could tell, Hiram. It was always there in your attitude and the way you glared at Virgil when he would not catch you doin' it."

"You've got a mighty big mouth today, Colonel," Hiram said between clenched teeth. He again wiped his hands on his pants.

Fred leaned across the table. "Want to make something of it?" he taunted. "Hiram, you know that I'm nothing like your brother. I don't let anyone push me around. No one. Not even the likes of you who pretend to be my friend."

"Pretend?" Hiram said, arching an eyebrow. "You think my friendship is all pretense?"

"Son, no one knows how to take anything you do or say, so how can I know whether your friendship is real or false?" Fred said, drumming his fingers on the top of the table.

"Fred, I am your friend and I hope I can depend on you as being mine," Hiram said. He sighed heavily. He slid a hand inside one of the pockets where he had placed the coins and ran his fingers through them, jangling them noisily.

"You have come to ask me for something, haven't you?" Fred said. He smiled cunningly at Hiram. "You didn't come just for a few games of poker or chitchat, did you?"

"Not to ask for something, just to see if you have recently sent men into the Everglades to try to find that Seminole island," Hiram admitted. He flicked sweat from his brow with his fingertips. "My brother thought he could peacefully coexist with them, but I'm not sure whether I can. If I stir up trouble, will you be there to cover my back?"

"What sort of trouble are you talking about?" Fred asked. He lifted his cigar from the ashtray and slipped it between his lips again.

He took a long, leisurely drag and let the smoke leave his mouth in casual circles.

"There's this lone Indian I've been seeing sneaking around way too close to my property," Hiram said, recalling the glimpses he'd caught of the Seminole in a canoe, far too close to his home.

Yes, *his* home.

He owned the plantation now, except for the portion that Lavinia had inherited from her husband.

"Has he caused you any actual trouble?" Fred asked, eyeing Hiram closely.

"Not really," Hiram said, shrugging. "It's just that I feel uncomfortable with him being so close to my property. Who's to say whether he might come some day with a whole passel of Injuns and take over everything, even Lavinia, for God's sake?"

"I imagine he'd be more interested in that golden-haired beauty than your land," Fred said. He laughed softly. "Even I'd come around if I knew there was a chance in hell she'd consider courting me. My wife has been dead now for five years. I'm ready to settle down again. Lavinia would be a wonderful choice."

Hiram leapt from his chair. He leaned down and glared into Fred's face. "Don't you think for one minute about coming around my place to court Lavinia."

"And you think she'd take a second glance at you with that one eye and that God-awful sweat?" Fred said, slowly rising from his chair to glare at Hiram. "Hiram, I think you'd better leave. All you brought with you today was confrontation. Don't come back until you are in a better frame of mind."

"The same goes for you, Fred," Hiram growled out. "Don'tcha come anywhere near my place or you might find the barrel of my shotgun staring you in your ugly face."

"I think you'd better take my advice, Hiram, and leave, or one of us will do something foolish, even more foolish than the words we are exchanging," Fred said tightly. "Calm down, Hiram. You're letting your brother's death get the best of you."

"He's got nothin' to do with anything I say or do," Hiram said. He turned and stomped toward the door. He stopped suddenly, whirled around, and glared at Fred. "Just remember what I said. You'd best heed my warning not to come to my place expectin' to see Lavinia. You see, Fred, she's mine now. All mine."

"Like hell she is," Fred said, guffawing at the nonsense that Hiram was speaking. Fred knew Lavinia well and knew she wouldn't take well to Hiram's attitude. The man sounded as if he thought he owned her, like one of his slaves.

Hiram gave Fred one more glare, then hurried from the cabin.

He mounted his horse and rode swiftly through the tall gates of the fort. The argument between him and Fred had stoked his courage to confront Lavinia at his first opportunity.

"Tonight," he mumbled to himself. "Yep, by gum, tonight."

Chapter Nine

They are not long,
The weeping and the laughter,
Love and desire and hate.

—Ernest Dowson

Quiet little drops of water fell from the paddle as each stroke pushed Dorey's canoe onward. Only the ripples of the water lapping at the opposite shore and the cry of a solitary bird broke the silence.

Dorey knew that she had already gone beyond the boundary of where her mother allowed her to travel in her canoe.

But everything was so beautiful and peaceful, it was hard to turn back.

Yet she knew she should.

She didn't want to do anything that might jeopardize her ability to enjoy these quiet times alone on the river.

Life had been so hard of late; being in her canoe carried her away from the sadness of it all.

She still couldn't believe that her father was dead.

But the fact that no one had found out who had done the ghastly deed made Dorey feel that she was no longer safe on the river, or even on the plantation itself.

Just as she started to turn back, she gasped and went pale. Two young braves in a canoe had suddenly appeared from behind some tall brush that leaned out over the water.

Before she knew what was happening, they had blocked her way, preventing her from going any farther.

She gasped when one of the young braves, who appeared to be no older than herself, raised a small bow notched with an arrow and aimed it directly at her.

She saw how small both the bow and arrow were, yet knew that even an arrow of that size could be lethal.

Having no choice but to lift her paddle out of the water, Dorey looked from one young brave to the other. They were dressed in breechclouts, their dark hair hanging down their backs to their waists.

"What do you want of me?" Dorey finally found the courage to ask. "Why are you stopping me? Why . . . are . . . you threatening me with your bow and arrow?"

Running Bear was the first to speak. "My brother and I have seen you before and are intrigued by your courage. You are not afraid to travel from your home and go among alligators and snakes . . . and Indians," he said.

"You speak in English," Dorey said, amazed at how perfectly he spoke her language. "Are you . . . Seminole? Are you from the clan who have made their home on Mystic Island?"

Deer Shadow slowly lowered his bow and arrow,

feeling that they weren't needed. The young white girl couldn't get away even if she tried.

"Yes, we are from Mystic Island," he said, studying her and seeing just how pretty she was. "We are Seminole. My name is Deer Shadow, and my brother is Running Bear. By what name are you called?"

"My name isn't any of your business," Dorey said stiffly. "But the fact that you are keeping me from returning home is. Get out of the way. I don't want to worry my mother."

"It is not our plan to allow you to go so soon," Running Bear said. He spoke firmly, yet not in a threatening way.

"Then what are you going to do to me?" Dorey asked, almost in tears. She struggled not to cry because she wished to show these boys that they did not frighten her. But the truth was that she was almost sick to her stomach with fear.

Yes, they were only young braves, surely no older than she, but there were two of them and they had weapons.

"We do not plan to harm you. We only wish to take you where we have prepared a place for us to sit and talk," Running Bear said. "But we cannot talk long today. We must return home soon. We are not allowed to leave our island except for a short time in search of small alligators and turtles."

"Will you let me go when you leave to return to your home?" Dorey asked, looking from one brave to the other. "You see, I don't want to be gone long enough to worry my mother. She's been through enough of late without having me to worry about."

"You are intriguing to us," Deer Shadow said. "We want to hear about your life. We will tell you, in turn, about our people and customs. Will you come with us now without screaming?"

"I should scream, but I know I have gone too far for anyone at my plantation to hear me," Dorey said, sighing heavily. "Where are you going to take me?"

"Just come with us and you shall see," Running Bear said, standing and gesturing with a hand for her to move from her canoe into theirs. "You will soon see that we have good intentions. We will not harm you. We have prepared well for your visit with us."

"You . . . have . . . prepared well?" Dorey said, stubbornly staying in her canoe, her hands clutching the seat tightly. "What do you mean?"

"You will come and see," Running Bear said, carefully stepping into her canoe. "Do not fight us. You are not as strong as we. Come. Climb into our canoe. We will take you where you will be comfortable for the time you spend away from your home. We made careful plans for the day we would finally see you again on the river. You have not been here for several days now."

"That is because my father was murdered and my mother is mourning his death and I am helping her through it," Dorey said. She winced when Running Bear reached out for her, then jerked his hand back quickly when Dorey leaned away from him. "You cannot keep me away from my mother. She needs me."

"We need you, too," Running Bear said, this time grabbing her by an arm and forcing her to her feet.

"Now go peacefully with me. You will see that we mean you no harm. We are your friends."

"Friends do not treat friends as you are treating me," Dorey said, now having no choice but to go over into the other canoe.

Once inside it, she sat down, her arms crossed defiantly across her chest. "Now what?" she demanded, hoping the fear building inside her wasn't revealed in her tone of voice. "Where are you taking me?"

Running Bear sat down in front of her, and his brother sat behind her.

They both lifted their paddles and turned the canoe around, directing it toward the spot where they had built their tree house.

Both boys' excitement was revealed in their eyes as they paddled the canoe briskly through the water.

"What are you going to do with me . . . or should I say . . . to me?" Dorey asked, looking over her shoulder at one of them, and then straight ahead at the other.

"You are not going to be harmed," Deer Shadow said, looking at her as he momentarily stopped paddling. "You might even enjoy it. *We* plan to."

A shiver raced up and down Dorey's spine at a thought that made her insides turn cold. She was all alone with two boys who might be seeking excitement in a way that made her feel ill.

And who was to say that they might not even kill her once their experiments were completed?

She hung her head, yet fought off the urge to

cry. She had disobeyed her mother by going much farther downriver than she ought, and now she was paying for it.

"We are going to keep you for only one night, and we will not harm you in any way," Running Bear said. "We have never been with a white person before; we just want to get to know you and learn of your ways. Then we will release you."

"You are going to hold me against my will for a full night?" Dorey gasped, turning pale at the thought of how that night might change her life.

"You are making a big mistake," she blurted out, slowly looking up into the eyes of Running Bear, who was studying her intently. "Let me go and I won't tell anyone what you have done. I promise. Please believe me. I need to go home to my mother."

"We will release you when we are ready to," Deer Shadow said, his voice suddenly tight. "Soon you will see that we have prepared well for your visit with us."

All was quiet for a while, and then Dorey saw a tree house built high above the river. "Are . . . you . . . taking me there?" she asked softly. "To . . . a tree house?"

"It was built just for you," Running Bear said, smiling at her. "You will see that you will not want for a thing."

"Except my freedom and my mother," Dorey said sarcastically, yet she could not help admiring the lovely tree house. She knew that these two young braves had spent much time and care building it with her in mind.

Something told her that she might not have anything to fear except the worry she would cause her mother.

"We just want to talk with you and spend time with you," Running Bear said. "You are a curiosity to us, and I am sure we are the same to you. You can ask and we will tell you about us and our people, and then you will tell us about your own."

"You could have asked politely, and then I would have come with you without being forced," Dorey said, thinking that she might really have done this, for she loved excitement in her life.

Even now, the longer she was with the young braves, the more she felt they were not the sort to hurt her!

"Just come with us and all will be well," Deer Shadow said as he and his brother beached the canoe just beneath the tree house and secured it to a rock.

Dorey did as they said and soon found herself high above the water in a very neatly constructed tree house. It had been outfitted with food, blankets, and mosquito netting. There was even a torch secured on one of the walls!

"You see that we have done all we could so that you would be comfortable," Running Bear said. "We had wanted to spend time with you today but it took us too long to find you. We are expected home. We must leave you here now without us."

Dorey went pale and felt sick to her stomach

again. These two boys had brought her here and now planned to leave her all alone in the swamp.

Her canoe had been abandoned; if they left in theirs, she would be at the mercy of the night creatures. If she tried to escape, she would have to travel alongside the river on foot.

"You can't leave me here by myself," she blurted out. "Please reconsider. Take me back to my canoe. Let me go home."

"We will return tomorrow morning, early," Deer Shadow said as Running Bear picked up two thongs and knelt in front of Dorey. "We must tie your wrists, and then your ankles. We do not want you running away."

"What?" Dorey cried as her wrists were secured by the leather thongs. "You are leaving me here, helpless?"

"You will be alright," Deer Shadow said. "We will leave the torch lit for you, and you will sleep beneath the netting to keep snakes and mosquitoes from getting to you. There is food that we are certain you will enjoy. Though your hands are tied, they are tied in front of you so that you can eat the food."

"You are insane," Dorey cried, trying hard to loosen the thongs at her wrists; those at her ankles were too tight for her to move at all. "Oh, surely I will die before you can get back here tomorrow. Nothing can protect me from the night creatures of the Everglades. Surely you know that."

They ignored her.

"If I do manage to stay alive, I will kill both of you at my first opportunity," Dorey screamed at them.

"You speak bravely, but we know girls cannot kill," Running Bear said, smiling. "Girls were not born to kill."

"We will return early tomorrow," Deer Shadow said, already making his way down the ladder that had been built for access to the tree house. "Come, brother. Mother will be worrying about us. So will our chief."

Dorey was suddenly alone.

As the sun began setting slowly on the horizon, everything was eerily quiet except for a strange bird call.

And then the more frightening screech of a panther filled the night air with its threat.

Dorey had heard about the white panther that roamed the Everglades.

Oh, what if it found her in the tree house?

Or what if snakes came into the house? The shield of netting would be useless to truly protect her!

She tried desperately to get her wrists free, knowing that her life surely depended on it!

Chapter Ten

That is happiness; to be
Dissolved into something
Complete and great.

—Willa Cather

Dusk was falling upon Mystic Island, painting orange across the treetops as the sunset glowed along the western horizon.

The usual huge outdoor fire that was lit each evening in the Wind Clan's village burned brightly into the heavens. It had been built to keep night creatures from stalking the sleeping Seminole.

Wolf Dancer had stepped from his home just in time to see Running Bear and Deer Shadow return from their outing.

He knew their mother had become alarmed that they had not yet returned home, and Wolf Dancer was also concerned for them. He had seen their mother, Moon Beam, step from her hut more than once to look toward the spot where the Wind Clan's pirogues were always beached.

For most of the day, Moon Beam had been busy in the communal garden and had not seemed to notice her children's lengthy absence.

But when she had returned home and they still

were not there, Wolf Dancer knew she was concerned, as was he. The swamp held much danger in its midst. Two young braves could disappear within it and never be found.

Moon Beam rushed outside and embraced both of her sons at the same time, clutching them near to her heart.

Wolf Dancer went to them just as the young braves' mother asked her sons where they had been for so long. They had done this more than once of late, she scolded.

When neither boy seemed ready to explain their strange behavior, Wolf Dancer placed a hand on each child's shoulder.

"Give your mother an answer," Wolf Dancer said, frowning from one brave to the other as the moon slid slowly up into the sky. At this moment he was taking on the duty of their father, who was no longer with them due to a lethal snakebite one moon ago.

The huge outdoor fire now cast a soft glow over the village. The smell of the food that had been cooked over the lodge fires was fading. The evening meal had long since passed, without the two young braves to participate in it. That alone had been cause for alarm, for they always were home for the evening meal.

Running Bear hung his head to avoid eye contact with his chief and his mother, as did Deer Shadow.

But though they would not meet Wolf Dancer's eyes, they knew they must reveal where they had been, and why.

Deer Shadow jerked his head up and gazed with wavering eyes at his chief's. "We meant no harm," he stammered. "It was something that seemed full of adventure and fun while we were putting our plan together. Since our father's death, everything has been so . . . so—"

"Tell me what you did," Wolf Dancer said tightly, interrupting Deer Shadow. "Now. And stop stammering like someone who does not know the skills of speaking. What have you braves done that makes you look and act so guilty? Is it something that will bring danger to our village?"

Almost in the same breath, Running Bear and Deer Shadow blurted out the truth. As they spoke, many of their friends and neighbors were coming from their homes to see what had caused their chief's voice to rise above its usual level.

"We know now that we should not have done it," Running Bear said, swallowing hard. "And we never meant to harm the girl, just to talk with her and share our customs with her. We were going to let her return to her home tomorrow."

"Do you mean you left this defenseless girl alone in your . . . your . . . tree house tonight?" Moon Beam gasped, her voice trembling with emotion. The white panther stalks the Everglades both day and night, as well as many other things that could . . . more than likely will . . . harm the poor child."

"I will not take the time to hear any more of your excuses about what you have wrongly done," Wolf Dancer said harshly. "Take me to her. Immediately!"

After having heard their description of the young girl, Wolf Dancer had no doubt who she was. He knew she must be the daughter of the woman who intrigued him so, for he had seen the child with her.

He could only imagine what was going on in this mother's mind . . . a crazed sort of grief over the unexplained disappearance of a beloved child.

He had to make this right for her. He only prayed he wasn't too late. It would take only one snakebite to end the girl's life.

And if that happened, he knew the child's mother would be inconsolable. She might even bring the soldiers from Fort James into his village, resulting in all of Wolf Dancer's people being removed to the reservation where so many other Seminole people now lived.

If he had to live there, penned up like an animal, everything within him—hope, trust, happiness—would die. His life would end as surely as if he had been shot by a poisoned arrow.

His people might pay dearly for the misguided acts of these two young braves.

"Take me to her," Wolf Dancer said, ready to leave. He stopped abruptly when he saw Joshua standing outside the hut that had been assigned to him, a home for as long as the black man wanted it.

Wolf Dancer hurried over to Joshua. He quickly explained to him what had happened.

He saw immediate fear in Joshua's eyes.

"Will you come with me?" Wolf Dancer asked, knowing that the black man was well enough now to accompany him. "The girl who has been wronged is one you know very well. It would be good if you were there to assure her that she is no longer in danger, that the two young braves who wronged her did so only out of curiosity, and that they acted without the knowledge of the Wind Clan as a whole."

Wolf Dancer hoped that Joshua would see the need of his being there when they found the wronged girl. He hoped Joshua could help calm her.

"Yessuh, I'll go with you," Joshua said.

He was now dressed far differently than he had ever before been dressed. He was no longer in raggedy clothes that the white owners of the plantation gave him. He wore the same type of buckskin as all the other men in the Seminole village.

He especially enjoyed wearing the tunic that had been made from Spanish moss. He liked the feel of it against his dark, smooth skin.

He also had exchanged his worn-out shoes for moccasins.

He now felt more Indian than black. And he felt special. He had a true friend now, and that friend was a powerful Seminole chief.

Joshua was the only man that Wolf Dancer asked to accompany him.

The two men, along with Running Bear and Deer Shadow, hurried to the beached pirogues while everyone else stayed behind, whispering about why two of their young braves would do something so foolhardy.

Moon Beam stood away from them all, ashamed.

At the tree house, beneath the flickering light of the one torch attached to the wall, Dorey was finally able to slide free of the thongs at her wrists, then quickly untie those at her ankles.

Full darkness had come, making the Everglades pitch-black and frightening.

Everywhere outside the tree house, Dorey could now hear the night sounds of the swamp, but she was not able to identify any of them.

"No matter how afraid I am, I must find my way home," Dorey whispered to herself.

Her heart pounded at the very thought of leaving what safety she might have high above the water and land, in the tree house the two Indian braves had erected.

"Why would they do this?" Dorey said, this time out loud. She was glad to hear her own voice in the darkness. Strange how that made her feel not so alone!

No matter why the boys had done this, Dorey knew she must find her way home. She didn't want to be in this tree house when the braves returned.

She'd show them a thing or two about abducting a white girl!

Perhaps they thought a girl her age would be easily kept at their tree house. She would prove them wrong.

Her knees trembling and weak, she grabbed the

torch and threw aside the netting that had at least kept the mosquitoes at bay. Then, stumbling on the hem of her dress, she made her way slowly down the steps that led from the tree house.

Finally she was back on the ground.

But suddenly she realized that in the darkness she was quite disoriented. She had no idea which way to go.

Now that she was looking at the shine of the water, where traces of moonglow crept through the leaves of the trees overhead, she saw that at this particular place, the avenues of water led in many different directions.

She had no idea which way to go in order to get home.

And she had no canoe to travel in.

Carrying the torch, she walked on whatever dry land she could find.

She saw eyes in the dark shadows of the trees. She feared she would not last long, out there in the swamp all alone.

Then she screamed as she slid unexpectedly into the water. The grasses of the marsh rose above her head while muck sucked at her feet.

After much scrambling, she was finally able to get back on dry land, although her shoes were soaked and felt strangely heavy on her feet as mud pulled at them with each step she took.

She winced and covered a scream behind a hand when she saw a group of strange lights rising into the air. By, the flickering light of the torch, which she had miraculously been able to hold on to when she slid into the water, revealed to her that what she had seen was only a swarm of mosquitoes.

Sighing, fighting off despair as well as mounting fear, Dorey stumbled onward, the skirt of her wet dress tangling around her legs, threatening to trip her again.

But she still managed to travel onward until she stumbled over something.

The torch revealed that it was her own canoe!

Before the young braves had gone home, they must have found her canoe. They had taken the time to partially hide it by burying it partway in the sand.

She thrust the handle of the torch into the sand, and, breathing hard, her heart pounding in her chest from both the effort and excitement of having found her canoe, she finally managed to uncover it.

She slid it into the water, glad that her paddle was still inside. Unfortunately, she still didn't know which way to go.

She tied the torch to the front end of the canoe, where it gave off enough light for her to begin paddling through the water.

She chose one of the three avenues of travel, hoping it would lead her back to the river.

She trembled as she traveled onward beneath trees where she could see snakes wrapped and coiled around the limbs. She was terrified that one would fall down on her at any moment.

Then she felt faint when she heard the sudden rush of movement as an animal leapt from a tree, a streak of black. She recognized a panther's shrill screech and was glad when she finally saw it slink off away from her canoe.

Relieved that it was no longer a threat, yet unsure of other dangers that might be lurking nearby, Dorey whispered a prayer to her dead father, asking him to somehow protect and help her.

Chapter Eleven

Man is the only animal that blushes,
Or needs to—

—Mark Twain

Ma'am, wake up," Twila said, feeling that she had already waited too long to come and tell her mistress the news about Dorey. "It's Dorey. She ain't come home and it's dark outside."

Those words awakened Lavinia with a start and caused a knot of fear in the pit of her stomach.

She gazed up at Twila, who held a candleholder with a lone candle in it, its flame flickering.

"She's not home yet?" Lavinia said, her voice full of fear.

Lavinia looked quickly at the windows beside her bed. She had opened the shutters early in the morning and had not closed them, which she didn't usually do until late evening.

When she saw how dark it was outside, she threw her blanket back, stood up, and scurried around the room, dressing in clothes she had discarded in order to rest more comfortably.

She had discovered of late that pretending to be ill and bed-ridden actually made her feel ill. Getting no exercise, and not going outside for fresh air, did that to her.

She was used to being out-of-doors for the better part of the day, supervising the staff or working in her garden. When her husband had been alive, he and Dorey joined her in the early evening, first to eat at the dining table and then to sit on the verandah in summer or beside a fire in winter.

Lavinia always loved the stories that her husband made up to tell Dorey when their daughter was smaller. After Dorey outgrew storytelling, they all played board games. Dorey was usually the victor, or thought she was.

Lavinia and Virgil had become practiced at pretending to lose, even though they both had begun to realize that wasn't a good thing for their daughter.

She needed true competition in order to get along in life with others.

When Virgil had first won a board game against Dorey, the child had been immensely disappointed, but then had begun to enjoy the competition more if she lost now and then.

Genuine competition made her want to play more often in order to show her parents that she could win without their giving the victory to her.

Yes, Dorey had been clever enough to figure out what they were doing long before they realized she was on to them.

"And now she might be lost in the swamps?" Lavinia said, her voice breaking with emotion as she slid the tail end of her long-sleeved white blouse into her skirt.

Lavinia would no longer hide away in her bedroom. Look where it had gotten her!

Flinging her golden hair over her shoulders, she went to the table beside her bed and pulled out the drawer. She grabbed up her tiny, pearl-handled pistol, loaded it, then thrust it into the pocket of her skirt.

Now she needed her sheathed knife. She had to be protected in as many ways as possible since she would surely have to go into the dangerous waters of the Everglades.

She opened another drawer and removed her knife, securing it at the left side of her skirt.

"Let's go, Twila," she said, hurrying to the door. Twila joined her as she left the room and ran to the staircase.

Lavinia was afraid that they might run into Hiram at any moment, but the house was quiet, although well lit by candles in wall sconces and beautiful crystal chandeliers.

"Where's Hiram?" Lavinia asked as Twila ran down the stairs beside her.

"He ain't come home yet," Twila said breathlessly as the foot of the winding staircase was finally reached. "I heard him mention Fort James to his overseer. That might be where he is."

"Well, it truly doesn't matter," Lavinia said, hurrying on to the front door. Just as she grabbed the doorknob, she stopped and gazed intently at Twila. "Why on earth didn't you come sooner to awaken me? You knew when Dorey was expected home. When that sun started setting, you should have come and told me she hadn't returned yet from her canoeing. Lordy be, Twila, she should have been home long ago. She knows the dangers of the Everglades. And so do you."

"I'se sorry, ma'am," Twila said, lowering her eyes.

"Then why didn't you come and awaken me sooner?" Lavinia asked, opening the door and peering out into the ghostly night.

"I was afraid to," Twila said, swallowing hard. "Massa Hiram would say it wasn't my place to come and tell you anything, and I didn't want to be whipped by Massa Hiram's whip. You knows he uses it when he gets de chance."

Lavinia turned to Twila and placed her hands on the child's frail shoulders. "Listen to me, Twila," she said flatly. "Now that my husband is gone, I'm in charge. I . . . I . . . just seem to have forgotten that I was. I never should have hidden away in my room like a scared kitten. I shall no longer do that. And just let Hiram try something with you, or me, or Dorey. I'll shoot him."

She turned and looked past Twila at the gun case hanging in the hall.

She hurried and opened the case, grabbed a rifle, loaded it, then went back to the door and opened it again.

"You come with me, Twila," she said. "You shall hold a lantern in the canoe as I paddle. We're going to search for Dorey."

"Me?" Twila said, wide-eyed. "I ain't nevah been in a canoe before."

"You won't be able to say that after tonight,

because you are going with me," Lavinia said. She determinedly took Twila by a hand and hurried with her out into the dark. "I need you to hold the lantern while we search for Dorey. I won't return home without her."

They ran to the stable that sat back from the house and hurried inside.

Lavinia snatched up one of the lanterns that the stable boy had lit for Hiram's return and ran with it down to the river, followed by Twila.

Soon they were traveling down the dark channel of water, Twila in the front, lighting the way with the lantern. The light revealed that her whole body was trembling with fear.

"You will be much safer with me, Twila, than at the plantation," Lavinia said to reassure the child.

Lavinia silently paddled down the cooling stretch of water that seemed to go on endlessly before her. Her eyes searched constantly through the darkness, and she shuddered as the canoe entered the Everglades.

When she heard the screech of a panther somewhere deep in the thickness of the trees, Lavinia fought off debilitating fear. She knew that more than one panther roamed this swampy land.

Lavinia did not fear the mysterious white panther. But there were other panthers out there, black ones that would not hesitate to pounce on her and Twila.

"Twila, keep that light high enough to penetrate the foliage alongside the water," Lavinia said, not missing a stroke with the paddle.

The rifle was close by, resting against the inside of the canoe, ready to fire, if needed.

"We've got to find Dorey," Lavinia went on. "We must!"

"I feel so guilty for havin' put off tellin' you that Dorey didn't come home when she should have," Twila said, tears spilling from her eyes and half blinding her. "But I am so afraid of Massa Hiram. I'm just waitin' for him to run me off your home now that my pappy is gone. You knows how he must hate me bein' there."

"Just remember that I also have a say in the matter," Lavinia said, again thrust back in time to the moment when she saw Hiram carrying Virgil in his arms.

Somehow it still did not seem real . . . that Virgil was gone from her life.

Heaven forbid if she were to lose her precious Dorey, too!

Chapter Twelve

Ask me no more; thy fate and
Mine are seal'd.
I strove against the stream and
All in vain.

—Alfred, Lord Tennyson

The flame of the torch which had been tied to the front of Dorey's canoe fluttered in the soft breeze, casting wavering light around the canoe and into the water.

As Dorey paddled onward with the light of the torch her only guide, and with fear her only companion, relief flooded her when she suddenly saw a golden glow up ahead in the low-hanging clouds. Surely that light came from the reflection of an outdoor fire.

She was even now aware of the savory smell of roasted meat, making her stomach growl fiercely. She had not taken time to eat the fruit the two young braves had left in the tree house for her.

The urge to escape had been the strongest drive she felt at the time, not for food.

Thus far she had escaped being attacked by panthers, alligators, or snakes, but she had almost lost hope of finding civilization again as she became more and more lost in the maze of swampy waterways.

Now she finally began to believe she might survive after all. Following the light in the sky, she paddled harder.

When she rounded a bend in the river, she saw an island that looked as though it had been magically placed there by God for her to find.

And then a thought came to her that gave her mixed feelings. This was surely the hidden island that so many people talked about.

This must be Mystic Island!

From what she knew, a lone clan of Seminole had escaped to this island when the American government began rounding up Indians to send them to reservations.

This Seminole clan had eluded the American soldiers, and had made their home where no one dared venture . . . where a white panther was rumored to keep guard over the island.

And now she had happened upon it.

Fear seemed to have numbed her insides at the thought of how she might be treated if the Seminole people were to see her so close to their private domain. But she had no choice except to land on the island and find her way to a place where she could hide until she figured out how to find her way back home.

Surely the island was large enough for one more person.

She grabbed the torch and lowered the flames into

the water, extinguishing them so that no one would notice her approach.

She paused awhile longer as she tried to get her bearings and decide where to beach the canoe. From what she could see beneath the fitful light of the moon, this was a large island.

But the view of the village itself was hidden by thick brush and tall trees, hung with beautiful lacy moss.

She had no idea where she should go on the island once she left the canoe, and only hoped that no one saw her.

She was afraid, yet knew she must find shelter on the island somehow. She must hide from her two captors, for surely the young braves made their home on Mystic Island.

There were no other Indian villages near her home.

Her pulse racing, her throat dry from fear, Dorey paddled onward.

Her fingers trembled as she clutched the paddle.

She had spotted a deserted section of sandy beach. There were no other canoes beached there, so it seemed unlikely that hers would be found.

After she had finally landed, she began to make her way through the thick brush. The moon came out from behind the clouds, providing enough light for her to see by.

It seemed forever before she came to a clearing, where she found herself at the edge of a huge garden. Shoulder-high corn was the most prominent crop growing there.

She found shelter amid the cornstalks as she ran

onward, then stopped and stared when she came to the edge of the cornfield and saw many dome-shaped homes, and a huge fire burning in the center of the village.

She could hear voices but she didn't see anyone. It seemed that everyone had retired for the night in their lodges.

That worked in Dorey's favor. There was a good chance she would be able to find a place to stay the night without being discovered.

She knew she didn't want to sleep on the ground, not where wild animals might sniff her out during the night.

She stepped farther from the cornfield, her eyes searching around her. And then she saw something promising.

It was another dome-shaped house, located just past the garden, but it was built high on a platform. A ladder leaned against it to provide access.

There was no lamplight coming from within, nor any fire, so she gathered that it wasn't a place where people lived.

With a sigh of relief, Dorey scampered up the steps of the ladder.

When she reached the door that led into the house, she hurried inside, then stopped and gazed slowly around her.

The moonlight coming through the open door revealed that this was a storage place of some sort, probably for harvested crops. During her quiet hours of reading in bed at night, she had found the study of Indians interesting, especially since her family had moved to the plantation, where Seminole people lived nearby.

During her reading about the Seminole, she had discovered that their harvested crops were stored in a place called a *garita*.

She was glad to have found not only a place to hide, but also one where there might be something to eat.

In the next moment she stifled a scream behind a hand as a mouse scampered from hiding. It fled through the door, just past Dorey's feet.

Grateful that she had had the sense to cover her mouth when she screamed, and relieved that the mouse had disappeared, Dorey crept further into the house. She found herself staring down at various kinds of melons stored among other foods there.

The sight made her belly growl, and without any more thought of being afraid, Dorey sat down on the wooden floor and reached for a delicious-looking golden melon.

She broke it open and gobbled up big bites of the juicy fruit. She thought she had never tasted anything so wonderfully delicious. But then again, never had she been so hungry either.

She felt blessed to have found this place.

Once her hunger was sated, Dorey realized just how much today's adventure had taken out of her. She was absolutely worn out.

In her exhaustion, her fear was forgotten.

She felt safe here, at least until tomorrow when the people of this village would begin their daily chores, which might include bringing crops up into their storage house.

But she would worry about that later.

Now she needed sleep.

She wouldn't even worry about mice. Usually mice were more afraid of humans than humans were afraid of them.

She searched around and found a pile of pelts and blankets.

She closed the door, then curled up in the blankets and fell asleep as the moon poured its light down through the cracks in the ceiling.

She would worry about tomorrow . . . tomorrow!

Chapter Thirteen

Man's love is of man's life
A thing apart,
'Tis woman's whole existence.

—Lord Byron

Lavinia was downhearted that she had found no trace of Dorey anywhere. And the hour was getting later and later.

She had traveled much farther from her home than she knew was safe. She paused in her paddling and hung her head.

The light from the lantern that Twila held revealed to the girl the despair on Lavinia's face. It matched the feeling of hopelessness that Twila, too, was feeling at having not found Dorey.

"She's gone, Twila," Lavinia said, her voice breaking. "She seems to have disappeared into thin air."

"Watch out, ma'am!" Twila suddenly screamed.

But it was already too late. A snake had uncoiled itself from an overhead limb and tumbled down onto Lavinia.

It quickly bit her on the arm, then slid away over the side of the canoe and into the water.

By the light of the lamp reflecting in the water, Twila watched, stunned, as the snake slithered away.

Then she turned and stared disbelievingly at Lavinia. Her mistress was clutching her arm where the snake had bitten her.

"Take the knife from my sheath, Twila," Lavinia said, already feeling dizzy from the poison spreading through her bloodstream. "Do . . . what . . . you've been . . . taught to do in case of a snakebite."

Twila still only stared.

But when Lavinia fell forward in a faint, her hand falling free of the snakebite, Twila knew exactly what she must do.

Her mammy and pappy, as well as Lavinia, had told her what to do if she was ever bitten by a snake.

Her heart pounding, hoping that she remembered those instructions correctly, and that she had the courage to do what she must in order to save Lavinia's life, Twila set the lantern on the floor of the canoe close to Lavinia. Then she fell to her knees beside her.

Twila slowly turned Lavinia over so that she lay on her back.

Lavinia's eyes were tightly closed, and Twila feared that she might already be dying. So many snakes in this area were poisonous.

She knew what she must do. And quickly!

Her fingers trembling, Twila first tore the sleeve of Lavinia's blouse away from the bite. Blood was oozing from it.

She then took Lavinia's knife from its sheath.

She gazed heavenward. "Sweet Jesus, have mercy and guide me to do what's right for Lavinia," she prayed. "Guide my hand, Jesus. Please guide my hand."

No matter how much praying she might do, Twila knew that nothing was going to stop her hand from trembling as she placed the blade to the wound.

She continued praying beneath her breath, over and over again, as she cut into Lavinia's delicate flesh.

Then she dropped the knife.

Trembling from her head to her toes, Twila leaned over and placed her mouth on the wound. She almost vomited from the vile taste of the blood. But she did what she knew must be done.

Twila sucked, then spit, sucked, then spit, until she had gotten all the venom she could from the wound.

She grabbed the paddle, sat down on the seat, and began drawing the paddle frantically through the water.

Everything was so dark around her. The light of the moon could not penetrate the thick foliage here, and the lantern made only a feeble glow. She feared she would be next to be attacked.

The river had narrowed somewhat, and she could see green eyes here and there peering at her from the darkness along the riverbank.

Twila had no skill to turn the canoe around, so she continued paddling the canoe forward. Her only hope was that eventually she might run into that island she had heard so much about . . . Mystic Island, the home of the Seminole.

She was more afraid of Lavinia dying than of coming face-to-face with Indians.

Fear held her in its grip, and Twila swallowed hard. She fought back more tears as she traveled down the river.

Her eyes widened when she saw the light of a torch up ahead; it was coming toward her on the river!

Someone else was on the river tonight, and she didn't care who it was, only prayed they would offer help.

Twila began screaming "Help" over and over again as she continued to paddle.

She felt hopeful now as the light from the torch in the other canoe came closer and closer. Finally she could make out someone sitting in that canoe.

And then her eyes widened and her heart soared with happiness. The torch revealed someone that she could hardly believe!

Her pappy!

He was in the canoe with an Indian warrior and two young boys.

She dropped the paddle and held the lantern up as high as she could so that her pappy and those with him could see her.

"Pappy!" she cried. "Pappy! I be here in de canoe. Pappy! You ain't dead!"

"Twila?"

Hearing her father's voice, knowing that he was alive after all, and oh, so close, Twila began crying and waving the lantern. "Pappy, oh, Pappy, it is me," she cried. "It's Twila!"

Wolf Dancer gazed at the child, astonished to see her there, alone, in waters that could be treacherous to adults, let alone children.

Had she escaped the plantation? Was she running away from her master?

The realization that this was Joshua's daughter made Wolf Dancer smile. With one more stroke of his paddle he brought his canoe up to the side of the one in which Twila was kneeling.

Joshua lifted Twila from it after she placed the lantern at the bottom of her canoe. He hugged her, assuring her that he was very much alive.

Now that the lantern was on the floor of the canoe, Wolf Dancer was stunned at who else he saw. It was the white woman.

She was stretched out on the bottom of the canoe, unconscious, one sleeve of her blouse ripped open, revealing a wound to his searching eyes.

"She was bit by a snake," Twila cried. "Please save her. Please?"

She clung to her father as he hugged her tightly. It was a miracle that in her desperation to find someone to help Lavinia, she had found her very own pappy, alive and well!

She gazed bashfully at the two young braves who sat together quietly at the far end of the canoe.

She then looked at her father again.

"I did what I could for Lavinia, Pappy, but was it enough?" Twila asked anxiously. "Is she gonna die? Please don't allow it."

Wolf Dancer understood the urgency of the situation now that he'd heard what had happened.

He moved into the canoe with Lavinia.

He nodded at Joshua. "Take the young braves and your daughter back to the village in my canoe. I will follow in this one," he said quickly.

"Please tell me she's not gonna die," Twila cried, looking down at Lavinia, and then up at the Indian.

"Just hush, darlin'," Joshua said. He understood the seriousness of this situation and knew not to disturb Wolf Dancer. "Chief Wolf Dancer knows what to do."

He put Twila on the seat behind him, then picked up the paddle and set out ahead of Wolf Dancer, paddling back toward the village.

Not missing a stroke with his paddle, Wolf Dancer sent his canoe swiftly through the water, his eyes glancing time and again at Lavinia. As long as he could see her breathing, he knew she was alive.

He looked up at Joshua, glad that he was strong enough to man the paddle as he continued ahead of Wolf Dancer's canoe. When Wolf Dancer had given him the job, he wasn't certain.

But he should have known that Joshua could do it. The former slave was very muscular and had regained most of his strength.

Wolf Dancer glared at the two young braves, then looked ahead again, focusing on the business at hand. He would see to the young braves later.

"Chil', why were you and Lavinia out at night in dese dangerous waters so far from home?" Joshua asked, still rhythmically pulling the paddle through the water.

"It's Dorey," Twila said, gulping hard at the

thought that she might never see her friend again. "She's missin'. She went canoein' and nevah came home again. Lavinia and I were lookin' for her."

"Dorey?" Joshua said, glancing quickly over his shoulder at Twila. "Chil', she's who we were lookin' for."

"You were?" Twila asked, her eyes widening. "How did you know . . . ?"

"It's quite a long story, and one that I'll tell you later," Joshua said.

He looked past her at the two young braves, whose faces were pale with guilt. He thought about Lavinia, wondering if he would ever hear the sweetness of her voice again, or her laughter. If she dies, he thought, those boys the same as killed her.

"Let's just get Lavinia where she can be seen to," Joshua said, putting the boys from his mind as best he could. "I just hope we be in time."

"Where we goin', Pappy?" Twila asked, looking ahead and into the darkness.

"To Mystic Island, tha's where," Joshua said. "And we're almost there. The shaman at Mystic Island will care for Lavinia. He'll make her well again. He's de one who saved your pappy from de arrow wound."

"You do seem well," Twila said. "I thought you were dead. Massa Hiram said that you were."

"Yep, I imagine tha's what dat man thought," Joshua said sarcastically. "But as you can see, I'se well."

"How'd you get wounded, Pappy? By who?" Twila asked.

"It's bes' that I tells you later, Twila," Joshua said thickly. "Lavinia is all tha's important for now. We must get her to de shaman so that he can save her."

Feeling eyes on her, Twila looked over her shoulder at the two young braves, who suddenly lowered their eyes again.

"Pappy, why did those two boys come with you and Chief Wolf Dancer while you were lookin' for Dorey?" Twila asked, gazing at her father as he looked over his shoulder at her.

He saw that she would not rest until she knew why the boys were there, so he proceeded to tell her.

"De boys stole her away and put her in a tree house."

Twila gasped, looking over her shoulder again at the young braves, who continued to avoid her eyes by looking down at the floor of the canoe.

"A tree house," Joshua repeated. "Dey built a house in a tree and took sweet Dorey there. They had planned to keep her there for a while."

"Why would dey do dat?" Twila asked.

"Because dey were all confused in their heads, dat's why," Joshua grumbled. "But somehow she got herself free, and dat's why we're looking for her. Now hush, Twila. I must put my mind on this paddling and getting the canoe to de island."

"I be quiet," Twila said softly, oh, so glad that her pappy had found her and Lavinia.

But it saddened her that Dorey was still out in the swamp somewhere all alone, in danger.

Twila was afraid that no one would ever see sweet Dorey again.

"Twila," Joshua said, breaking the silence this time. "I was gonna come for you and your mammy soon, but until now, I didn't have enough strength to do dat. I'm glad you's safely away from Hiram Price. You's never goin dere again. I'll go soon and rescue yore mammy from the tyrant, too."

Twila suddenly broke into tears. "Pappy, you cain't do that," she sobbed. "You cain't go for Mammy. She ain't alive no more."

Josuha flinched as though he had been shot. He froze. His heart seemed to have suddenly been wrenched from his chest. "Yore mammy . . . is . . . dead?" he gasped, then seeing Wolf Dancer coming up quickly behind him in the other canoe, he continued on toward the island.

"Massa Hiram killed Mammy," Twila cried, then went on and told him how she had died, and why.

Joshua cursed beneath his breath, swearing that he would see to that evil man's death.

"He'll pay, Twila," Joshua swore. "Daughter, he'll pay for that sin against yore mammy. I'll see to dat, personally."

Twila wiped the tears from her eyes just as she saw a glow of orange in the sky. It came from the outdoor fire in the Seminole village, which burned high and bright.

She was a little afraid, for she had heard ghastly tales of what the red men did to people they hated. But she made herself remember that neither she nor her pappy had done anything against these Indians, to make the Seminole want to harm them.

In fact, she had came face-to-face with their chief and she believed him to be a man of kindness.

No. She wasn't afraid, only anxious. She longed to see Lavinia awake and smiling again!

Oh, how badly she wanted to see Dorey!

Chapter Fourteen

Be mine, as I am yours,
Forever.

—*Robert Graves*

As soon as the canoes touched the shore of Mystic Island, Wolf Dancer gathered Lavinia in his arms and ran through the thick vegetation.

He couldn't believe that the gods had crossed his path with hers in such a way. He had thought about her so often, and so badly wanted her to be his.

He knew her snakebite could be lethal, but he would not believe that he had just received her into his arms only to lose her to death's grip. He had lost his precious bride to the jaws of an alligator after they'd spent only one night together as man and wife. He would not even consider losing this woman.

As soon as he reached the outskirts of the village, Wolf Dancer took Lavinia to Shining Soul's hut.

He hurried inside with his precious unconscious burden still snugly held against his powerful chest, his muscled arms holding her securely.

Joshua and Twila ran into the lodge behind Wolf Dancer, but stopped just inside the door when they saw Shining Soul rise to his feet.

"She is suffering from a snakebite," Wolf Dancer explained. He gently placed Lavinia on a thick pallet of furs near the softly burning fire in the center of the room.

"What is her name?" Shining Soul asked as he reached for his bag of medicines, stopping only long enough to put on his magic owl hat. He would need all the magic he could conjure up this time, for the woman looked as though she might already be too near death to save.

"Lavinia," Wolf Dancer said. "Her name is Lavinia Price. She is the mistress of the huge, pillared white plantation house that I told you about. The woman and her husband moved into it not so long ago."

"If she has a husband, why did you not take her to him?" Shining Soul asked, casting Wolf Dancer a half glance as he positioned himself beside Lavinia. "Would not her husband have wanted to care for her?"

"Her husband no longer lives," Wolf Dancer said thickly. "But were he still alive, I would still have brought her to you for your special medicines. I do not believe a white man's medicine would be able to save her from such a bite as this. I have faith in you, only you, Shining Soul."

"I will do as my magic allows me to do," Shining Soul said, already preparing powdered sumac leaves and the root of the pallaganghy together in one of his wooden vials.

He poured some warm water into the mixture and stirred, then gently began applying the concoction to Lavinia's open wound.

Not planning to leave the side of the woman anytime soon, Wolf Dancer sat down and folded his legs before him. He wanted to be there should she awaken, to make certain she was not afraid of her surroundings.

His eyes never left Lavinia as he watched for movement beneath her lids that might be a sign she was awakening. It was important for her to awaken soon, or she might not wake again, ever.

He worried when she continued to sleep soundly, and he noticed how pale she had become since the snakebite.

Although she was a white woman with golden hair and pale skin, when he had first seen her he had observed that she had been slightly tanned by the sun. Obviously she often worked outside beneath the sun in her garden of flowers.

He had noticed those brown dots across the bridge of her nose that he knew whites called "freckles." He found them fascinating and thought they seemed to make Lavinia look more innocent and beautiful.

Joshua and Twila stood just inside the door. Joshua gently clasped Twila's small hand.

"Pappy, why does that strange-looking Indian wear an owl on his head?" Twila whispered only loudly enough for her father to hear. "And look at his strange robe. It looks like something made by magic with drawings of things you only see in the sky."

"As for the owl, I sees it as a magic owl," Joshua whispered back as he leaned down closer to Twila's ear.

He did not want to disturb the magic of the shaman, magic that had worked very well on Joshua himself.

"I was told by Wolf Dancer, when I asked him about the owl hat, that the owl is the Seminole symbol for a doctor," Joshua explained. "Just watch him, Twila. You will see a man of infinite wisdom and patience. I have never felt a touch as gentle as Shining Soul's. If anyone can save our Lavinia, he's de one."

"You do think Lavinia is going to live?" Twila asked, still seeing how quietly her mistress lay.

Twila's eyes widened when she saw what the old shaman was applying to the wound. It looked like the chalk that she and Dorey had used when they played school.

Dorey. Tears sprang to Twila's eyes to think she'd never see her best friend in the world again! She hated the thought of those two boys mistreating Dorey!

"Daughter, we bes' leave now," Joshua said, his eyes wide as he watched Shining Soul.

The shaman was cleaning the roots of reeds and mashing them into a pulp. He then placed the pulp on Lavinia's wound to draw out foreign substances from it.

The sumac leaves and roots of the pallaganghy

were taken in equal parts and crushed separately again until they were almost a powder.

These were mixed with sumac berries, then all of this was placed in a small pot in the flames of the lodge fire. The mixture would simmer until it was ready for use later.

Joshua knew that in time the shaman would also take another root called the *ouissoucatcki* and grind it into a thin powdery substance. Shining Soul had given it to Joshua to increase his strength, and he would give it to Lavinia when she was finally awake. He would place this mixture in warm water for her to drink.

"Do we have to go, Pappy?" Twila whined as she looked up into his dark eyes. "I'se so worried about Lavinia, I don't think I could stand bein' away from her."

"We aren't needed here, Twila. It's bes' that we go to my home and wait to hear how Lavinia is doin'," Joshua said, already taking Twila by the hand and leading her outside.

"Pappy, you have a house here on Mystic Island?" Twila asked, her eyes wide as they walked away from the shaman's lodge. "A house of yore very own?"

"Yes'm," Joshua said proudly. "And it's a mighty fine one, Twila. You'll see. It's a home like ours back at the plantation nevah was. I wished your mammy could be here to live in it with us."

"And Dorey," Twila said, sobbing. "Where is she, Pappy? Where can Dorey be? Those boys! They should be punished, that's fo' sure."

"I'm certain they're in a mighty bunch of trouble," Joshua said, walking onward with Twila.

Inside the shaman's lodge, Wolf Dancer continued to sit silently by as Shining Soul worked his magic on Lavinia. As he watched, he vowed that after Shining Soul made her well, Wolf Dancer would never let her go!

He doubted that she would want to return to the danger waiting for her back at the plantation. Its new owner was a man who had killed her husband in order to have her!

That man would never be allowed to get near her again.

Surely she would not want to go there after she discovered the truth about her husband's death.

The only person she had left to care about was her daughter. And Dorey was lost in the swamp.

Lavinia was lying somewhere between life and death because of the young braves who had made plans to abduct a white child for their own entertainment. When he and Joshua and the boys had reached the tree house earlier that evening, they had found it empty. Somehow their prisoner had escaped.

He would make sure Running Bear and Deer Shadow understood the wrong they had done, but his main concern now was seeing that Lavinia was alright, and finding the lost child.

Tomorrow he would resume searching for the daughter named Dorey. He would make certain many canoes of warriors were sent out to hunt for her, and he would instruct some of these warriors to go on land and search there, too.

He did not want to think that Dorey might have been swallowed up by the treachery of the Everglades.

He would not think of that possibility. He would believe that the child would be found, just as he believed that his shaman would work a miracle on the child's mother.

He sat quietly by as Shining Soul continued to minister to Lavinia's wound. As he watched he was convinced that this woman was the loveliest on this earth, and she deserved far better than what life had thus far handed her.

She deserved to be happy.

She deserved to have her daughter with her again.

She deserved a husband who would never let her down, in any respect.

And she deserved to see the man who had killed her husband dead.

Wolf Dancer had assigned himself her protector, and he would not let her down.

Now if only she would survive to accept him as such!

Chapter Fifteen

There is a fullness of all things,
Even of sleep and of love.

—Homer

Dorey stood at the door of the *garita*. She had been awakened by a commotion in the village. Afraid that it might be something that would put her in danger, she had crept to the door and peered outside.

The moon had slid behind clouds just as she looked out, making it almost impossible to see.

But the glow from the huge outdoor fire had at least given her a view of a tall Indian carrying a woman to a lodge.

She had seen others, as well, but it was too dark to make anyone out.

She could only conclude that someone in the village had been injured, or had become ill.

Perhaps the hut the woman had been carried to was the home of the village doctor, or the wife of the man carrying her.

The one thing that puzzled Dorey was that when the Indian carried the woman past the huge fire, it had looked as though her skin and hair were pale.

But Dorey had quickly discounted that impression, for she knew, from having heard it said, that no whites were welcome at the Seminole village on Mystic Island.

That was what frightened her. When she made herself known to the inhabitants, which she knew she must do tomorrow, since she had no idea how to get back to her home, how would she be treated?

Would she be sent away with no guidance as to which way to go?

There were so many waterways through the swamp, she was afraid that one of them might lead her into even more dangerous territory than this Indian village. Was she going to die, alone and afraid, amid the Everglades?

Tears of regret filled her eyes. Why had she recklessly traveled so much farther than her mother ever allowed?

Dorey hung her head, wiped her eyes, and went back to hide inside the food hut again.

She curled up in the warm pelts and blankets that she had found in the *garita*. She gathered them all around her, shivering when she recalled that more than one mouse had come up and sniffed at the blankets while she was lying there.

She had to place a hand to her mouth to stifle a scream when she had seen a mouse dreadfully close to her face. When the moon was not hidden behind clouds, she had seen the mouse's beady eyes staring into hers.

She had been so relieved when it lost interest in her and found its way into a storage bin of grain.

So tired, so displeased with herself and the predicament she found herself in, Dorey sighed.

She again closed her eyes and welcomed escape in the black void of sleep.

Not far away, in a hut where soft flames burned in the firepit, a snack of corn cakes was being eaten by Joshua and Twila. Twila sat beside her father, looking slowly around her.

"Pappy, this house the Seminole gave you is so nice, and you say it is yours for as long as you wish to remain on Mystic Island?" Twila crunched on a corn cake, filling the empty void in her belly. She had missed the evening meal when she and Lavinia had left the mansion so hurriedly to look for Dorey.

"Chief Wolf Dancer is a kind man," Joshua said. He stretched his long, lean legs out before him; the new buckskin breeches fit him snugly. "He took me to his shaman, who made me well, and he gave me this home and as much food and as many blankets as I want. They are all free, Twila. I doesn't have to pay anything fo' them. It's like heaven, ain't it, daughter?"

"Pure heaven," Twila sighed, as she looked around her at a bed made of blankets and pelts, enough for her father to give her some for herself when they were ready to sleep.

There were other things of comfort, too: benches upon which to sit if a person so desired, and mats of various colors spread over the wood floor.

There were eating utensils, and jugs of water.

And there was even a bow and a quiver of arrows!

That alone proved how much these people trusted and cared for her pappy!

"I still can't believe that this is all yours, Pappy, for as long as you wish it to be," Twila said. She swallowed her last bite of corn cake. "Can I stay with you? Can we be a family again? Or will it be forbidden? Will I be sent away? Will I have to return to that horrible plantation? With Dorey no longer there and Lavinia ill, perhaps too ill to return there herself, I want to stay here with you, Pappy."

She shivered, then reached for a blanket and wrapped it around her shoulders. "If'n I return to that place where Massa Hiram is in charge of everythin', I don't think I'll last long, Pappy," she murmured. "Without you and Lavinia there to protect me, I 'magine I'd not last for long. Massa Hiram sho' nuff likes his whip and usin' it on we poh slaves."

She broke into hard tears. "Oh, Pappy, where is sweet Dorey?" she cried. "Where could she be? Those mean boys. They did this to our Dorey. They should be the ones at the end of Massa Hiram's nasty whip. I'd laugh while they were bein' whipped, I would."

"Now, now, daughter, don't talk like that," Joshua scolded. "No one deserves to be at the end of that horrible man's whip." He laughed throatily. "But that whip did do one good deed. It took the evil man's eye, it did. I saw it happen. I had to fight off laughin' out loud when I saw that eyeball pop from its socket. What a sight. Yes'm, what a sight."

"I saw it, too," Twila said. "Lordie be, I thought

he'd wet his breeches right on the spot like I'se seen the poh chillen he's whipped do."

"We don't have to worry 'bout that one-eyed scoundrel ever again, Twila," Joshua said. He reached out and wrapped her in his arms. "I know de young chief will allow you to stay with yore pappy and let you share dis house with me. I knows it, Twila."

"That would be pure heaven, Pappy," Twila said, snuggling closer to him. "Now if only we knew Dorey was somewhere safe and that Lavinia would soon be well, we'd have a reason to smile 'gain, Pappy. Wouldn't we?"

"Yes, chil', we've got plenty to smile about, thanks to de young chief," Joshua said thickly. He softly rocked Twila in his arms. "He saved my life, and we've become fast friends. Now dat I know how my sweet wife died, I want to make Hiram pay for not only that crime, but, oh, so many others. Hiram Price is a man without a heart."

"When you speak of him now, you don' call him massa," Twila said, gazing up into her father's dark eyes.

"Tha's cuz he ain't that no mo' to either of us, Twila," Joshua said, gently holding her away from him. He looked her square in the eye. "We're as free as the birds that fly in the sky, Twila. We're free!"

Twila began crying again. "If only Mammy could be with us," she sobbed. "I miss her so much. And Dorey. I'se so afraid for her. There are so many things in the swamp that could kill her." She visibly shuddered. "The white panther. What if dat white devil pounced on our Dorey and . . . and killed her? So many have said how elusive it is, and surely deadlier than anything else in the Everglades, or anywheres else, fo' that matter."

"Chil', stop yore cryin' and frettin' and thinkin' such thoughts," Joshua said. He wiped the tears on her brown cheeks dry with the palms of his hands.

"Pappy, Dorey knew not to go far in her canoe when she went explorin'," Twila said. She snuggled again in her father's arms, relishing their strength wrapped around her. "But today mus' have been different. She went way too far. And now she might've died after escapin' the tree house those mean boys put her in."

"Darlin' Twila, the search for Dorey will resume tomorrow, but tonight, the main concern is Lavinia," he said. "But I trust de shaman will make her well. He has magical powers. I know that as fact, because dat shaman used his powers to get me well. Your pappy was almost on death's doorstep from the wound made by dat arrow. When Hiram shoved me in de river, my blood turned dat river red. Dat evil man laughed as I floated away down de river, fightin' off unconsciousness every inch of de way. He truly thought I was a dead man."

"I'm so glad that you are alright, Pappy," Twila said as she stretched out on her blankets, and Joshua covered her with another one as her eyes began drifting closed. "Pappy, I'm so tired, and so glad to be with you again."

"Sweet Twila, if you had not been in dat canoe with Lavinia, I'd have come fo' you," Joshua said softly. He stroked her hair. "I'd 'ave nevah left you with dat tyrant for any longer than I had to. Every minute I was away from you was pure torture. One nevah knows from one minute to de next what to expect from dat one-eyed demon. How he murdered yore mammy is proof o' dat."

"Mammy, oh, Mammy," Twila whispered as she fell asleep in her father's shadow. His eyes gazed at her as she slept.

"You'll meet your mammy again, sweet chil', as will your pappy, too," he whispered as he stroked his fingers through her long, black hair. "When we all go to heaven, Twila. When we all go to heaven."

Chapter Sixteen

Alas, how love can trifle
With itself!

—William Shakespeare

Lavinia awakened slowly to faint lamplight and the glow of a fire nearby.

She soon realized how feverish she was. Her whole body felt as though it were on fire. Panic filled her at the thought of how ill she was.

Her vision was blurry, yet she could make out two Indian men sitting one on each side of where she lay.

As she slowly came out of the haze and was able to see somewhat better, she noticed that one Indian was younger than the other.

Then her heart seemed to skip several beats. She recognized the younger, more handsome Indian.

She had no doubt that he was the one she had seen resting on a limb of the old oak tree.

Wolf Dancer's heart had pounded inside his chest when he saw Lavinia first struggling to see. Now she was gazing at him intently.

No doubt she was remembering that she had seen him more than once near her home.

Did she also recall . . . the white panther?

He would not think about that. All he cared about was knowing that she was on the road to recovery. He wanted her to feel comfortable with her surroundings and the people who were caring for her.

He was glad that he didn't see fear in her eyes, but instead the same curiosity that had appeared on her face the other times she had seen him watching her. He wanted her to realize that she was most definitely with friends, and soon she would also understand that she was with a man who wanted more than friendship from her.

Yes! He wanted her to be his, so that he could protect her from all future harm.

"What . . . happened . . . ?" Lavinia asked softly, struggling to remember what had brought her to this time and place . . . to him.

Although she was able to recall that she'd seen him more than once near her home, she could not recall much more. Everything else seemed to be blocked from her mind.

She suspected her confusion was a result of the fever that was raging inside her body. She had had soaring temperatures before and knew that they sapped not only her strength but also her memory.

Now that she was so near to the Indian, she was even more awed by him than before. Up close he was much more handsome than from a distance, and she saw such kindness, such caring, in his eyes.

For some reason, she felt safer now than ever before in her life, even safer than she had felt with Virgil.

Although Virgil had been a kind and wonderful man, he had had many weaknesses.

She felt guilty for having such thoughts and cast them from her mind when the Indian moved closer to her and placed the palm of his hand gently on her brow, then drew it away.

She was surprised when he began speaking in perfect English to her.

"You have much fever," Wolf Dancer said gently. "But it should soon be gone. My shaman, who would be called a doctor in your world, sits on your other side. His name is Shining Soul, and he is the one who will make you well and happy again."

He paused, then said, "I am called by the name Wolf Dancer. I am chief of the Wind Clan of Seminole. You are now on my people's island, which is named Mystic Island. All that you have to know now is that you are with friends."

"Mystic Island? Who . . . brought me here?" Lavinia asked, searching his eyes. "Was it not you?"

"Yes, it was I," Wolf Dancer said. "I found you unconscious in a canoe with your small companion who goes by the name Twila. A snake had dropped down from a tree overhead and bitten you."

"I . . . don't . . . remember." Lavinia said, trying hard to recall the events he spoke of. "I don't seem to remember anything about it. Why was I in a canoe with Twila?"

It frustrated her that she could remember so many things past, yet she could not conjure up even a glimmer of memory concerning a trip in a canoe with Twila. She had never gone canoeing with Twila before, so why would she have . . . ?

Suddenly images came to her in quick flashes, and what she remembered made her wince and want to cry out in despair.

Her daughter! She had left the sanctuary of her bedroom to search for Dorey when her daughter had not returned from canoeing.

She now recalled how dark it had been while she was in the canoe, looking desperately for Dorey. She remembered the anguish of each stroke of the paddle through the black water. Despite her efforts, she had never seemed to get any closer to Dorey.

"My Dorey," she suddenly sobbed, tears flooding her eyes. She turned her eyes away from Wolf Dancer. "Oh, Lord, Dorey."

And then she looked quickly back at Wolf Dancer. "Surely Twila told you why we were on the river after dark," she blurted out, trying to see some hopeful sign in the handsome Indian's eyes as she continued telling him what she remembered about that night.

But when she had finished telling him all that she recalled, and he still gave no indication that Dorey had been found, she wanted to curl up and close her eyes and never wake up again.

Seeing her despair and understanding it, because he had suffered such feelings himself, Wolf Dancer wanted to sweep Lavinia into his arms and hold her close to his heart and comfort her.

But he knew that was not the proper thing to do, especially since they were strangers.

Furthermore, he was an Indian and she was white. Such relationships were forbidden in the white world. If an Indian was known to desire a white woman, he would be hunted down by whites and destroyed, perhaps even tortured before being slain.

He could not allow himself to reveal his feelings to her. Not yet.

At this moment, the most important thing to do was comfort her about her daughter and convince her that he would find her and bring her back safely.

"This is what I know . . ." Wolf Dancer said; then he told her all that he'd learned about Dorey; how she had been abducted, by whom, and how she had disappeared.

"No," Lavinia cried, tears again flooding her eyes. "My Dorey is out there in the swamp . . . where . . . there are so many dangers?"

"The search for your daughter will resume at the break of dawn," Wolf Dancer said, still longing to take Lavinia in his arms. He had to remind himself that this was not the time to do so.

Yet in time she would allow herself to welcome his embrace, for he knew that she had feelings for him.

He knew even before she knew!

Shining Soul brought her a wooden cup of white liquid. "Drink this," he said. He held it to her lips with one hand, holding her head up with the other so that she could swallow more easily. "This will ease more than one pain inside you," he said reassuringly.

"It will take away your worry, and allow you to sleep."

Lavinia welcomed anything that could help relieve this gnawing pain of loss, even if it meant drinking something unknown to her. It was better than being awake and knowing that her daughter was out in the Everglades all alone, perhaps even . . .

Her eyes drifted slowly closed as Shining Soul handed the half-empty cup to Wolf Dancer, then gently eased Lavinia's head back down on the pelts.

He reached for a blanket and covered her with it, then sat up again, watching her.

"When she awakens, I hope to have her daughter sitting beside her, waiting to be held in her arms," Wolf Dancer said. "Thank you, Shining Soul, for caring for the woman. She doesn't deserve all of the pain she has been forced to endure these past days. I hope to alleviate at least some of it by bringing her daughter back to her."

"If she does not see her daughter again, she herself may not survive, for it seems that the child is her world," Shining Soul said thickly.

"She deserves far more than she has been given in this world," Wolf Dancer said, slowly rising. "I must go now and inform her friends that she awakened for a short while. I will assure them again that she will be alright."

After leaving Shining Soul, Wolf Dancer went to Joshua's hut and spoke his name outside the closed door. Joshua hurried over and opened it.

He gazed into Wolf Dancer's eyes, the moon's

glow giving him enough light to see by. "Have you brought me news about Lavinia?" he asked, his voice drawn with anxiety.

"She awakened," Wolf Dancer said, seeing how that news lit up Joshua's dark eyes. "But she is asleep again."

"But she is gonna be alright?" Joshua prodded as Twila awakened and came to stand beside him. She reached out and took one of his hands.

"She spoke to me," Wolf Dancer said. "Then I explained to her about her daughter. I told her that I would be searching for the child early in the morning. Then she went to sleep."

He did not tell Joshua and Twila the worst of what had happened, that Lavinia had to be sedated so that she could sleep again.

Sleep was what she needed until better news was brought to her!

"But she is going to be alright?" Twila burst out, searching Wolf Dancer's eyes as he gazed down at her.

"I assure you, she will be alright," Wolf Dancer said. He placed a gentle hand on Twila's shoulder. "I must go now and get some rest, for the morning hours are not far away."

"I will go with you when you leave in the morning," Joshua said. "I want to help search for Dorey."

"I want to go, too," Twila added quickly. "She is my best friend. I want to help find her."

"We'll see," Joshua said, smiling down at her.

"Until tomorrow," Wolf Dancer said, then turned to walk away.

Joshua and Twila called their thanks after him. He gave them a soft smile over his shoulder, then went on his way toward home.

When he passed Shining Soul's hut, he wanted to go and spend the night there, but he knew that rest would benefit him more than sitting and gazing at the sleeping woman whom he now knew he loved with all his being.

Chapter Seventeen

There are two things to aim at in life;
First, to get what you want;
And after that, to enjoy it!

—Logan Smith

After placing his horse in the stable, Hiram stumbled through the dark until he found the steps to his front porch.

He had drunk from his flask of whiskey all the way home from his poker game. He had already imbibed a great deal while playing, and when the flask was empty, he found himself too drunk to continue on. He'd slid off his horse, passed out, and awoke who knew how many hours later.

Now he stumbled on the bottom step, fell, laughed throatily, got up and made it to the second step, then fell again. He was still drunk.

Dizzy, his legs like rubber, he sat down on the step and lowered his face into his hands, then started and opened his eyes quickly when he heard the growl of thunder in the distance.

Hating storms, he rose shakily to his feet and stumbled up the steps and inside the house to the foyer.

Teetering, he glanced up the winding staircase,

thinking it would be quite a feat to tackle in his condition.

But wanting to sleep on a mattress, not a sofa, he grabbed hold of the banister, steadied himself, and began the slow climb.

The wax candles sputtered in the sconces along the staircase wall; the candles had almost burned down.

Still stumbling and now cursing beneath his breath, Hiram continued up the stairs until he finally reached the second-floor landing.

He suddenly recalled what his plans had been before he loaded up on whiskey and passed out.

He had planned to go to Lavinia's bedroom, awaken her, then tell her she had been wrong to avoid him for so long. It was time for her to face up to Virgil's death and consider taking on another husband . . . him!

He was so drunk he wasn't thinking clearly; without stopping to consider how Lavinia would react were he to awaken her almost at daybreak, Hiram wiped the sweat from his brow, then ran both hands up and down the front of his breeches so the sweat would be absorbed there. He had seen Lavinia wince when he touched her with his sweaty hands.

Tonight would be different in many ways. He had decided not only to awaken her, but also to have his way with her. Surely she was as hungry to have a man in her bed as he was for the feel of a woman's soft flesh against his own.

He had often watched as Lavinia went hand in hand to her bedroom with her husband, closing the door and shutting out the world beyond it, which included Hiram Price.

He had closed his one eye and allowed himself to envision what they were doing behind that closed door.

His brother's loud groans of pleasure had reached Hiram, making his hunger for Lavinia almost unbearable.

But he had never heard any sounds coming from Lavinia.

He had assumed that her husband had not been man enough to give her the sort of pleasure she wanted.

Perhaps even tonight she had gone to bed with unfulfilled needs.

"I'll show you what you missed when your husband was alive," Hiram said beneath his breath, stumbling toward Lavinia's closed bedroom door.

The candles along this corridor were also sputtering, the wicks now floating in what was left of what had been tall, stately candles. Reaching Lavinia's door, Hiram stopped, attempting to balancing himself while his head began spinning again.

He grabbed for the door frame and held tightly to it to keep from falling. This was the worst time of all to be this drunk, when he was ready to make a beautiful woman his.

He was becoming sober enough to realize that he'd begun sweating again. He growled as he wiped the wetness from his face, and then ran his hands desperately up and down the legs of his breeches to dry the sweat that he despised even more than Lavinia did.

He had to live with it day in and day out, while she had only to look at it when she was with him.

But even knowing her distaste for the sweat, and perhaps even the man who was cursed with it, nothing would dissuade Hiram from going into her bedroom and letting her know who was boss.

If she didn't cooperate, by gum, he'd go for his whip.

Surely one look at that whip would make her change her mind. She would recognize that a man's loving was preferable to a whipping that might leave scars on her lovely flesh for the rest of her life.

He smiled wickedly as he recalled the many scars he had left on the brown-skinned slaves at the plantation.

And by gum, he planned to add more and more. He'd do whatever it took to show the slaves that he was their master.

His heart began to pound as he placed a hand on the doorknob. Just being this close to Lavinia awakened that part of him that had been denied a woman's touch for far too long.

His loins were on fire and ached unmercifully.

He had grown tired of the big-breasted, perfumed bodies of the prostitutes that were housed in every town he frequented.

Cribs.

Yep, they called those houses cribs.

The whores flaunted their "wares" in windows at the front of the cribs, beckoning for men to come and take their pleasure from them.

None of them compared with Lavinia.

He wanted sweetness when he made love to a woman, and Lavinia was all sweetness!

His sweaty palm slipped on the doorknob, making it difficult to get the door open.

But finally!

The door creaked open!

The room was black inside. The shutters were closed at all of the windows, not allowing any moonlight in to bathe Lavinia's body.

But that didn't matter. He'd feel around and find her.

He'd climb into the bed with her, and should she try to fight him off, he was not too drunk to use his strength to subdue her.

"Lavinia?" he murmured. He laughed beneath his breath. She would be shocked that he'd ignored her warning never to open her bedroom door when it was closed.

"Sweet Lavinia, it's time for you to put an end to your mourning," Hiram said, weaving as he walked into the room, moving in the direction of her bed. "Ol' Hiram is here to make sure you do. I'm gonna give you lovin', Lavinia. I'll show you what a real man is and how your husband lacked the skills of pleasuring a lady. Just you wait and see. Hiram is here for you, Lavinia. Only you."

His knees made sudden contact with the side of the bed, throwing him totally off balance. He laughed as he fell onto the bed, his hands reaching out to stop himself from landing on top of Lavinia.

The strange thing was that he knew he had fallen

near where Lavinia should have been sleeping, yet he did not feel her. His sudden untimely appearance should have awakened and frightened her.

She should be screaming. But the room remained totally silent. He couldn't even hear Lavinia breathing.

"Lavinia?" Hiram mumbled as he steadied himself. He ran his hands all around him, searching for her.

It suddenly came to him like a bolt of lightning that she wasn't there. She wasn't in her bed!

And he hadn't seen her downstairs.

If she'd been awake and heard his clumsy entrance, she would have scolded him for coming home drunk as a skunk!

The thunder rumbled again, and this time much closer, so close, in fact, that he could glimpse the flash of lightning through the slats of the shutters.

This tiny bit of light was all it took for Hiram to see that he was right. Lavinia wasn't there!

Stunned to realize that she wasn't in her bed at this time of night, Hiram stumbled up and went out to the corridor. He leaned against the top railing of the staircase and shouted Lavinia's name.

He shouted loudly enough for her to hear him wherever she might be in the house.

But still there was only silence around him.

"Where are you, Lavinia?" he cried.

He felt a strange emptiness in the pit of his stomach. Had she left him and the plantation to seek a new life elsewhere?

That thought made him want to vomit at first. Then he was overcome by an anger he had rarely felt before, the sort that encompasses a soul.

He stumbled back into her bedroom, opened the shutters at one of the windows, then raised the sash and thrust his head out. "Lavinia, where are you?" he bellowed, his voice echoing back at him.

He gazed heavenward, glad at least that the storm had moved off.

Then he shouted Lavinia's name, over and over again, until his voice was hoarse.

Totally exhausted now, and feeling strangely empty, he stumbled from her room and went to his own, where he fell across his bed. He soon passed out.

Outside, his voice had traveled to the slaves' cabins, and they had gathered together in front of their homes.

They all huddled in one large group, trembling at the fury they'd heard in Hiram's voice.

Fearing the man with every fiber of their being, and knowing that he would take his anger out on the black folk at his plantation, the slaves debated what they should do.

Even Franklin Owen, the white overseer hired by Hiram, came and stood among them, his hands on his hips as he looked from one to the other.

"It's time we show that man a thing or two," Franklin said, his bright red hair picking up the light of a lantern held by one of the slaves. "I've had enough of Hiram Price. He ain't nothin' like his brother Virgil. This man is out for blood if anyone so much as looks at him sideways. I feel too threatened to stick around, and my skin ain't even black like yours. Hiram is a madman. Didn't you just hear him shouting like someone gone crazed?"

"He was shoutin' for Miz Lavinia," one of the women said. "What has happened to her? Where could she be?"

"I saw her leave in a canoe with Twila," another woman said. "As far as I know, they still gone. Even Dorey. All that's left in that big plantation house is those who work there, and Massa Hiram hisself."

"Don't you see?" Franklin said, placing his fists on his hips as he gazed from one slave to another. "Lavinia left because she was afraid of Hiram. Surely she took both children with her."

"But where could dey have gone?" asked Caleb, a tall black man. His wife Nada stood beside him, clinging to his arm.

"I don't know and I'm not stickin' around to find out," Franklin said. He lifted his suitcase. "I'm leavin' now. You all are welcome to go with me. You know that I came by hired buggy but I'll be forced to leave on foot. I can't take the time to arrange for transportation. You can leave on foot with me. I'll see that nothin' bad happens to you as long as you are with me. When we get separated, you are on your own, but at least you will have escaped Hiram. Those of you who want to go with me, step forward. Those that don't, return to your cabins and pay the price when that madman sobers up and sees that some of his slaves and his overseer are gone. Just remember this. You know as well as I that he kills for the pleasure of doin' it."

Caleb looked around the circle of worried men and women. "I ain't goin', nor is my wife Nada," he said stiffly. "I believe that Massa Hiram will not beat us for the wrongdoings of others."

"And surely if we stay, our massa will treat us better," another man said, holding his wife protectively to his side.

"That's your decision. You'll have to live with it," Franklin said. He gestured with a hand. "Come on. Those who want to go with me, come. We'll get far down the road before Hiram wakes up and finds us gone."

Several slaves hurried to follow Franklin as he walked past the huge house and onto the gravel drive that led away from the plantation. Those who stayed behind scurried back inside their cabins.

Caleb smiled at Nada as they stood in the light of a candle in their cabin. "We's done right, Mama," he said. "We's done right."

He looked over his shoulder at his two sons, who were staring back at him, their eyes wide with fear.

That was when Caleb doubted the sanity of what he had just done. But he would stay firm and hope for the best.

He prayed to himself that Lavinia would return home. When she was there, Hiram Price at least maintained the appearance of sanity.

Chapter Eighteen

All for love and nothing for reward.
                    —Edmund Spenser

The morning sun filtered down through cracks in the domed ceiling of the *garita*, settling onto Dorey's face and awakening her with a start.

She leapt to her feet with alarm. When she looked around, she remembered where she was, and why.

She began to tremble, for never had she been as afraid as now. Surely with daylight she would be discovered, for someone in this village would come to the storage house, either to take something from it or bring something there after the women began working in the garden.

But for now, there seemed to be only a stirring of people down below in the village as the Seminole awoke to a new day.

She was so afraid of being discovered. What would these people do to her when they found a stranger in their midst?

If only she could find a way to get back home. Surely by now her mother knew that Dorey had not returned to the plantation. Yet when her mother did realize Dorey was missing, she would be so distraught, she might make herself sick with worry.

Dorey must find a way to get home, and today. She didn't want to cause her mother any more grief than she had to.

Dorey wondered if her mother would go to Fort James to ask Colonel Cox for help locating her daughter. Dorey's father had never had anything good to say about that man. The colonel was known for his corruption.

No, Dorey doubted that her mother would seek his help. Instead, she would probably set out on the river, alone, to try to find Dorey. If her mother found Dorey's abandoned canoe, she would think the worst . . . that her daughter was more than likely dead!

"But, Mama, I'm not," she whispered.

She went to the door and leaned out just far enough so she could look down upon the village. The hut where she had spent the night was higher than all the other buildings except one.

She gazed at the unique home, which was two-storied, yet otherwise similar to the other huts in the village. She wondered if the larger home was the chief's. Wouldn't a chief have better lodging than everyone else?

If so, the chief's home was not far from where Dorey now stood.

"Surely if I'm caught, I'll be taken to the chief," Dorey whispered, still staring at the two-storied building.

She had heard her father speak of a Chief Wolf Dancer, who was said to be young and kind, though they had never actually met. Her father had believed it was best to keep his new neighbors "at arm's length," as he had put it.

Dorey decided she would watch the activity in the village, and at her first opportunity, she would flee back to the river.

She knew it would be easier to find her way back home in daylight. If she could only choose the right waterway that would lead to the main part of Bone River, she could find her way home easily!

She was feeling so hungry, her stomach was growling. She turned and eyed the stores of food that lay everywhere around her.

Now that it was daylight and she could see it all, she was astounded. Last night she had only been able to search with her hands for something she could eat.

When she had found the melons, their golden color revealed to her by the beams of moonlight that came through the cracks in the roof overhead, she thought she had never tasted anything so good. It had been so juicy and delicious, she now hungered for more of the same.

But before she could eat, she must take care of another pressing need. She had to relieve herself, but where could she do that?

She just couldn't find it in herself to do it where the food was stored.

That only left her one other choice!

She must hurry down the ladder to the ground

and rush into the brush, then scramble back up into the *garita* without anyone seeing her.

Her pulse racing, she stepped to the door and peered outside.

She looked near and far for anyone who might catch her on the steps. Fortunately, she saw that hardly anyone was outside yet.

Dorey said a soft prayer before leaving, then hurried down as quickly as possible, attended to her business, and scrambled back up the ladder.

Eager to eat, Dorey plopped down on the floor and broke open a melon, the juice dripping all over her skirt, as it had done last night. She savored the sweet flesh as she chewed and swallowed it.

Then she saw something else that looked interesting: green beans, freshly picked and strung together on a string. Although they would not be as good as when cooked in meat broth, they were another form of nourishment, which she needed to keep her strength up for all that lay ahead of her. She might not be able to find her way home right away. If she got lost farther in the Everglades, she might not have anything fit to eat for days.

She crawled over to the beans and plucked one and then another from the string and ate them. They were hard and crunchy, yet she knew they were good for her, something her mother had always stressed when it came time to sit at the dining table.

Dorey was the sort of child who sometimes just toyed with her food.

But today?

She wished that her mother could see how eagerly

she was eating. And everything she chose was very nutritious.

As she sat there, chewing on the green beans, she was scarcely aware of the increasing sound of voices as people came out of their lodges to begin the day's activities.

All she could think about was finding her way back home. But first she had to find a way to leave the village without being seen.

Until that moment, she had forgotten one important thing: the two young braves who had abducted her and taken her to the tree house.

Surely they would be going to their hideaway this morning. They would discover that she had escaped. They would surely begin looking for her and might see her as she tried to find her way home.

But no matter what, she would be leaving this island. She would just pray that God would be her companion and look out for her. He was all she had to depend on.

Chapter Nineteen

My love for you is mixed throughout my
body,
So hurry to see your lady, like a falcon
Swooping down to its papyrus marsh.
    —Love Songs of The New Kingdom

Joshua! Twila!" Lavinia exclaimed excitedly as she awakened and found them sitting together beside her bed.

Then she saw someone else. Her insides felt strange, a feeling she had never before felt, as she found Wolf Dancer sitting on her other side, his eyes full of concern for her.

She would never forget his loving care of her. It went beyond his just wanting to be certain she didn't die from the snakebite.

She knew when she had seen him that first time in the tree that he felt something special for her.

She had actually felt a connection to him, then, and she felt it now as he sat close beside her. She wanted to reach out and touch him, just to know that he was actually so close to her.

These strange feelings he aroused in her were the ones she should have felt for her husband.

But sad to say, she hadn't felt anything but kindness and affection toward Virgil.

But now?

A host of beautiful emotions seemed to have been awakened inside her at the mere sight of Wolf Dancer.

And he was a proud Seminole chief! His pride in being chief was evident in his demeanor.

"Your fever is gone," Wolf Dancer said, smiling at her and feeling deeply for her, especially now that he had seen how she felt toward those whose skin was black. Her pleasure in seeing Joshua and Twila proved that she was not a prejudiced woman.

She could possibly feel something for him, a Seminole Indian.

He had felt something for her for some time now.

Wolf Dancer had missed seeing Lavinia these past days, when she had not been visible even at the window. He had feared she might have died.

"Yes, your fever is gone," he repeated, so very glad she was alive and well. "And your eyes are clear. How do you feel?"

"I feel wonderful," Lavinia said, slowly sitting up and drawing a blanket around her shoulders. "Thanks to you and your shaman, I believe I am going to live."

Then she gazed at Joshua and Twila. "Joshua, oh, Joshua, you are alive!" she said, reaching out to take one of his hands in hers. "I thought—"

"We all thought he was dead," Twila said, taking her father's other hand and smiling up into his dark eyes. "But he ain't. He was only wounded."

Twila turned grateful eyes to Wolf Dancer. "Chief Wolf Dancer not only saved you, Miz Lavinia, but also my pappy," she murmured. "He found him in a canoe, unconscious, with that dreadful arrow in his shoulder that Massa Hiram shot him with."

"What?" Lavinia gasped. "Hiram . . . shot you, Joshua?"

Realizing that it might not be best to reveal too much to Lavinia while she was still weak from her wound, Joshua decided not to tell her that Hiram had shot not only him but also her husband.

"Yes'm, he done shot me," Joshua said tightly. "He's no good, dat man. Rest now, Lavinia. Don't fret none 'bout what dat man did. I'se goin' to tell you all 'bout it later."

She understood and agreed.

Although she was so much better, she still felt weak and even disoriented at times.

"Yes, later. For now, all that is important, Joshua, is that you are alive," she murmured.

She turned smiling eyes to Twila. "And you, you sweet thing," she said, reaching out and placing a gentle hand on Twila's cheek. "I'm so glad to see you safely with your pappy."

And then sudden alarm entered her eyes and heart and she gripped Joshua's hand harder. "Oh, Lord," she cried. "What of Dorey? Twila, after I was bitten and fell unconscious, did you . . . did . . . you see . . . did you find . . . Dorey?"

But she already knew the answer without hearing it. If Dorey had been found, and was safe, she would be there at her mother's bedside.

Realizing that, Lavinia slowly took her hand from Joshua's and turned her gaze away from them all as tears spilled from her eyes.

"You don't need to say it, Twila," she sobbed. "I already know the answer. If my daughter had been found, she'd be here with me."

Seeing Lavinia's despair, feeling it deep inside his own heart, Wolf Dancer reached a hand out and gently placed it beneath Lavinia's chin.

He slowly turned her face so that they could look into each other's eyes. "Lavinia, we were searching for Dorey when we found you unconscious in your canoe," Wolf Dancer said thickly.

He saw puzzlement in her eyes behind the shine of her tears, and he understood. The circumstances behind Dorey's disappearance were difficult to comprehend. He wasn't certain he could even make it clear to her, himself, were he to tell her from the beginning how the two young braves had abducted Dorey, and why.

"Please tell me everything," Lavinia said, searching his eyes. "I . . . I . . . am alright. I need to hear it. I want to know what you know about Dorey. You do know what's happened to her, don't you? It's there in your eyes and in your voice. Please, oh, please tell me she is alright."

"I cannot tell you that because I myself do not know how she is," Wolf Dancer said.

His reply made her wince and brought even more tears to her eyes. He placed gentle hands to her face and wiped the tears away.

"I am not certain you are well enough to hear

what I am about to tell you," he said, his voice tight. "Perhaps you might want to wait until later."

"No," Lavinia said, swallowing hard. "I want to hear whatever you know, now. This is my daughter we are talking about. If anything has happened to her, I . . . need . . . to know."

She reached a desperate hand to Wolf Dancer and clutched one of his hands. "You must tell me," she said urgently. "Please tell me now."

He knew he had no choice but to tell her what he knew, even though it might turn her against the two young braves who'd caused such sorrow, and possibly against himself and his entire band.

"There are two young Seminole braves . . ." he began and didn't stop until it was all said, even the worst of it—that Dorey seemed to have disappeared into the Everglades and had not been seen again since the boys left her alone in the tree house.

"No!" Lavinia cried, turning away from everyone and sobbing. "No. She can't be dead. Not . . . my . . . Dorey."

Then she turned back to Wolf Dancer. "It is my fault," she cried. "I never should have given her permission to leave our home, especially alone . . . yet I have always trusted that she would be alright."

Then a sudden fire replaced the guilt in her eyes. She sat up straight and gazed directly at Wolf Dancer. "And . . . those . . . two boys?" she demanded. "Where are they? Are they being punished? Do they know the wrong they have done my daughter . . . and me? I may never see my precious Dorey again!"

"The young braves have been shamed for what they did, and they are out in the swamps even as we speak, helping to search for your daughter," Wolf Dancer said, understanding her need for vengeance.

He was going to wait awhile longer before making a decision about what the young braves must do to atone for their reckless behavior.

"Lavinia, for now, all that is important is finding your daughter," Wolf Dancer quickly added.

Tears filled Lavinia's eyes again. "Where can my daughter be?" she asked, feeling sick to her stomach because she was so upset. "Could she have made it back home in the dark during the treacherous hours of night? Or . . . is she lost? Could she have died in the Everglades all alone?"

Suddenly a voice spoke up from outside the shaman's lodge. Shining Soul was away for the moment, saying prayers in private, so Wolf Dancer went to the door and opened it, finding one of his most trusted warriors standing outside.

"Singing Waters, you have left your sentry post," Wolf Dancer said. He gazed intently into his warrior's eyes, seeing trouble in them. "What brings you to your chief?"

"A small canoe has been found beached at the far side of the island," Singing Waters said. "It is not one of our canoes, and no one was found anywhere near it."

Wolf Dancer was filled with sudden alarm, for he had always feared the day when whites might find his village and invade it.

He stepped outside, quickly looked beyond Singing

Waters, and slowly scanned the village. When he saw nothing unusual, he turned back to Singing Waters. "Go," he commanded. "Get several warriors. Tell them what you have seen and instruct them to search every part of Mystic Island."

After Singing Waters left to do his chief's bidding, a new thought came to Wolf Dancer. Could that canoe be the one in which Dorey had traveled? Could Dorey even now be on the island, hiding and afraid?

He went to Lavinia and knelt beside her. "A canoe was found beached on the opposite side of the island," he said, and saw her eyes light up at the possibility he'd just been considering.

"Could it be Dorey's?" she gasped. Wanting to see the canoe herself, she started to get up, but her weak knees buckled and she fell back down onto the bed of pelts.

"If it is, she will be found," Wolf Dancer reassured her. "I will go myself and search the island, to see if she is here. But you must not get your hopes up. The empty canoe might have floated down the river on its own, and the waves might have carried it onto the sandy beach of my island."

He nodded at Joshua. "Come with me," he said. "We shall look together."

Joshua's eyes lit up as he went to stand beside Wolf Dancer.

Lavinia smiled up at Wolf Dancer. "Thank you," she murmured. She found it incredible that this young chief could be so kind to her, when it was whites like herself who had forced his Seminole band into isolation, and others onto reservations. She wished she could somehow find a way to make it up to them, especially Wolf Dancer and his people.

Twila settled down close to Lavinia and held her hand.

"She'll be fine, Miz Lavinia," Twila said optimistically. "I just can't imagine anything happening to our Dorey. She's a strong person. She'll be alright, I just knows it."

"Me too," Lavinia said, yet she was not sure at all that her daughter was even still alive.

Chapter Twenty

Give me a kiss and to that kiss a score.
                    —*Robert Herrick*

The morning air was suddenly filled with a woman's scream. The sound filled Lavinia with alarm.

She looked up questioningly at Wolf Dancer. They could all hear the woman shouting that there was a stranger in the *garita,* in the food supply!

Wolf Dancer and Lavinia exchanged quick glances, both suddenly thinking the same thing, yet not saying it out loud in case it was a false hope. Could the stranger be Dorey?

"I shall go and see," Wolf Dancer said, leaving with Joshua.

Somehow, Lavinia found the strength to get out of bed and make her way to the door. Just as she stepped outside she saw a warrior leading Dorey toward Wolf Dancer. Her daughter's eyes were filled with fear, yet she appeared unharmed.

Lavinia's eyes lit up when Dorey spotted her, and then Dorey saw Twila. She was shocked to see them there. She had spent the night so afraid and alone, and all along, her mother and her best friend in the world had been so near!

"Mama," Dorey cried as she ran toward her, her arms outstretched. "Oh, Mama, I'm so sorry that I didn't listen to you."

"It's alright," Lavinia murmured as Dorey flung herself into her arms and clung to her. "Everything is going to be fine now that I know you are safe and well."

"But you?" Dorey asked, stepping away from her mother and seeing how pale she was. She had felt the weakness of her mother's embrace, and knew that something was wrong. "Mama, how did you ... how did Twila and Joshua get here? Mama, are you alright?" She stopped and stared at the Indian robe her mother wore instead of her own clothes. "Mama, tell me why you are here and whether you are alright."

Wolf Dancer was happy for both the mother and child, that they were reunited and nothing had happened to Dorey while she was lost and alone in the Everglades. But he noticed that Lavinia was struggling to stand. He knew it was too soon for her to be on her feet for any length of time.

Yet he also knew she was well enough to leave the shaman's lodge so that it would be free for others who were ill and needed his magical touch.

"Come with me," he said, hurrying to Lavinia's side and sweeping an arm around her waist. He was glad to feel her relax against him, glad to know she accepted his touch.

He wanted much more than this, and now believed

that she wanted the same. It was in her eyes when she gazed into his. It was in her voice when she talked with him.

"You aren't taking me back into Shining Soul's hut?" Lavinia asked, relishing the strength of his arm around her waist as he walked beside her.

"You are well enough to give up the shaman's care," Wolf Dancer said. He glanced over at Dorey, who fell into step beside her mother, while Joshua and Twila walked behind them.

Then he looked at Lavinia again. "I am taking you to my own home. It is spacious. You will be comfortable there, as will your daughter. There is room enough for us all there."

Dorey was taking all of this in, realizing there was more than just respect between her mother and this handsome man. She believed he must be Chief Wolf Dancer, for he had an air of command about him.

As they made their way through the village, people stepped aside, their eyes on him, showing affection and love. He walked onward toward the larger two-storied home Dorey had seen from the *garita*. She had assumed that this was the chief's home, and she had been right.

"Dorey, oh, Dorey, where have you been?" Lavinia asked as Dorey stepped closer to her side. "I was so afraid for you. Twila and I looked for you in the swamp, but there was no sign of you or your canoe anywhere. And then . . . I . . . had the misfortune of being bitten by a snake. If not for Twila, who sucked the poison out of my wound, and then

Wolf Dancer, who rescued me and took me to his shaman, I would be dead."

"I'm so sorry, Mama," Dorey said, swallowing hard. "I had not meant to travel so far, and then suddenly I was taken captive by two young braves."

"I know all about what they did, and I am sorry you had to go through such an experience," Lavinia said, sliding her free arm around Dorey's tiny waist. "But now we are all going to be alright. Even Joshua. Did you see him, Dorey? Wolf Dancer saved him after he was shot down by an arrow."

Having been so excited to see her mother, Dorey had been aware of nothing else. Now she realized that Joshua was there and that he was alive, when all along no one thought they would ever see him again.

She looked over her shoulder at Joshua and Twila. "I am so happy that you are alright, Joshua," she murmured. "We all thought—"

"That I was dead," Joshua finished, interrupting her. "I would be, if not for Wolf Dancer and Shining Soul. They saved me, Dorey, just as they have saved your mammy."

"Mama, I can't believe that you left your room to go into the Everglades looking for me," Dorey said, gazing up at Lavinia. "What about Uncle Hiram? If he knows you left your room, he will expect many things of you. Mama, what are you going to do about Hiram and his plans for you?"

"Hiram is no longer a threat to any of us," Lavinia said, her voice a little weak. She was finding each step harder to take, and she realized just how tired walking was making her.

"What do you mean, Mama?" Dorey asked.

"I'll explain later," Lavinia said, gasping in alarm when her knees began buckling.

She was so glad when Wolf Dancer realized what was happening and reached out for her. He took her quickly up into his arms and carried her the rest of the way; everyone else followed quietly behind them.

When Wolf Dancer reached the door of his house, he turned to Joshua. "Go inside with the children, and we will eat and talk as Lavinia rests," he suggested. He looked at Dorey. "This will be your home as well as your mother's for as long as you wish to stay here in my village."

Dorey was stunned to see that her mother had deep feelings for the Indian chief, perhaps even deeper than Dorey had first thought. Their attraction was evident in the way her mother looked into the chief's eyes and the way he held her so tenderly. Dorey realized that while she'd been away from her mother, lost and afraid, Lavinia had grown close to this man who had saved her from the horrible snakebite.

It made Dorey feel warm inside to see her mother so happy with this man. Dorey could hardly wait for Hiram to know that Lavinia had a new protector, so he could forget about ever having her himself!

Suddenly all that had been wrong in their lives since her father's death was righted. Knowing that her mother had never truly loved her husband in a passionate way, Dorey could accept the idea that her mother had fallen in love so quickly after his death.

"We be glad to come and sit for a while inside your home," Joshua said, speaking for himself and Twila.

"And I thank you for being so kind to me and my mother," Dorey blurted out.

Lavinia clung to Wolf Dancer's neck, feeling a contentment that had long been foreign to her. She was especially happy that he welcomed her daughter with open arms, because if all went well, she never wanted to return to the world she had left behind.

She was in love for the first time in her life. She felt its sweetness all through her body.

"Let us go inside now," Wolf Dancer said. He opened the front door and stepped aside to allow the others to enter first.

And then he went inside, where his morning fire was burning in the firepit of the large, central room. The home consisted of several rooms, including one on the second floor far to the left side, away from where the smoke spiraled up to the smoke hole above.

As everyone stood aside and slowly admired the many comforts of his home, Wolf Dancer carried Lavinia to his bed of pelts near the firepit. He had never felt comfortable sleeping away from his central fire and the front door. He didn't like the idea that someone could come in during the night and he would not be the wiser if he were sleeping far away from the door.

And soon he hoped to share this bed and room with Lavinia as his wife!

For now, it was enough that she was there with

him, away from that madman Hiram Price. He was glad that her daughter had been found, too, safe and happy to be reunited with her mother.

He saw nothing standing in the way of his hopes. He would not have to work hard to get Lavinia's daughter's acceptance, for he could see that she wanted only her mother's happiness.

After getting Lavinia comfortable on his bed, Wolf Dancer went back to where the others still stood. They seemed to be awaiting his permission to sit on the mats, filled with the down of cattails, that were positioned around the fire.

"Sit," Wolf Dancer said, gesturing toward the mats. "Be comfortable. And, Joshua, know that you and your daughter are welcome here anytime you wish to visit Lavinia."

He turned and smiled at Dorey. "Your mother will want you here with her," he said softly. He reached a hand out for here. "Come and sit beside her. She has worried so much about you."

"Thank you," Dorey said, smiling as she went over and settled down on a pelt beside her mother, while Joshua and Twila made themselves comfortable beside the fire.

"Mama, I was so worried about leaving you alone with . . . with . . . Uncle Hiram," Dorey said, swallowing hard.

"You never have to worry about Hiram again," Lavinia said, taking one of Dorey's hands. "I've made a decision, Dorey. I don't ever want to return to that plantation, or that house where I never felt much happiness."

"Where will we go, Mama?" Dorey asked, her eyes wide.

"For now, we'll just leave it at that . . . that we aren't going back there. We will work things out later," Lavinia murmured. "For now I feel at peace here with Wolf Dancer and his people. Until I am stronger, we will stay here and know that we have nothing to fear."

"What if Uncle Hiram hunts for us and finds us here?" Dorey asked, searching her mother's eyes. "You know he'll be so angry—"

"Let him be angry," Lavinia said. She brought Dorey's hand to her lips and gently kissed its palm. "Just be happy that we have found each other and that we are all alright."

"But you, Mama," Dorey said, her eyes filling with tears. "You could have died."

"Yes, but I didn't," Lavinia said, gazing over at Wolf Dancer as he came and knelt beside Dorey, a cup in his hand.

"Drink this," he said, handing it to Lavinia. "You should drink a lot of water in order to make your body completely well and strong again."

"It's only water?" Lavinia asked, easing her hand from Dorey's and leaning on an elbow. "I remember something Shining Soul gave me that made me sleep."

"That was only because you needed sleep at the time," Wolf Dancer said. "Now you want to stay awake and spend time with those you love."

Lavinia smiled sweetly at him, took the cup, and swallowed the water, enjoying its cold sweetness.

Then she handed the empty cup back to Wolf Dancer. "Thank you so much for all that you have done for me and my loved ones," she murmured.

"You do not have to keep thanking me for something I did from the heart," Wolf Dancer said, setting the empty cup aside. He sat down beside Dorey. "Now do you feel like talking, or do you think you should rest?" he asked Lavinia.

"At this moment I am very much awake, for I feel more alive now than I ever have in my life," Lavinia said, smiling into his eyes. She felt so much for him now, it almost frightened her.

She knew it was forbidden for a white woman to care for a man with red skin. She had heard of women being murdered after falling in love with Indians.

But she truly didn't care about going back to life as she had known it. She was finding everything about the Seminole village fascinating. And she could never fall in love with anyone else, because she now knew she loved this handsome, wonderful Seminole chief.

"Mama, do you think those two boys will try to bother me while I stay here?" Dorey blurted out.

Wolf Dancer responded to that question before Lavinia had a chance. "They will never cause you trouble again," he vowed. "They know better."

"You can trust Wolf Dancer's word, Dorey," Lavinia said. "You have nothing to fear while you are here in the Seminole village. You are even safer here than back at the plantation. As long as Hiram has breath in his lungs, he will not stop wanting everything for himself, and that includes me. We will not give him the chance to hurt us, Dorey."

"But what if he finds out where we are and comes for us?" Dorey asked.

"He doesn't have the courage to stand face-to-face with any Seminole warrior, especially Wolf Dancer, their chief," Lavinia said, then sighed. "I am much more tired than I thought."

"Then you should sleep," Wolf Dancer said. He reached a hand out for Dorey. "Come. Sit beside the fire with your friends."

Dorey leaned over and kissed her mother's brow, then went and sat beside Twila and began chattering about all that each had experienced, while Wolf Dancer remained beside Lavinia until he saw she was asleep.

He could not take his eyes off her.

She was his world now.

Chapter Twenty-one

She was a phantom of delight
When first she gleamed upon
My sight.

— William Wordsworth

The next day Lavinia was enjoying the morning meal with everyone she loved, sharing hominy corn cakes and a variety of fish.

It seemed unreal to her that Wolf Dancer should be sitting with her and her friends, talking casually with them, even though he was a powerful Seminole chief.

But he had opened his lodge to her and her friends. He had never behaved as though he were better than anyone else, not even Joshua or Twila, whom most whites would look down on.

Yes, Wolf Dancer was someone very special, kind and caring toward all he knew.

The more Lavinia learned about him, the more she loved him.

She had never thought such a love was possible, or that she would meet such a man as Wolf Dancer.

She felt that he cared deeply for her as well. Sometimes she would catch him looking at her with such intensity, and he always treated her with great gentleness.

He was more gentle than her father had been, and he had been everything to Lavinia when she was a child.

Now? If only she knew for certain how Wolf Dancer felt about her! Did he love her too, even though they met so recently? She felt this was a man she would be happy to share her life with forever.

"Joshua, I believe it is time for you to tell Lavinia all that you told me about her husband's death, how he truly died . . . by whose hand," Wolf Dancer said thickly as he gazed at Joshua. "She is strong enough now to hear the truth."

Lavinia's hand clutched a wooden cup in her hand, which held a drink called *cazina*, a bitter-tasting infusion made from a weed that the Wind Clan gathered on the island.

Wolf Dancer had told everyone as he handed them cups of *cazina* that this was a very healthy brew for all who drank it. Lavinia found that despite its bitterness, she thought it was delicious.

"Joshua, what do you know that you have not told me?" Lavinia asked, setting her half-empty cup aside. "I . . . I . . . want to know."

She gazed at him intently as he lowered his eyes, seemingly avoiding not only her question but also her eyes.

"Joshua, please?" she begged in a tone Joshua knew well, a voice of such sweetness that he could not help responding to it.

He slowly lifted his eyes and returned her steady gaze. "It ain't a nice thing to tell, nor to hear, Lavinia," he said, his voice drawn. "But you mus' know, and it is time for you to be told. I'se the one to tell you, Lavinia, for I witnessed it all first-hand."

"Witnessed what?" Lavinia asked, realizing that the lodge had grown stone quiet, except for the popping and crackling of the fire. Everyone's eyes were on Joshua.

"I saw Hiram murder your husband," Joshua finally blurted out. "Lavinia, I seen it with mine own two eyes. Hiram drew back a bowstring with an arrow in it, and then shot Massa Virgil in the chest."

"Lord," Lavinia gasped, feeling suddenly dizzy. "No. Oh, no. Why . . . how . . . ? Virgil's own brother killed him?"

"He sho' 'nuff did," Joshua said, wanting to reach out and steady her when he saw how distraught she was.

"Lord, oh, Lord, how could Hiram do that?" Lavinia cried. "My Virgil. My dear, kind Virgil. I knew that Hiram was jealous of everything Virgil had. My husband was more capable and intelligent than Hiram ever could be. But to . . . to . . . kill him?"

"He killed him in order to take control of the plantation and the slaves, and . . . even . . . you, Lavinia," Joshua said softly. "Yes'm, he plans to have you all to hisself now that Massa Virgil is gone."

Lavinia sat quietly for a few minutes, absorbing all that she had been told.

She glanced over at Wolf Dancer, whose eyes were on her, a protective softness in their depths.

She wanted to go into his arms and lose herself in the wonders of his embrace.

But she knew that this was not the time, not when she had just learned the true fate of her husband. It wouldn't be proper to receive solace from Wolf Dancer when she had just learned the awful fate of the man who had so recently been her husband.

Wolf Dancer saw how she gazed into his eyes. He could tell that she needed him, yet he knew she must struggle through these horrible moments on her own. She had to prove to herself that she was strong enough to withstand this pain.

Lavinia swallowed hard, wiped tears from her eyes, then reached for Dorey's hand.

Dorey had sat quietly as she listened to Joshua's revelation; she hadn't seemed all that shocked at the news of how her father had died. Now Lavinia realized that her daughter must have been told the truth.

"Dorey, are you alright?" Lavinia asked. She was amazed that Dorey was showing such strength of character. In the past few days her daughter's whole world had changed, had been turned upside down.

"Mama, are you?" Dorey asked, searching her mother's eyes. "You just learned the full horror of what happened to Papa. Are . . . you . . . alright?"

"Dorey, I am learning day by day how things in one's life change, and so quickly that one cannot be prepared for it," Lavinia said. She affectionately squeezed Dorey's hand.

"Some of the things I've learned are so horrible I've felt that I can't go on," Lavinia said. "But there are other times, when I've discovered there are more wonderful things than bad ones in my life, and wonderful people whom you suddenly meet and love."

She glanced quickly at Wolf Dancer. She blushed and lowered her eyes when she found him gazing at her.

He knew to whom she was referring when she spoke of discovering new love. He knew now without a doubt that she loved him.

But Lavinia was struggling with the guilt she felt for thinking about new love at this time, when only moments ago she had learned the details of her husband's death. She slowly turned her face so that when she raised her chin and looked straight ahead, she wouldn't be looking directly at this man who had stolen her heart.

"Joshua, did Hiram see you?" she asked softly. "Is that why he shot you with an arrow as well?"

"Dat's de reason, a'right," Joshua said dryly. "I came upon de killin' and tried to get away before Hiram knew I had been witness to his crime. But he done seen me. I didn't get turned quick enough to run away before de evil man saw me and shot dat poisoned arrow into my shoulder. I . . . fell . . . into de Bone River and done floated away, hanging on to life as hard as I could. Hiram thought he had done shot me dead, for there was a lot of blood from de wound. He saw de river turning red with my blood.

I'll nevah in my life forget dat lunatic laugh he laughed as I floated down de river."

"How horrible," Lavinia said, shuddering as she imagined the events Joshua was describing. Then she looked at him again. "Joshua, what happened after that? You are here now and well. How is that possible?"

"You knows already that Wolf Dancer saved me," Joshua said, giving Wolf Dancer a grateful smile.

"Yes, I know that, but how . . . where . . . did he find you?" Lavinia asked.

"I found a canoe floatin' in the river, empty," Joshua said. "I managed to climb into it. I laid myself down on de bottom, with dat arrow still stickin' outta me. I falls asleep. Den when I wakes up I finds Wolf Dancer there. He had put me in his canoe and was already on his way to his village with me. He took me to the shaman's home, same as you. It is because of Wolf Dancer and de shaman dat I am here today, able to tell you everythin'."

"And we have since become fast friends," Wolf Dancer said, drawing all eyes to him. "Lavinia, Joshua and I have been making plans about how to make Hiram pay for what he did, but we wanted to first get you and Joshua's family away from the plantation, as well as any slaves who were not too afraid to leave."

"But things happened to change your plans, didn't they?" Lavinia murmured. "You didn't have to go for me, Dorey, or Twila. It seems we found our way to you, each in a different fashion."

Wolf Dancer smiled at Lavinia. "One by one you were brought into my life," he said thickly. "And now all of you, except for Joshua's wife, are safe here in my village."

Tears came to Lavinia's eyes. "Poor Lorna," she murmured. "Hiram has much to answer for."

"His days are now numbered on this earth," Wolf Dancer replied, reaching over and taking one of Lavinia's hands. "We will make him pay for the crimes committed against your families."

"But how?" Lavinia asked, looking quickly up at Wolf Dancer, savoring the touch of his hand. "Hiram has a powerful friend in Colonel Cox. If anything happened to Hiram, surely the colonel would retaliate."

"I wonder if Colonel Cox is really all that friendly with Hiram," Wolf Dancer said. "I doubt Hiram has any true friends."

"You are probably right," Lavinia said, nodding. "I imagine the only reason the colonel puts up with Hiram's nonsense is because Hiram goes and plays poker with him. From what I have heard, except for a few times, the colonel always cleans him out. That is surely the only reason he allows Hiram anywhere near him . . . to get his money."

"I know you are anxious to see that man get his comeuppance, and I am willing to see that it is done, but, Lavinia, you must grow stronger before we take action. You do wish to go with us, do you not?" Wolf Dancer asked.

"Yes, I want to be there," Lavinia said firmly. "I only wish I had stepped in earlier and stopped his cruelty, but I truly didn't realize that he was such an evil man. And . . . he was my husband's brother. Virgil tried to make up for all of the wrongs Hiram did to others. But now that his brother is no longer there to stop him, Hiram is showing his true colors."

Lavinia got up and went to Joshua, who was now standing, preparing to leave the house with Twila. She flung herself into his massive arms and clung to him. "I am so sorry about Lorna and what Hiram did to you," she sobbed. "I wish I had known the true evil of that man. He would never have been around long enough to kill my husband . . . and . . . your beloved wife. I would have sent him away no matter how much my husband argued against my doing it. You see, the main part of our wealth came from my side of the family, not his, but I never spoke of that to my husband. I didn't want to make him uncomfortable over it. I didn't want to take his pride away."

"You'se done right by him, Lavinia," Joshua reassured her as he stroked her hair with his long, callused fingers. "You'se done right by him."

Wolf Dancer watched the emotional scene, and saw how deeply Lavinia was being comforted by Joshua. Wolf Dancer ached to have her in his own arms.

He longed to be her protector . . . the one who made sure no sadness touched her life.

He wanted more than those things.

He wanted her as his wife! He wanted to have children with her.

Chapter Twenty-two

Man is in love and loves what vanishes,
What more is there to say?
                    —*William Butler Yeats*

Hiram groaned as he awakened with a fierce headache. He hated even opening his eye, but he knew he had stayed in the house long enough, drinking away his disappointment and anger that Lavinia had disappeared from the plantation.

He didn't for one minute think she had been forced to leave. He knew how much she despised him.

He was certain that she had taken advantage of his being gone for so long playing poker at the fort. Yet her disappearance was odd, for she had left without even taking any of her clothes. Perhaps she had planned this with someone, a man he had never known about, for she hadn't ridden off on any of their horses, and the buggy was still in the stable.

He hadn't checked the canoes, for he doubted she would have chosen that mode of transportation. The Bone River would only take her into the Everglades.

Yep, he thought bitterly to himself, surely even when Virgil was alive, Lavinia had had a man waiting to make her his.

She had probably met him on one of her shopping expeditions in the various small towns surrounding their plantation. She had no doubt just been waiting for the right opportunity to make her escape as soon as Hiram left.

"I stayed away too long," he growled as he tossed the blanket off himself.

But he'd had no idea what she was planning!

She was a tricky one.

He wondered if Virgil had had even an inkling of what a two-timing wench he'd married.

Grumbling, he left the bed and went to a window to throw open the shutters. His bedroom reeked of unpleasant odors. As usual, there was the sweat that always covered him. Combined with it was the vile stench of alcohol spilling from his mouth with each breath he took. And though he had not smoked a cigar after coming home, his clothes still smelled terribly of smoke.

Hiram leaned out the window just enough to take a deep breath of fresh air.

But he got more than that. He realized that it was eerily quiet outside the mansion.

Usually there was a lot of activity as slaves came and went from the fields. And the women, even though they hated being enslaved, sang while working in the tobacco fields, especially now at harvesttime.

He heard no songs. He heard no laughter of the slave children. He . . . heard . . . nothing.

Only silence!

His heart began to race as he leaned farther out and looked in all directions. He saw only a few slaves working the fields. He saw no children running and playing.

Smoke was spiraling from only a few of the slaves' cabins. He should see it coming from all of them. Each morning the slaves built their cook fires in the cabin stoves and started cooking their beans slowly over the flames before they left for work; beans were the only staple he handed out to them. They were lucky if they got any meat to add to the beans, for he thought that an unnecessary extravagance.

"They don't deserve anything extra," he grumbled to himself. And especially not today when they were lazing around inside their homes, probably thinking that he was still gone.

"I'll show 'em a thing or two. I'll teach 'em how wrong it is not to do their duties even in my absence," he growled to himself.

He stepped away from the window, gazed down at his wrinkled shirt and breeches, and saw that he had not removed his shoes before falling into bed in his drunken stupor.

And even though he reeked of sweat and tobacco, and had not shaved for two days, nor bathed, Hiram left his room.

Still unsteady from having drunk too much these past days, he stumbled down the massive staircase.

As he took each step, hanging on to the banister to keep from falling, he still heard no sounds, not even in the house, where servants should be busy doing their chores.

Nor did he smell the food that should be cooking in the kitchen.

As he continued down the stairs, he grew angrier and angrier, for still there was no one in sight, nor did he hear anything. It was as though the house were empty of servants, but how could that be?

They knew better than to desert him, for he would search them out and kill them if they did! Yet . . . yet . . . he believed that was exactly what had happened.

Had Lavinia given them permission to leave? Had she freed the slaves before she left?

Finally at the foot of the stairs, he frowned as he looked frantically around, still hoping he was wrong about having been deserted by the people he depended on for his way of life.

When he still didn't see or hear anyone, he stamped through the house, searching and growing angrier by the minute. He stopped suddenly when he heard soft crying.

He followed the sound and pulled open the door that led into the kitchen pantry. He found the servants who usually worked in the house huddled there, crying. It took only a moment to realize that Twila was not among them.

The servants shrank away from him, their dark eyes wide as he yanked his belt from the waist of his breeches.

"You tell me what's going on," he shouted, holding the belt between his hands and snapping it threateningly as he looked from one to the other. "Why aren't you working? Where is everyone who should be out in the fields? I saw only a few. And where is Twila?"

"Massa Hiram, please don't hurt us," one of the younger servants said, trembling. "Please don't make us tell you what you will hate to hear."

"What will I hate to hear?" Hiram shouted, suddenly lashing the belt across the belly of the woman who had been brave enough to speak to him. "You'd better tell me the rest of it, or I'll do even worse to you."

The young woman cried hard as she clutched her belly. She was too distraught to respond to Hiram. She was afraid she'd say the wrong thing and be hit again.

"I'll tell you," one of the older women said as she stepped in front of the crying slave. "Just don' whip this gal again."

"Well, then, say it," Hiram shouted. "And you'd better be quick about it, do you hear?"

"Yes, suh, I'se understand," she said, still standing tall and straight as she gazed directly into his one eye. "Many of your slaves are gone, but there are enough left to tend the fields. Massa Hiram, they are afraid of what you might do to us because the others have left. And Massa Hiram, we have no idea where Twila has gone. She's just gone."

Hiram was shocked at the thought of so many of his slaves running away. Surely they were long gone by now. They'd had plenty of time to get away as he lay in his bed in a drunken stupor.

"Your overseer also left," the woman quickly added. "Those who are workin' the fields are doin' it out of loyalty to you, Massa Hiram. And they are doin' fine without the whip of the overseer."

Hiram stood there for a moment longer, absorbing all that he had been told. He was stunned that his overseer had walked out on him. If you couldn't depend on your overseer, who was paid well for his services, then who could you depend on?

"I appreciate your tellin' me everything," Hiram said, looking from one slave to another. "Now get out of this pantry and get to work. I'll be expecting some mighty good food on my dining table after I return from speaking with Colonel Cox at the fort."

He leaned into each of the servants' faces in turn, hoping to intimidate them into obeying him.

"If you leave, I won't be far behind," he warned. "As for those who have already left, they'll pay for their disobedience. I'm going to find them. Do you hear? I'm going to find them! They are gone for now. But you're still here. And I expect you to obey me, same as always. Do you understand?"

They all nodded, then filed past him out of the pantry.

They scurried through the house, returning to their usual chores, each one different.

"That's more like it," Hiram muttered.

He went to his gun cabinet, unlocked it, and took a rifle from it, too rattled by all that had happened to miss the rifle Lavinia had taken.

He grabbed a pocketful of bullets, then went outside and stood at the edge of the tobacco field.

He mentally counted how many slaves were still there, stunned at how many had deserted him.

He hurried to one of the heftiest men and grabbed him by the arm. "In which direction did those slaves who deserted me go?" he asked, his jaw tight.

"North," the man said, pointing in that direction.

That meant that the runaway slaves had not gone into the Everglades to hide. They were headed out of Florida.

His jaw tightened as he stepped away from the slave and stood with his hands on his hips. He just couldn't let the runaway slaves go.

Surely with the colonel's help, they could be found. If so, he'd punish them good and then give them the hardest work he could come up with.

"Get back to work," he said, turning and glaring at those who had stopped to stare at him. "Now. Do you hear? Now. And don't you think of tryin' to escape while I'm gone. I'll be back soon. You'd best be here."

They all nodded quickly and returned to their harvesting of the tobacco.

Hiram ran to the stable and threw a saddle onto his best steed, a white mare, and mounted it. Then he rode off, ignoring the hunger that ate away at his gut. He'd already lost too much time by lying in bed, wallowing in self-pity for having lost Lavinia.

Once he reached Fort Adams, Hiram wasted no time in getting to Colonel Cox's office.

He saw the look the colonel gave him and understood the reason for it. Hiram had never allowed himself to look so disheveled in the presence of others.

But that was the least of his concerns. He wanted his slaves back and would go to any length to reclaim them.

"Well, now, look what the cat dragged in," Colonel Cox said, gazing at Hiram over his desk. "Lord, man, have you forgotten how to shave and bathe? And look at your clothes. Aren't those the same duds you wore when we were playing poker the other night?"

He sniffed and frowned. "And do you know how bad you stink?" he said, waving a hand toward Hiram. "Step back. Do you hear? Step back away from my desk and then tell me why you're here so you can leave. I don't savor havin' your company in this condition."

"I need help," Hiram said, ignoring Cox's command to step back. Instead, he placed the palms of his hands on the desk and leaned even closer to the colonel. "Fred, did you hear me? I need your help."

"What's happened?" Colonel Cox asked, arching an eyebrow. He placed his fingertips together before him.

"Disaster," Hiram said, suddenly sinking into a chair across the desk from the colonel. "The worst of it is that Lavinia is gone. She wasn't there when I returned home from the fort. And then after I awakened from sleeping off my drunken stupor, I

discovered that more than half of my slaves have
fled the plantation. They're headed north, out of
Florida. I need your help, Fred. I need it now. With
you and your soldiers' help, I can get my slaves
back. But I think Lavinia is gone forever. I've got to
forget about her."

"And so you've discovered the pitfalls of bein' a
slave owner, have you?" Fred said, relaxing into his
chair and chuckling. "You know, I have never
thought much of owning slaves, but there are many,
like you, who do. Well, that's nothing to do with
me. I've got no orders to chase after runaways. No,
Hiram, I won't help you get those slaves back. Had
you treated them humanely, I doubt they'd have
left. So be on your way, Hiram. I've better things to
do than waste my time on you."

"Not even if it's to go after Chief Wolf Dancer?"
Hiram taunted, knowing how much the colonel
would like to get his hands on the only chief in the
area who had outwitted the military.

"But you said the slaves went north," Colonel
Cox replied, arching an eyebrow. "Which is it?
North or in the direction of the chief's island?"

"I'm not sure," Hiram said. "Who's to say
whether that slave who told me the runaways went
north told me the truth? Maybe they went in the
opposite direction. In any case, this would be a
good opportunity to go looking for that island."

"I told you I don't believe in slavery, and I don't
ever want to try and find that island," Colonel Cox
grumbled. "I wouldn't send my regiment into that

swampy mess for any reason. There are too many mysterious things going on in the Everglades. Nope. I won't send any of my men to fight against the likes of mysterious white panthers, nor floating and flying ghostly apparitions. It's much safer staying away from there. Anyway, Chief Wolf Dancer hasn't caused me any problems. I see no need to attack him, and I especially don't want any of my men to come face-to-face with that white panther that stalks anything with two legs."

"That white panther is only a myth," Hiram said, laughing. "It's only a tale made up to scare whites outta the swamp and away from the Indians' island."

He leaned farther over the desk. "I'm begging you," he said thickly. "My whole life is going to be changed if I don't get those slaves back. I'm accepting that I've lost Lavinia. But I don't want to lose my tobacco. It's ready to harvest. It takes a lot of work to get it harvested."

"Then go and do it yourself," Colonel Cox said, laughing. "And if you need those slaves so badly, you go into the Everglades yourself and find them. But consider this: If they did go there, by now they are probably dead, killed by snakes, alligators, the panther, or the swampy water itself."

Hiram glared at the colonel with his one eye, then turned and left angrily.

He didn't see Colonel Cox standing at a window watching him, smiling, as Hiram rode away on his steed, not so much angry as embarrassed by defeat.

"Virgil, it's because of you," Hiram cried to the heavens. "You had the loyalty of the slaves. You taught them to hate me, didn't you, Virgil? I hope you're rotting in hell!"

For the first time he could remember, tears sprang to Hiram's eyes.

Chapter Twenty-three

A pity beyond all telling
Is hid in the heart of love.
                    —*William Butler Yeats*

A youthful voice sounded outside of Wolf Dancer's closed door, interrupting Joshua in the middle of a sentence.

Joshua glanced over at Wolf Dancer, who rose to his feet and walked to the door.

Wolf Dancer looked over his shoulder at Dorey. He recognized the voice as belonging to Running Bear and wondered how she was going to react to seeing the two young braves who had caused her such alarm and fear. He was sure that she too had recognized the voice.

Wolf Dancer had expected the two boys to come this morning to offer an apology to Dorey for the way they had treated her.

Thus far they had avoided her, and Wolf Dancer had decided not to rush the issue. He wanted to give the boys enough time to realize what they had done. He wanted the apology to Dorey to be sincere.

Dorey had stiffened when she recognized the voice and now saw Wolf Dancer glance over his shoulder at her. She wasn't sure how to interpret that look, but she knew how she felt: uneasy!

She had yet to come face-to-face with her young assailants, and she wasn't sure how she would react to the sight of them.

She sat still, filled with anxiety at what might happen in these next few moments. She hoped that when she saw those boys again she wouldn't be filled with hatred. She wanted to forget that the incident had ever happened, for she knew she must learn to get along with the two boys as well as all the other Seminole people, at least until her mother made other plans for their future.

Something told Dorey that Lavinia was so in love with Wolf Dancer that she might never want to leave him.

She had seen that love in her mother's eyes whenever she was around Wolf Dancer. She had seen it in the chief's eyes as well.

They were certainly in love, even though it was forbidden for a white woman to love a red man. But she and her mother were no longer among whites! They were with the peace-loving Seminole.

And if Dorey had her way about their future, she would stay in this village. While she was with Wolf Dancer, she felt safe. She had known she could trust him the moment she heard the kindness in his voice.

And he treated Dorey's mother with such gentle care that she felt he might be the very one to put everything right in her mother's world.

Her mother had not loved the man she'd married. She deserved to find a man she could love now.

Lavinia's insides tightened as Wolf Dancer opened the door and peered outside. From where she sat, she could see past him to the two young braves standing there.

She could only conclude that these were the two boys who had abducted Dorey. They had yet to come and apologize to her. Surely that was why they were here now.

She glanced over at Dorey to see how she was reacting and found her daughter looking at the young braves, too. Lavinia saw a mixture of feelings in Dorey's eyes, but the overriding emotion was anger.

And Dorey had cause to be angry. She could have died in the murky waters of the Everglades.

Just as Lavinia had been bitten by a snake, Dorey could have been bitten, too, and she would not have survived the bite because she had been left alone to fend for herself!

Lavinia was surprised when Wolf Dancer welcomed the two young braves kindly—she thought they should have been reprimanded and made to apologize.

But she loved Wolf Dancer and everything about him, so she believed that however he had decided to treat the young men was surely best. He was a man of much intelligence, and also patience.

But she couldn't help feeling he had been patient enough with those two young men as far as she was concerned. She would enjoy giving them a piece of her mind.

But she knew it was not her place to speak up, or scold them. Wolf Dancer would take care of this.

Wolf Dancer stepped outside with Running Bear and Deer Shadow. He saw the uneasiness in their eyes as they looked up at him.

"My chief, Deer Shadow and I would like to apologize to Dorey, and then we would like to invite her to join in the fun with us and our friends this morning," Running Bear said as he peered around Wolf Dancer and made eye contact with Dorey, who was staring angrily at him.

Wolf Dancer looked from one boy to the other, then placed a hand on the bare shoulder of each. "You know the wrong that you did, do you not?" he asked, his jaw tight. "You know that it could have ended in tragedy?"

Both braves nodded anxiously.

"We are very sorry to have gone against all that my mother and father, and . . . you . . . have taught us," Running Bear said. "We did not want to harm Dorey, only to spend time with her. We know nothing of her world. We have been on the island since we were born. Do you not understand why we wanted to learn about the white world? We were going to tell her of our ways, too. It would have been an exchange of knowledge between us."

He lowered his eyes. "We should not have waited until it was so late in the day to take her to our tree house," he said, swallowing hard.

Then he looked quickly up into Wolf Dancer's eyes. "If we had brought her to the tree house at an earlier hour, we could have talked and then released her and let her return to her home before night fell," he said. "As it was, she came in her canoe too late for us to talk at length with her. That is why we left her there alone."

"But we regret having done it," Deer Shadow blurted out. "We have learned our lesson. You can trust us, Chief Wolf Dancer. We will never go against the rules of our people again. But . . . but . . . we do want the girl's friendship now, for as long as she will be at our village. If she accepts our apology and wants to join our fun, will you allow it?"

Wolf Dancer had listened intently to what had been said, and he had heard true regret in the braves' voices. He knew it was important for the young people to put this unfortunate incident behind them. If Wolf Dancer had his way, both Dorey and her mother would not want to return to the life they had left behind, but instead would spend their futures with him and his Seminole people.

He turned and gazed at Dorey. "You have heard," he said quietly. "Do you hear the sincerity in their voices? They regret what they did to you. Can you accept their apology, or would you rather not join them in their fun today?"

Dorey had not been able to quell her excitement at the idea of joining the children in their games. She had seen the fun they had while she had silently observed them.

She understood why the young braves had captured her.

She herself had hungered for knowledge of the Seminole.

That was why she had sought answers in the books in her father's study.

She rose to her feet, and as her mother, Twila, and Joshua watched, she went and stood beside Wolf Dancer. She could not help feeling nervous about what she was going to do, for although she did want to forgive these young men, she might never forget her fear while she was alone in the tree house, and later in the *garita*.

"Are you truly sorry for what you did?" she asked guardedly, looking from one boy to the other. She saw the humbleness of their expressions, and she knew deep inside that they did regret their actions.

"We are very sorry," Running Bear said, tears shining in his eyes. "Will you let us make it up to you? Will you come and meet our friends and join in our games?"

Deer Shadow suddenly pulled out his right arm, which he had kept behind him, and smiled broadly as he reached out to Dorey and showed her what he had kept hidden.

"We made these game darts just for you," Deer Shadow said, proudly displaying the darts, which had been made from corncobs and feathers.

"They are for me?" Dorey said, her eyes widening as she gazed at the beautifully colored feathers on the darts.

"For always," Deer Shadow said, holding them closer to her. "Please take them and come with us to play darts with our friends."

Dorey slowly reached a hand out toward him, then smiled as he laid the lovely darts in her palm. "They are very pretty," she murmured. She looked from one boy to the other. "Are they truly mine?"

"Yes, and we have made another set for your black friend," Running Bear said as he brought out the darts he had hidden behind his back. "Will she come, too?"

Twila had heard everything, and her heart skipped a beat when she saw the darts that the young braves had made especially for her.

She scampered to her feet and went to stand beside Dorey. When Running Bear held the darts closer to her, she slowly opened her hand and accepted them.

"Thank you," she murmured, her eyes bright with excitement.

Dorey turned and smiled at her mother. "May I go and play with the children?" she asked. She turned to Joshua. "May Twila?"

Both parents quickly nodded.

Lavinia sighed with a mixture of relief and happiness as she watched Dorey and Twila join the two young braves. They were all soon laughing together as they ran and joined the others who were waiting for them.

Wolf Dancer closed the door and sat down beside Lavinia.

"It is a good day," he said, gently taking her hand in his. "You do believe the boys were sincere?"

"The gifts they made for Dorey and Twila proved their sincerity," Lavinia said, relishing the touch of Wolf Dancer's hand in hers. It seemed that suddenly everything in her and her daughter's world was being righted.

Even Joshua and Twila's lives held much more

promise than they ever could have at the plantation. They were now as free as anyone could ever want to be. They were among people who did not scorn them because of the color of their skin. They were treated as equals by the Seminole.

Joshua had sat quietly by, watching and listening to everything, glad to see that Wolf Dancer and Lavinia seemed so happy.

Joshua had noticed the undercurrents between Wolf Dancer and Lavinia from the first moment they had come together. Surely something more than friendship was developing between them. Both were widowed, and they were very obviously attracted to one another.

Sensing that these two people wanted to be alone, Joshua rose to his feet and walked to the door. "I'se needed in the cornfield," he said, opening the door. "It is harvesttime back at the plantation. It is harvesttime here as well. I will go and help harvest de corn."

"Joshua, that is kind, but not necessary," Wolf Dancer said, smiling up at him, and understanding what was behind Joshua's planned exit. Joshua was a wise man and had seen how Wolf Dancer and Lavinia felt about one another. He sought to give them privacy.

"I'se good in de fields," Joshua said, nodding and smiling. "Jest you two sit there and enjoy one another's company."

Joshua hurried outside, closing the door behind him.

Suddenly there was silence in the room as Lavinia and Wolf Dancer gazed into one another's eyes.

GET UP TO 4 FREE BOOKS!

You can have the best romance delivered to your door for less than what you'd pay in a bookstore or online. Sign up for one of our book clubs today, and we'll send you **FREE* BOOKS** just for trying it out...**with no obligation to buy, ever!**

HISTORICAL ROMANCE BOOK CLUB

Travel from the Scottish Highlands to the American West, the decadent ballrooms of Regency England to Viking ships. Your shipments will include authors such as CONNIE MASON, CASSIE EDWARDS, LYNSAY SANDS, LEIGH GREENWOOD, and many, many more.

LOVE SPELL BOOK CLUB

Bring a little magic into your life with the romances of Love Spell—fun contemporaries, paranormals, time-travels, futuristics, and more. Your shipments will include authors such as KATIE MACALISTER, SUSAN GRANT, NINA BANGS, SANDRA HILL, and more.

As a book club member you also receive the following special benefits:

- **30% OFF all orders through our website & telecenter!**
  (Plus, you still get 1 book FREE for every 5 books you buy!)
- **Exclusive access to special discounts!**
- **Convenient home delivery and 10 days to return any books you don't want to keep.**

There is no minimum number of books to buy, and you may cancel membership at any time. See back to sign up!

*Please include $2.00 for shipping and handling.

YES! ☐

Sign me up for the **Historical Romance Book Club** and send my TWO FREE BOOKS! If I choose to stay in the club, I will pay only $8.50* each month, a savings of $5.48!

YES! ☐

Sign me up for the **Love Spell Book Club** and send my TWO FREE BOOKS! If I choose to stay in the club, I will pay only $8.50* each month, a savings of $5.48!

NAME: _____

ADDRESS: _____

_____

TELEPHONE: _____

E-MAIL: _____

☐ I WANT TO PAY BY CREDIT CARD.

☐ VISA   ☐ MasterCard   ☐ DISCOVER

ACCOUNT #: _____

EXPIRATION DATE: _____

SIGNATURE: _____

Send this card along with $2.00 shipping & handling for each club you wish to join, to:

**Romance Book Clubs
1 Mechanic Street
Norwalk, CT 06850-3431**

Or fax (must include credit card information!) to: 610.995.9274.
You can also sign up online at www.dorchesterpub.com.

*Plus $2.00 for shipping. Offer open to residents of the U.S. and Canada only.
Canadian residents please call 1.800.481.9191 for pricing information.
If under 18, a parent or guardian must sign. Terms, prices and conditions subject to change. Subscription subject
to acceptance. Dorchester Publishing reserves the right to reject any order or cancel any subscription.

JOIN NOW!

Lavinia felt so much for Wolf Dancer, yet she was a little afraid of those feelings.

Although she thought he was falling in love with her, too, it seemed too soon after her husband's death to admit to such passion. How could she explain that she and her husband had never truly been in love? They had loved, but only in a gentle, caring way.

"I am surprised that corn is grown in the Everglades," she blurted out, wanting something, anything, to talk about. She needed some time before acting on her feelings for Wolf Dancer, and she felt that he needed the same thing. They both wanted to be sure of what they felt for one another.

But she knew that if he so much as kissed her, she would be truly lost to him.

"The ground of this island is very fertile. Many crops are grown here," Wolf Dancer said.

He understood Lavinia's need to talk.

If it was up to him, though, he would take her in his arms at this very moment and kiss her; his body cried out for hers. But he wanted her to be certain before she gave in to her feelings.

"And I've noticed that you have various kinds of meat which are cooked by your women," Lavinia said softly. "Among them . . . is turtle meat, which I never thought was good to eat."

"Turtle meat is a very good food source for my people, as is the tender meat of young alligator tails," Wolf Dancer said, and noted how the latter made Lavinia shudder.

"I imagine you need to raise your own crops and catch your own meat because you do not feel safe to go beyond the Everglades to trade," Lavinia said. She saw a sudden hardness enter his eyes.

"Wolf Dancer, I know that you said the white soldiers are afraid to come this far into the swamp, but I still can't help being afraid that they might come looking for me and Dorey when Hiram discovers that we are gone," she said. "I don't believe Hiram will let us go all that easily. I truly expect him to fight to get me back."

"My warriors have been alerted to this possibility," Wolf Dancer said. "They are posted at the most vulnerable points of the Everglades. No one will be allowed to get near my village, especially not your evil brother-in-law."

The longer she sat there alone with Wolf Dancer, the more Lavinia felt like an awkward girl in the presence of this powerful, handsome Indian chief.

"I am sorry about your husband's death," Wolf Dancer said, bringing Lavinia out of her deep thoughts. "I know how the shock of his death made you feel, for I felt the same when my wife died shortly after we were married. One day an alligator came out of nowhere and my wife, Golden Dawn, was taken from me."

"I'm so sorry that you experienced such a terrible loss," Lavinia said, turning to sit directly in front of him. "It's hard when one loses a spouse."

"My wife lives on in my memory, Lavinia" Wolf Dancer said, taking her other hand and holding both in his. "As long as we continue to remember our loved ones, their spirits will live on within us."

"That is so beautiful," Lavinia said, fighting off tears that were burning in the corners of her eyes.

"My woman," Wolf Dancer said as he released one of her hands so that he could reach up and draw his fingers through her luscious, golden hair. "We are all one . . . no matter what the color of our skin outside. Inside, our souls recognize each other as kindred spirits."

"Tell me more," Lavinia asked, sitting closer to him.

"We are all connected," he said thickly. "All people have similar needs and desires. We are all the same, but different. Each of us is one of a kind, special and unique. We all come from the same Master of Breath, who is our creator. Yet we are all born into this world without understanding why we are here. This is the knowledge each one of us must seek."

"I feel such a connection with you and your people, although we have only recently become aware of each other's existence," Lavinia murmured. "That first time, when I saw you in the tree, I was not afraid, but instantly drawn to you."

"You have also seen the white panther," he said, searching her eyes for her reaction. He could see that she was surprised he would speak of it, confirming the existence of the mystical creature.

"The white panther is something that everyone has learned to avoid," he went on, now wanting to change the subject. This was not the time to share the magic that he held within his heart. It was something that might frighten her away from him.

And he could not chance that.

He needed and wanted her.

She also needed him!

"The panther stalks the night like a white ghost," he quickly added. "But no one has ever seen it enter our village. Surely it is because Shining Soul's magic keeps it away."

Lavinia was confused by his words. Whenever she had seen the white panther, she had always seen Wolf Dancer soon after. She gazed intently into eyes that were every bit as green as the panther's. Until now, she had wondered if what she had seen was real, or just her imagination?

Now she knew it hadn't been her imagination; he had told her that he knew she had seen the panther. Was there, as she suspected, some connection between Wolf Dancer and the panther?

Had he mentioned the panther to test her? Was he waiting, even now, for her reaction?

She decided that it was best not to discuss the panther with him just now.

Hopefully, one day she would understand how the panther and Wolf Dancer might be one and the same. For now, she would not think about it. Whatever the truth might be, she loved him no less!

Yet she would ask him about the unusual color of his eyes. All of his people's eyes were dark brown.

"Your eyes are such a beautiful color of green," she murmured.

"Long ago there was a marriage between my great-great-grandfather and a white woman whose eyes were green," he said, hoping what he was telling her would be enough to quell her curiosity, at least for now. "I am the only one of my family whose eyes were the same as my great-great-grandmother's."

"They are very beautiful," Lavinia said, relieved that he had such a reasonable explanation. Had he not told her this, she would always associate those green eyes . . . with the panther's!

"Yours are the color of violets, and also beautiful," Wolf Dancer said, again running his fingers through her golden hair. "Your eyes and hair both fascinate me. As does your past. Will you share it with me?"

She told Wolf Dancer about her life as a wife and mother, that she was from Georgia, and that her parents and Virgil Price's parents had arranged a marriage between them in order to keep the wealth within their two families.

She confessed to having never loved Virgil, admitted that they just respected and were fond of one another.

She explained how Virgil's brother Hiram had always been a troublemaker. He had wanted the arranged marriage to be between himself and Lavinia.

But he'd resented Virgil even before that, because Virgil was a fine-looking man, a gentleman in all respects, while Hiram was a beastly, ugly man, who always reeked of perspiration.

"Hiram's hands are always dripping with sweat,"

she said, shuddering at the very thought of him touching her with those hands.

She went on to tell how Hiram's resentment had grown through the years.

"Virgil, who was gentle with everyone, felt sorry for his brother because of Hiram's offensiveness and invited him to come with us to Florida. When we moved here, Virgil shared everything with his brother."

She swallowed hard and lowered her eyes, then gazed into Wolf Dancer's again. "Of course, it has been proven that what my husband did for Hiram wasn't enough for him," she said coldly. "He wanted it all, especially his brother's wife. And now, because of his brother's death, Hiram has it all—except his brother's wife."

She slowly shook her head. "The resentment never left Hiram, even after his brother gave him so much," she said. "He was driven to kill Virgil in order to have everything that legally belonged to his brother. But he forgot that his brother was the smart one when it came to handling business transactions. Hiram was a bungler. Things will soon fall apart at the plantation. And Hiram has already lost what was most valuable of all to him . . . me."

"I am so sorry about the way your life has turned out. How sad it is to lose a husband at such a young age," Wolf Dancer said, taking her hands in his. "I wasn't married long enough to have a child. But I have had my people to fill the void in my life left by the sudden death of my wife."

"I feel so blessed to have my daughter," Lavinia murmured. "She has been such a blessing to me at a time in my life when I was filled with despair. I lost my husband, and I hate keeping slaves. Each day since my husband's death, I have pondered what to do about the slaves."

She paused, then said, "Something has to be done about Hiram, and I most definitely want a role in seeing that he gets his comeuppance."

"Your husband's death will be avenged," Wolf Dancer said tightly. "I will see that it happens."

"Yes, Hiram must pay for what he has done, but I don't want to draw you or your people into this fight," she said, freeing one of her hands so that she could place it gently on his face. "Your world seems so perfect here on your hidden island."

She started to get up, but fell back down from weakness.

Wolf Dancer caught her, then both were drawn together in a magical kiss . . . their first!

Lavinia couldn't believe this was happening. The kiss made her feel truly alive for the first time in her life.

Wolf Dancer was completely captivated by this woman. He would never allow any harm to come her way again, and he would most definitely make Hiram Price pay for the wrongs he had done this woman and those who slaved in the fields for him.

But for now, it was only the two of them. He wanted more than a kiss, and had to remind himself it was too soon to show her just how much he loved her.

Soon, yes soon, he would make love with her. He wanted to be the one to awaken all of that pent-up passion inside her!

Chapter Twenty-four

I drew them with . . . bands of love.
—Old Testament, Hosea 11:4

As Lavinia stood at the window of the bedroom she occupied in Wolf Dancer's home, gazing out at a beautiful day, she found it hard to believe that her world had changed so much so quickly. Only a short while ago she had a husband and comfortable marriage. But both had been destroyed by one man.

Hiram.

Even while Virgil had been alive, Lavinia had felt threatened by Hiram's presence on the plantation. Although he had only one eye, he used it to mentally undress her, especially when Virgil wasn't around.

And now?

Her husband was dead.

Hiram was alone at the mansion.

And Lavinia was where she hoped to be for the rest of her life.

Although she was used to a huge home, servants, and more riches than she could count, she found this simple village stimulating in oh, so many ways!

She gazed out at the lush trees at the far edge of the village. The beautiful Spanish moss hung from their limbs like lace. She could smell the fragrance of roses and knew that many of them grew wild in Florida. She also smelled wild gardenias, and inhaled more deeply, for they were her favorite flower of all.

A wooden basin of water had been brought to her a short while ago so she could bathe. With her toilette complete, she now wore one of the lovely doeskin dresses that the women of the village had brought for her to wear.

Her own clothes had been ruined when Twila cut the sleeve away from the snakebite so she could tend to it.

"Twila," she whispered.

Yes, Twila had saved her life, and now Lavinia hoped to repay her by seeing that she was free and happy for the rest of her days.

Dorey was with Twila already this morning, having found many friends among the children. They seemed especially fond of the two young braves, Running Bear and Deer Shadow.

"So young," she whispered, smiling. "Puppy love."

She found it amazing that the girls could forget so quickly what the two young braves had done to Dorey. But the aftereffects of Dorey's misadventure had benefited them all.

And Joshua!

Even Joshua was happier now that he and Twila were reunited.

He had a home of his own now, which he shared with his daughter. And he was free. He rose early from his bed each morning now and joined the others in the garden, helping with the harvest, which would be completed soon.

Lavinia could hear him now as he sang while working, his deep voice carrying in the wind to her open window.

Yes, he enjoyed working in the garden, for he was doing so as a free man, not a slave! No one was forcing him to do anything. No one stood over him with a pistol holstered at his waist, or a whip in his hand.

"Yes, Joshua, you are free forevermore," she whispered. When a familiar voice spoke her name from the other side of her closed bedroom door, she felt a strange giddiness.

Wolf Dancer.

Everyone had shared the morning meal already, and when the girls and Joshua had left, and Wolf Dancer had been called from his home by one of his warriors, Lavinia had taken the time to go to her room and tidy her bed.

She found the pallet of furs surprisingly comfortable. And she loved the soft mats that were spread across the wood floor.

In fact, she enjoyed everything about this house that was made so differently from any other she had ever seen. It was constructed mainly from palmetto leaves and other things brought in from the forest, and she found it was actually cooler than the plantation house had been.

It was not a huge mansion, but it did have two stories, and the upstairs was so beautiful at night with the stars overhead.

"Lavinia? I would like to take you for a ride in my canoe," Wolf Dancer said as he stood waiting for her to open the door. "Are you well enough?"

"I am very well, kind sir," she said, smiling. She opened the door and found herself being gazed upon by the most handsome man she'd ever seen. Today he wore only a breechclout, and his usual moccasins.

This brief attire made her blush, yet she could not help admiring the muscles it revealed.

His body rippled with lean strength, and his smile almost melted her as he gave her his own look of admiration.

"And, yes, I would love to go with you in your canoe," she finally blurted out. For a moment she had been rendered speechless by the sight of him. Sometimes she still couldn't believe that she was with this man she had admired from afar in those days when she had seen him sitting casually in the tree or paddling down the river in his canoe.

But this was all real enough, and she felt more alive now than ever before in her life.

And she did feel strong today, even almost totally well, thanks to Wolf Dancer and Shining Soul.

"I would like to show you why the river was named Bone River long ago by the people who settled here before we Seminole," he said. His eyes took in just how beautiful she looked in the doeskin dress, which had beaded designs of forest flowers sewn across the front. "Also I would like to show you where my people go to collect shells to make wampum."

"It all sounds so interesting, and, yes, I would love to go," Lavinia said, stepping out of the room and walking with Wolf Dancer through his house and outside into the sunlight. She gazed up at him. "I have heard the term 'wampum' used, but have no idea what it means."

"The word wampum actually refers to strings of special shells which are found along the shore here. They are used to finalize agreements," Wolf Dancer said. "It is the same as white people's currency and is very valuable to the Seminole."

He walked with her through the village, where many people were busy with their chores.

Lavinia caught sight of Dorey and Twila as they played with several children, a mixture of girls and boys. They seemed to belong now, having been accepted by the Seminole adults and children as a part of the community.

She looked far to her left and saw Joshua gathering corn in a wicker basket along with others working alongside him.

"Tonight Spirit Talker, our people's storyteller, will tell stories of our people's ancestors. We will all gather beneath the stars beside the large outdoor fire," Wolf Dancer said, smiling down at Lavinia. "Spirit Talker is my people's spirit guide to the old ways. The children listen to each and every word, learning much from him."

They left the village and walked through the trees and brush until they came to the beached canoes.

Wolf Dancer lifted her and gently placed her in his canoe, which was larger than the others, but not too large to be manned by just one person.

Thrilled to be with Wolf Dancer alone like this, Lavinia watched him shove the canoe out into the water. Then he leapt aboard, and began pulling the paddle through the water.

Lavinia held on to the seat as Wolf Dancer took the canoe out deeper, then guided it down the center of the river beneath the low-hanging limbs of the willows and mossy oaks.

The sun spiraled its way through the thick vegetation overhead, twinkling like diamonds in the water, and becoming many more suns as the reflection floated away in many directions in the wake of the canoe.

Lavinia was glad that he was not going in the direction of her home, but instead farther into the swamp.

Although she knew this was the Everglades and that many mysteries lay within the swamp, she was not afraid, because she was with a man who knew these waters better than anyone else.

Lavinia could hear the screeching of birds and the cries of animals as they traveled on. She looked up and saw birds that she had never seen before. Then over on the shore, she spotted the shine of eyes through the vegetation, and wondered what animal it was, and whether it would be safe to leave the canoe when they reached their destination.

"There are so many animals and birds here that I am not familiar with," Lavinia blurted out, unable to keep down the fear that was creeping into her heart. "Will it be safe to beach the canoe so . . . so . . . far from your village?"

"I know all the animals that live in this area, and while you are with me, you have nothing to fear. They all know me and know they have nothing to fear from me," Wolf Dancer said.

He looked over his shoulder at her, yet did not miss a stroke in the water as they traveled onward.

"I have respect for living beings, whether they stand upright or prowl the forest, whether they swim in the river or send roots into the earth," he said.

"You think of trees as beings?" Lavinia asked, marveling anew over the complexities of this man.

For a brief moment she thought of seeing the white panther, and then Wolf Dancer, on the limb of the old oak near her house.

Yes, Wolf Dancer was someone unique, and someone she might be afraid of if she had not been given the chance to know him.

But the opposite was true. She felt safer while with him than she had ever felt with anyone else, even her beloved father. Her father had been an ordinary man who did ordinary things.

Wolf Dancer was not ordinary in any sense, and he was the man she now loved with all her being.

There was not one aspect of him that frightened her, not even the part of him that seemed linked to the white panther.

She recalled having seen something curious back

at the village and decided to ask him about it. "Wolf Dancer, I saw something the women were doing at your village that fascinated me," she said, glad to have something to talk about other than mysteries.

"What was that?" he asked, glancing at her over his shoulder.

"I saw women stringing what looked like green beans on threads," she said. "Why is that? We have always had green beans in our family garden, but never did we string them on thread."

"It is the custom among my people. We find that stringing the beans is a good way to store them in the *garita*," Wolf Dancer said, this time paying more attention to where he was guiding the canoe. He now directed it toward a long, sandy beach. "After the beans have been strung on thread, the women dry them in the sun for several days. Once they are prepared in this way, the beans will keep for months. When other food is scarce, we always have beans available. The women soak them overnight and then cook them up in tasty, nourishing stews." He turned back to smile at Lavinia. "Moon Beam will be glad to show you how to string the beans and how to prepare many dishes with them."

"I want to learn how to do that and everything else your women do each day," Lavinia said. Then she was distracted from their conversation by a strange sight. She saw piles of bones, all sorts of bones, along the shore where Wolf Dancer was carefully guiding the canoe.

"Those bones," she said, just as Wolf Dancer

beached the canoe. "Where on earth did so many bones come from? And what creatures are they from?"

"These bones have been here for many, many moons," Wolf Dancer said, going back and sitting beside Lavinia. "No one goes among them, for it is forbidden to disturb the dead."

"Are they animal bones, or . . ." Lavinia was unable to finish her sentence. She just could not imagine those bones being human, for there were so many.

And she could not tell by their shape if they were human or not.

All she did know was that they had been bleached white by the sun.

"These bones have been washed ashore and have come together in these large stacks long ago," Wolf Dancer said. "No one really knows for sure, but I would say that some are human bones from shipwrecks of long ago."

"But this is only a narrow, shallow river. How could ships ever travel on it?" Lavinia asked, looking over at Wolf Dancer who now sat beside her.

She could smell the clean scent of him.

She could almost feel his heartbeat, for surely it was pounding as rapidly as hers now that they were so close together.

"I would guess that the bones washed up from the sea over the course of many, many years," Wolf Dancer said thoughtfully. "They make a fearful sight, do they not? That is why my people avoid this island whenever they can. They are afraid of touching the bones."

"I most certainly would not want to touch them," Lavinia said, shivering.

Wolf Dancer slid an arm around her waist and drew her close. "While you are with me you have nothing to fear from anything or anyone," he said. "But I can see how uncomfortable you are here. I will now take you to another beach where there are many beautiful shells. There we will beach the canoe and walk along the sand. I have brought a small basket for you to gather shells, if you wish."

"I would love to," she said, her pulse racing because his lips were so close and his arm was wrapped so protectively and lovingly around her waist. "Wolf Dancer, oh, Wolf Dancer, will you please kiss me? I cannot stand another moment without knowing the wonder of your lips against mine. But if you think I am brazen for asking—"

He twined his fingers through her golden hair and swept her closer to him, his lips finding hers in a wondrous, all-consuming kiss.

Lavinia had never found such bliss, such sweetness, in any man's kiss. She twined her arms around his neck and returned the kiss, then jerked suddenly away from him when she heard the loud call of a bird. She looked up and found a huge, white, long-legged heron flying down, alarmingly close to them.

"She is only curious," Wolf Dancer said as he leaned away from Lavinia and gazed up at the lovely bird. "Not too many people come this far into the swamp. She is only used to seeing those bones."

When he heard Lavinia gasp, he chuckled, brushed a kiss across her brow, then went back to where he had left the paddle resting against the side of the canoe.

"I will take you now to where you can choose which wampum shells you wish for your own necklace, and also for your daughter and Twila," he said, already paddling the canoe away from the bones.

Lavinia found herself relaxing more as they drew away from the bones, but when she saw him guide his canoe toward land again nearby, she wasn't certain she was ready to go ashore, not this close to the skeletal remains.

But when she caught sight of the many beautiful shells that lay everywhere on the white sand, she gasped in pleasure. She was glad when he beached the canoe and handed her the basket.

Together they walked among the shells, some of which were actually in the shape of beads. And there were so many varied colors to choose from.

"These shells have floated in from the ocean, up the river on the tide," Wolf Dancer said, pointing to one shell and then another.

"Please tell me about these different shells," Lavinia said, glad that full strength had returned to her legs so that she could enjoy these special moments with the man she loved. "Each one is beautiful in its own way."

"Let me see if I can find the shells we use to make wampum," Wolf Dancer said, stopping and kneeling to run his fingers through the sand, unearthing several more shells that the sand had hidden from view. "The white wampum beads come from the inner spiral of this shell." He held it out so she could see.

"The purple wampum is taken from the shiny inside of a hard-shell clam. Whether purple or white, the shell beads are ground smooth and then used to decorate bracelets or belts. My people prize them as a sign of wealth."

"There is so much to learn," she murmured. "But I do find it interesting."

She began earnestly gathering shells, feeling utterly content. Wolf Dancer had told her more than once that she was safe with him, so she allowed herself to relax completely.

"Wolf Dancer, for the first time since I left my parents' home to be a wife, I feel free, and oh, so alive," she murmured. "I cared for my husband, but so often I felt trapped in that huge white mansion. I was only able to get out of the house to spend time in my garden, which I loved, and to go into town occasionally for some brief shopping expeditions. But I never traveled with my husband when he left to tend to business, and he was sometimes gone for weeks upon weeks. Yes, I did feel truly trapped."

Wolf Dancer was uneasy about her comment on being free, that she was so happy in her newfound freedom.

Did that mean she would never be happy when married? Perhaps she would not even want to marry again.

He had to change her mind if that was the case, for he now knew that life would never be the way as he dreamed if he could not share it with her.

After her basket was brimful of shells and

beads, they stopped and sat on the sand beside the water.

They watched all sorts of birds and butterflies soaring here and there. Lavinia found herself studying their intriguing, colorful markings.

"I have never been as happy as I feel now," Lavinia murmured, setting her basket on the sand.

Wolf Dancer reached for her and drew her into his arms. He kissed her passionately, but Lavinia stiffened in his arms when she heard a noise close by.

Her eyes flew open and she saw something over Wolf Dancer's shoulder that terrified her.

"An alligator!" she screamed, just as the beast moved quickly through the water toward them.

Wolf Dancer relived another time, another alligator, another woman that he had loved with all his heart but hadn't been able to save. He couldn't allow it to happen again.

Lavinia felt frozen to the ground as she watched Wolf Dancer leap up and grab a large, thick, sharp stick that lay close by. He put himself between Lavinia and the alligator, and just as the beast charged out of the water, its mouth wide open, Wolf Dancer ran toward it and rammed the stick down its throat. The alligator quickly sank into the water, and was soon dead.

Wolf Dancer hurried back to Lavinia. He grabbed her up into his arms. "I am sorry for having put you in harm's way when I have vowed so often to keep you safe," he said, holding her close.

She was still so stunned by his bravery, she couldn't speak. When she was finally able to find words, she clung to him and thanked him over and over again.

"No thanks are ever necessary when I do things for you," Wolf Dancer said fervently. "But I would truly like to kiss you again."

She smiled sweetly at him, twined her arms around his neck, then kissed him.

When he returned the kiss, she felt as though she were floating above herself, it was so beautiful and sweet.

She had finally, truly found her place in this world, and she would never let anything or anyone stand in the way of this newfound happiness.

Especially not Hiram Price.

Yet she could not help wondering what Hiram was thinking now that he knew she was gone, and of her own free will.

She would do all that she could to make certain he had no opportunity to find her and destroy her world all over again.

Chapter Twenty-five

My soul thirsteth for thee,
My flesh longeth for thee.
　　　　　　—Old Testament, Psalms 63:1

The stench of rum was heavy in the air of his study as Hiram paced the floor, an almost empty bottle clutched tightly in his right hand.

He had spent a good portion of the night drinking and trying to make decisions that seemed to elude him.

It was morning now and he could hear the remaining slaves already dutifully in the field, humming and singing as though there wasn't anything wrong.

But Hiram knew that there was plenty wrong. His whole world had been turned upside down, and all because of his crazy doings. When he had killed his brother, he had expected everything to finally go his way, but nothing had turned out right.

Lavinia had fled with her daughter and Twila to parts unknown. Although she had thought she was being clever by pretending to be ill after her husband's death, Hiram had known all along that she had stayed in her room to avoid coming face-to-face with him.

He had hoped she would accept Hiram as part of her life and forget her ill feelings toward him.

But he knew now that he'd only been fooling himself when he'd thought she might actually marry him after her husband was gone. Instead, she had gone to great lengths to avoid him.

He now knew that it was more important to her to escape him than to live in a beautiful mansion with all the luxuries she would ever desire. She had fled without claiming any of this as hers.

He expected that she was even now at her favorite aunt's house outside Atlanta. She had spoken fondly of this aunt often.

Hiram thought he could go to Atlanta and plead with Lavinia to return home, and promise not to broach the idea of marriage. He could say she could run the house as she saw fit. He could tell her he just didn't want to live alone.

But he had his pride and would not beg that woman for anything.

He smiled wickedly.

Yes, he would have all of this to himself, and be happy for it.

That meant if he wanted a wife, he would have to go looking for one, and today was the first day of his search.

He would make certain the slaves were happy enough in their surroundings to remain while he was gone, even though there was no overseer. He had never given one thought to the slaves' happiness before.

But now?

Now they were all he had to keep his plantation going. The tobacco fields were all but bare now, with the harvest almost complete. After he took the tobacco to market and got paid for it, he would decide whether or not to stay in that business, or sell the slaves off and try something else.

He would no longer think of Lavinia or the fact that she seemed to have chosen to give up everything in order to escape him!

"I don't need her," he grumbled. He slammed the bottle down on his desk. "With my money, I can get any lady I want."

But he had one more thing to do before heading into town. He intended to put up posters letting the local women know that he was looking for a wife. There were many widowed women, and often they were left penniless.

Frowning, and cursing beneath his breath, Hiram took the stairs two at a time. When he reached the second-floor landing, he didn't pause before going into Lavinia's bedroom.

Just seeing her belongings made him angry all over again. He felt deeply hurt, too. He had wanted Lavinia as far back as when they were teenagers in Atlanta.

But his brother, with his sculpted face and suave manners, had been the lucky one. And now his brother was gone and Hiram still didn't have Lavinia.

He couldn't help it. Wanting her was eating away at him like a cancer. Even losing his eye had not been as devastating as knowing that he would never have the woman he loved, and had even killed for.

He went into a sudden fit of rage.

He went to Lavinia's chifforobe and grabbed an armful of her clothes from it. He tore up what he could with his bare hands, then took scissors from her sewing basket and destroyed the rest. He continued until none of her beautiful clothes were left in one piece.

His heart pounding, his jaw tight, he went to a window and threw the shutters open, raised the window, then took the tattered remains and pitched them from the window to the ground below, all the while shouting obscenities.

He stopped and stiffened when he saw that the slaves had stopped working and were looking up at him with wide, frightened eyes. Surely they had heard his rantings and seen him throwing the clothes out the window.

"What'cha lookin' at?" he shouted. He doubled a hand into a tight fist and waved it above his head. "Get back to work. Do you hear? Or I'll bring my whip out and set your skin aflame with it!"

They immediately went back to work, and he began to regret threatening them. There was the harvest to consider. He certainly couldn't do it all by himself.

But he still couldn't contain his anger. He broke everything in the room that could be broken, then ran down the stairs.

Dripping wet with sweat, and stinking from the mixture of perspiration and rum, he continued his rampage throughout the house. He broke anything that reminded him of Lavinia . . . all the things she had loved and enjoyed.

Even though he didn't expect her to return and see what he'd done, he still got pleasure from doing it. When he was finished, he stood back and surveyed the destruction.

He wiped sweat from his brow with the palm of a hand, smiling when he saw just how far he had gone. Nothing Lavinia had loved was left intact.

Nothing!

And after he found a woman he could bring into this house as his wife, he'd let her choose pretty things of her own to decorate the rooms.

Wanting to get on with finding a bride, Hiram went to the kitchen and poured some fresh, cold water from a pitcher into a basin. He splashed his face with it, then straightened his back and ran his fingers through his hair.

He hurried to the gun cabinet in the front hall, grabbed his rifle, and ran outside with it. He already had his pistol holstered at the right side of his waist, and had sheathed a knife at the other side.

He planned to go to the newspaper office in the nearest town and persuade them to print some posters that he could tack up here and there in town.

Surely, in time some pretty, lonely thing would see one of those posters and come to investigate. He knew that once she saw the huge plantation house, the fields and slaves, he would have himself a bride.

The woman wouldn't even care that he had only

one eye and that he sweated "like a pig," as some had described it.

Yep, the woman would see how she would be coddled as his wife. He would give her all the pretty clothes her little heart desired!

He hurried outside to the fields. He told each group of slaves that he would be leaving, but he wouldn't be gone for long.

"I trust you," he said, looking from one to the other. "I depend on your being here when I return."

Wide-eyed, fear in the depths of their dark eyes, they all nodded.

"Don't disappoint me," Hiram said over his shoulder as he hurried to the stable. "You'll get good food, more'n you've ever seen before, once this harvest is completed. You won't regret being loyal to Hiram Price."

He went inside the stable, prepared his white mare for riding, then swung himself into the saddle and rode away from the plantation.

"I'm going to find myself a lady!" he cried to the heavens. "And to hell with Lavinia!"

Chapter Twenty-six

Thou shalt love and be loved by me, forever;
A hand like this hand shall throw open
The gates of new life to thee!
—Robert Browning

Although exhausted from her first full day of activity, Lavinia sat beside Wolf Dancer beneath a beautiful sky bright with a dazzling array of stars and a full moon.

The night air had become chilly, so Lavinia held a blanket snugly around her shoulders, while Wolf Dancer was wrapped in his own.

The fire burned brightly in the center of the village. Beside it sat many mothers and fathers as they watched their children at play while they awaited Spirit Talker's arrival.

Food had been shared by the fire, and much talk and laughter. The children had played all afternoon and into the early evening.

Lavinia was glad that Dorey and Twila fit in with the Seminole children so well. They had forgiven the two young braves for what they'd done to Dorey, and the four were fast friends now.

Lavinia watched the children playing a game with sticks.

"That is called a whirl and catch game," Wolf Dancer said as he leaned closer to Lavinia.

He was filled with love for this woman, far more than he had ever thought possible.

They had shared a wonderful day today. The basket of shells they had collected sat in his house waiting to be made into necklaces.

They had shared more than one kiss before returning to the village, but they had not made love, although his body ached to have her.

But he felt it was best to wait until she was stronger before making love. And he wanted to be certain that she felt the same way as he.

As difficult as it might be, he would not initiate lovemaking tonight after the stories had been told. Just by looking into her eyes, he could see how tired she was from all the activities of the day.

She was only sitting beside him now for her daughter's sake. More than once since he and Lavinia had returned from their outing, Dorey had voiced her eagerness to hear the stories with the other children tonight.

Once the stories were told, Wolf Dancer would take Lavinia to his home and tuck her snugly in her bed. He expected her to be asleep before he left the room to go to his own bed.

One day soon he hoped they would share the same bed as man and wife.

"It looks like such a simple game the children are playing, but they seem to be enjoying it," Lavinia said. She smiled at Wolf Dancer. "Will you explain it to me? I want to understand it in case Dorey talks to me about it later."

"Whirl and catch is a favorite game with the boys and girls," Wolf Dancer said, watching the children as Lavinia listened to his explanation. "It is played with ten short sticks. As you see, the sticks are thrown in the air, one at a time, and each child tries to catch them. The person who catches the most wins the game."

Lavinia mentally counted how many Dorey had already caught and noticed that her daughter was disappointed when at the end of the game, she had only two sticks.

Wolf Dancer had also seen how few Dorey had caught. "She will learn to be faster and catch more sticks," he said. He now watched Twila, who had caught four of the sticks and was giggling because she had outdone her friend.

Wolf Dancer was glad when Dorey laughed good-naturedly, accepting that she was not as fast as the others, not even Twila.

This demonstrated her unselfish nature to him. It was a trait loved and admired by all.

Lavinia sighed. The air was still filled with the aromas of the food that had been cooked earlier by the women. She was full, yet comfortably so, and she felt sleepy. She hoped she could stay awake until the stories were all told.

She still tasted the bear ribs she'd eaten for dinner. She had hesitated before taking her first bite, for she had never eaten bear meat before.

But she'd found that it tasted better than any other meat she had ever eaten. She had also enjoyed the hot corn cakes that had been covered with a jelly she was told was called *conte*.

When she had asked one of the women how this jelly was made, the woman had eagerly responded that it was made from the roots of a wild rose bush, which grew on Mystic island. The roots were carefully ground into a pulp, to which water was added. The paste was then air dried and saved for later use. The woman explained that she mixed the powdered root with water and honey to make the delicious jelly.

Lavinia planned to make her own *conte* one day, to show Wolf Dancer that she could be a good cook. She had just never had to cook while living first with her parents in Atlanta, and then with her wealthy husband.

But now, away from all of those luxuries, she would enjoy learning such womanly skills.

At that moment an elderly man stepped from his home near the central fire. His gray hair dragged on the ground behind him as he walked to a small platform, upon which were thick bear pelts.

The children scattered and found their places sitting on blankets that had been spread earlier.

Some mothers had given their children netting to tuck around themselves, so they would not be bitten by mosquitoes.

Lavinia had to smile when she saw Dorey and Twila sharing mosquito netting with the other girls. Running Bear and Deer Shadow were sitting near them with braves of their own age, who chose not to use netting.

Lavinia could only surmise that they had refused the netting because they thought it might make them look weak in the eyes of the girls.

"The Spirit Talker is such an old man," Lavinia whispered to Wolf Dancer as the storyteller made himself comfortable on the platform. It was raised high above, so that everyone would have to look up at him as he told his stories.

"Most Spirit Talkers are elderly, for they must have lived a long life in order to have knowledge of all things," Wolf Dancer said just loud enough for Lavinia to hear. "Our Spirit Talker is a legendary storyteller, and all listen to him in respectful silence."

"What is his true name?" Lavinia asked, watching the elderly man as he tucked his buckskin robe around him, his legs folded beneath him on the platform.

She was fascinated by his long, long hair and watched as the Spirit Talker wound it into a tall bun atop his head, securing it with short sticks stuck into it.

"He was born with the name Star Gazer. That is because his mother gave birth to him outside her home beneath the stars. She wanted to be sure that when he opened his eyes for the first time, he would first see the stars," Wolf Dancer explained. "His mother had had a vision of her firstborn being the village Spirit Talker when he grew into adulthood. She felt that the name Star Gazer fit the child whose life was already mapped out for him."

"What if he had not wanted to be the storyteller when he grew into a man?" Lavinia asked. "What then would his mother have done?"

"There was no question that he would be as his mother willed him to be," Wolf Dancer said. "You see, it was said that Star Gazer felt the calling himself the first time he heard stories being told around the night fire by our people's storyteller."

"What happened to that man?" Lavinia asked softly, hoping she wasn't disturbing anyone around her with her curiosity about Wolf Dancer's people.

"The one who was our people's Spirit Talker was already elderly, yet he lived long enough for Star Gazer to reach the age that he could take over his duties," Wolf Dancer said. "You see, each Spirit Talker must do his best to retell the stories as close to the original version as possible. It is a great responsibility, and the best storytellers are greatly admired."

"It sounds like he might be as much admired and loved as the village chief," Lavinia said, hoping she wasn't offending Wolf Dancer.

"A storyteller and chief are both loved and admired, but never in the same way," Wolf Dancer said.

He was not insulted by Lavinia's comparison, for he, too, would have wondered the same were he not Seminole.

"Star Gazer has devoted his life to the Wind Clan, just as I have, and for that he has earned our people's love," he said. "He keeps our history and traditions alive. But a chief is responsible for the future of his clan. Through prayer, sacrifice and careful thought, he guides the lives of his people. The storyteller prays to the Master of Breath, the same as a chief, but there is one difference. If necessary, the chief must be willing to lay down his life if such be necessary for the survival of his people, whereas nothing akin to that is ever required of a Spirit Talker."

"You . . . would . . . sacrifice yourself?" Lavinia asked, paling at the thought.

"Yes, if it meant the survival of my people," Wolf Dancer said thickly.

When he saw how Lavinia's face drained of color, he smiled and reached beneath the blanket, taking her the hand. "No sacrifice will have to be made here on Mystic Island, so do not fret, my woman, that our future together might be endangered," he said.

"Our . . . future . . . ?" Lavinia asked, her heart racing at the implication of what he had just said.

"Our future as man and wife," Wolf Dancer said, and noted that her eyes widened even more. "You will marry me, will you not?"

Lavinia was stunned speechless by the sudden question, although she had dreamed of this moment after realizing the nature of their feelings for one another.

"You will become my wife?" Wolf Dancer repeated, placing a hand beneath her chin and directing her eyes to his. "I want to protect not only you but also your daughter. I want to love you forever."

Lavinia suddenly became aware that they were sitting among others. She realized that the Spirit Talker was beginning his first tale of the evening.

She looked quickly around to see if anyone had heard Wolf Dancer's proposal of marriage. When she saw that he had spoken so quietly that only she had heard, she turned and smiled into his eyes.

"I will gladly become your wife," she said softly. "Although we have only known one another a short time, I knew right away that I had fallen in love with you. I think it happened the first time I saw you resting in the tree near my house. I dreamed of you often after that."

She didn't mention the white panther, and doubted she would ever question him about it. The creature was too mysterious to talk about, and she felt that if there was some association between him and the panther, he might rather not speak of it.

If he ever wished to talk to her about these mysteries, she wanted him to know that he could tell her anything. Even if he revealed something she could never understand, she would not love him less for it.

"We will marry soon," Wolf Dancer said, still holding her hand as they turned their attention to the tale being told.

Lavinia at first found it hard to concentrate on anything but what they had just agreed upon.

But the more she listened to the Spirit Talker, the more engrossed she became. He made his story so interesting, she couldn't help listening intently, and marveled at his ability.

After a short while, the Spirit Talker drew the first story to a close and started another one. It was about a grandmother spider who stole the sun.

Lavinia settled in more closely to Wolf Dancer. Both now snuggled under the same blanket as they listened together to the words of the elderly storyteller.

"When the world was young, there was blackness on one side," the Spirit Talker said as his eyes moved from child to child. "Nobody on that side of the world could see beyond the nose on his face. One day Mother spider suggested that their new world needed light. Possum said he would go to the other side, where there was light, and steal some, because those people there were too selfish to share it with the world. Fox said he would go. His tail was thick enough to hide some of that light and bring it home to everyone on this side of the world. Possum frowned at Fox. He wanted to be the one to go and get the sun, and so he tried. When he got to the other side, he found the sun high up in a tree. Possum climbed up and grabbed a piece of the sun, which he quickly hid in his tail. But he soon discovered that the light was very hot. It burned all the fur off his tail. From that time on, the possum's tail has been bare. He went home with his burned tail and without the light. Mother spider said that she would go and get the light. She grabbed a pot and then, carrying the pot, spun a web that reached to the other side of the world. Then she crawled on that web until she was able to grab some of the light and put it in her pot. Then she carried it home along the path of her web. Everyone celebrated, for their side of the world finally had light!"

The children applauded and asked for more, but Spirit Talker said that was enough stories until the next time. Then he left and returned to his home.

Dorey ran over to Lavinia. "Mama, did you hear the story?" she asked excitedly. "Wasn't it interesting?"

"Yes, dear, I found it quite fascinating," Lavinia murmured, smoothing a lock of her daughter's hair back from her eyes.

"Mama, Twila wants me to stay the night with her," Dorey blurted out. "May I? Joshua said it was alright."

"I see nothing wrong with that," Lavinia said, smiling at her daughter's excitement. "Enjoy yourself, Dorey."

"I shall, Mama," Dorey said, her eyes bright. "Thank you."

Lavinia watched Dorey run over and take Twila by the hand. Then the two girls skipped toward Joshua's is and Twila's hut.

"I think you need to go to bed," Wolf Dancer said, removing the blanket from around their shoulders. He gazed into her weary eyes. "Did you do too much in one day?"

"It was a wonderful day," Lavinia said as she slowly rose to her feet. "One I shall remember forever."

"I want each and every day to be that unforgettable for you," Wolf Dancer replied. He placed an arm around her waist and walked her toward their home, others behind them collecting their own blankets and dispersing, too.

"If I am with you, they shall be," Lavinia said with a shy smile.

She accompanied him to his hut, and was soon asleep in her bed of blankets and pelts. Wolf Dancer sat beside her, marveling at how the world had become a better place since he had met this woman.

She was all sweetness.

When she smiled or laughed, her joy reached right inside his soul, warming it as nothing had ever before been able to.

But there was still a problem: a certain man that Wolf Dancer knew must be dealt with to assure the continuing contentment of this . . . his . . . woman.

He knew that if Hiram Price ever discovered where she was, he would find his way to Mystic Island, and perhaps bring the whole United States cavalry with him. Wolf Dancer could not allow that to happen.

As soon as Lavinia had the strength, he and she would do what they must to ensure her happiness on Mystic Island, and her safety.

"That man will not be a danger to anyone much longer," he whispered. "And soon, my woman, we will make love. How I need you, and I feel that your needs match my own. Perhaps even tomorrow . . . ?"

Chapter Twenty-seven

When love could teach a monarch to be wise,
And gospel-light first dawn'd from
Bullen's eyes.

—Thomas Gray

Lavinia awakened feeling refreshed, even renewed, after her outing with Wolf Dancer the day before.

She would never forget how understanding and gentle he'd been when she told him how tired she was after hearing the Spirit Talker's stories.

She sat up on her bed of pelts and stretched her arms lazily above her head, yawned, then smiled as she recalled how gently Wolf Dancer had tucked her in.

She knew he had sat beside her as she fell asleep. It was wonderful to know that she could trust him so much.

She had seen the need in his eyes yesterday as he gazed into hers. She had wondered if he had seen that she felt the same needs.

But neither of them had made any motion to assuage those needs. They both knew it would happen sometime.

And the fact that they had made a commitment

to one another, to be married, made her heart swim with pure joy.

Although she had been married before, to a wonderful, gentle man, this love she felt for Wolf Dancer was brand new. She felt a deep passion for Wolf Dancer, something she had never experienced before for any man.

And the knowledge that he loved her so much he wanted her to be his wife made tears of joy fill her eyes.

She had felt a connection between them from the moment they first made eye contact. At first she'd thought it might be her imagination. But now she knew that his love for her was real. She wanted to shout her joy to the treetops.

This life with him would be so different from her life with Virgil. She and Wolf Dancer shared a true connection, and had passionate feelings for one another.

To be fulfilled in this way was something she had never expected in her life. But now she would belong to the most wonderful, gentle, caring, loving man in the world.

She glanced over at the basket of shells, remembering the special time spent with Wolf Dancer.

Then she noticed other things in the room that had not been there yesterday: a beautiful doeskin dress embellished with beads on the front, and a pair of new moccasins on the floor mats.

Also there was a basin of fresh water and a cloth with which to bathe herself.

She had been told that Moon Beam would bring

these things for her. It seemed that the woman felt she owed Lavinia much because her two sons had wronged Dorey.

Lavinia would correct this misconception, for the lovely woman owed Lavinia nothing except friendship, which Lavinia openly welcomed. It would be good to have a special friend among these people. She hoped to live among them for the rest of her life. She would enjoy learning the ways of the Seminole, not only from Wolf Dancer but also from this friend.

A mischievous glint appeared in Lavinia's eyes as she looked at the lovely dress. She glanced out the window and saw that it was barely dawn. Surely Wolf Dancer would still be asleep.

She wondered what he might think if he found her at his bedside when he awakened.

If she hurried, she could wash up, put on the dress, and get into his room before he woke up.

If he found her sitting there, surely he would understand why she had come so early in the morning to his bedside.

She felt wonderful today, without an ache in her body. Her wound was feeling much better. In fact, she couldn't feel any pain in it whatsoever.

Would Wolf Dancer think her a hussy if she approached him to make love for the first time? She didn't think so.

"We love each other," she whispered to herself as she rose from her bed. "It is time to share the magic wonder of our love."

She hurried through her bath, slid the beautiful, soft dress over her head, then did the best she could with her long hair. She had no brush so she moved her fingers through it until she finally got the witches' knots out and the blond strands fell gently across her shoulders and down her back.

Having never approached a man in such a way, she felt a strange knot in the pit of her stomach. She swallowed hard, closed her eyes, and took a deep, nervous breath, then left her room.

She tiptoed down the hall, even though she knew no one else was there to hear her.

Dorey had spent the night with Twila and Joshua. The house was totally hers and Wolf Dancer's, to do as they pleased with their privacy!

Her pulse raced as she crept down the stairs. She could feel the heat of a blush rush to her cheeks.

She placed the palms of her hands there and tried to cool her flesh with them. She didn't want Wolf Dancer to awaken and find her blushing like a timid child.

She wanted him to see her love for him, her need. She hoped he would open his arms to her and welcome her into his bed.

She could even envision him removing the dress and moccasins as he gazed at her with those mystifying green eyes.

She could almost feel his lips where no man's lips had been before—on her aching breasts. Her husband had been timid in his own way and had never kissed her anywhere except her mouth. He had not even caressed her breasts, as she knew most men were wont to do.

She had not hungered for any of those things, even

though she knew it was a natural thing for a man to worship a woman's body, especially his wife's.

But all that Virgil had wanted was the release her body provided. She had always lain there, almost lifeless, as he thrust endlessly into her until he finally attained what he sought from her.

He had always spent only another moment in her bed, which he took to give her a quick peck on her cheek, and then he departed for his own room. He would leave Lavinia feeling strangely used, and with a longing that she doubted would ever be fulfilled. She had discovered shortly after they were married that her husband knew only what to do to find the release his body cried out for.

Now it was Lavinia whose body cried out for release. For the first time in her life, she wanted to be with a man in every way. And she did not think she was brazen for feeling such things. Wanting to be loved was not shameful!

Having bolstered her courage enough to proceed with her plan, Lavinia slowly approached Wolf Dancer's bed.

The light was dim coming from the window, since it was still so early in the morning. But there was enough light to see across the room where Wolf Dancer lay.

She hadn't expected to find him sleeping in the nude, as she now saw he was. She could not stop another blush from rushing to her cheeks, for she felt as though she had invaded his privacy. Surely Wolf Dancer did not expect a woman to come to his bed unannounced, especially at this time of day.

She knew she should go back to her room, but the sight of him caused her to stand there frozen, her eyes taking in every inch of his beautiful, bronzed body.

His long black hair was spread out beneath his head, framing his sculpted face. The muscles of his shoulders and arms bulged, even relaxed in sleep.

She ached to run her hands over those muscles, and feel them against her own flesh!

She let her eyes roam slowly lower, marveling at his muscled chest, past his flat belly, to see something that made her knees almost buckle. Her gaze froze on that part of him that God had been so generous with.

She had only seen one other man naked and that had been her husband.

Now that she saw this man in the nude, she understood the vast difference possible between two males.

And this man, whose bronzed body was so beautiful, was not even awake or aroused. When he was fully excited, surely he could give a woman such loving that she would never want it to end.

"What am I thinking?" Lavinia whispered to herself, framing her face between her hands at the realization of where her mind had shamefully taken her.

But she couldn't help herself. Her body was reacting in many strange, yet sensually exciting ways. She now knew that she couldn't leave this place without finding out what it was really like to be loved.

She knew just how much Wolf Dancer loved her; perhaps he would demonstrate it in ways that she had never known were possible.

Suddenly his eyes opened and he was staring at her with those beautiful green eyes. Gazing at her in wonder, he slowly leaned up on an elbow.

"I'm sorry," Lavinia murmured. Her pulse raced so hard, she was afraid he might hear her heart beating.

"I didn't mean . . ." she quickly began, before he had the chance to speak. Then she halted, feeling too awkward to say anything else, or even remember what she had planned to say.

Wolf Dancer was not really surprised to find her there. When they had parted last night, they had left something undone between them.

It seemed that Lavinia had awakened feeling those needs that had been left unanswered when she had gone to bed without him.

"Come to me," Wolf Dancer said, standing, the muscles of his legs flexing as he took a step toward her. "I was just dreaming about you."

"You were?" Lavinia asked, her voice sounding strange to her now in its huskiness. But everything about her body was suddenly different.

She smiled sheepishly. "I had to come," she murmured. "Was I wrong to?"

"In my dream I beckoned to you to come," Wolf Dancer said huskily as his passion for her filled his very soul. "You heard me calling for you. You answered my call."

"When I awakened, you were the first thing I thought of. Last night when we parted, I was so tired I could not have . . ." she began.

Yet she could not finish. It seemed too brazen. This man wasn't her husband.

"You could not do what last night?" Wolf Dancer urged, smiling at her as he stepped closer. "Make love?"

"You must think me so brazen," Lavinia murmured, lowering her eyes.

When she felt his hand beneath her chin, slowly raising it so that their eyes could meet, she knew he was now close enough that she could reach out and embrace him.

She could even smell his clean scent and realized he was freshly bathed.

She now knew that he had been awake long before she had risen and had taken his usual early-morning swim in the creek that bisected the island a short distance away.

She also knew that after that swim he made his morning prayers. She knew these things because he had told her.

"You knew that I would come, didn't you?" Lavinia asked, searching his eyes. "You weren't asleep at all when I stepped into the room."

"No, I was not asleep the moment you arrived, but only resting my eyes until you approached, as I beckoned you to do," he said. "You are here. And you are beautiful. The dress? Moon Beam placed it in your room for you last night before I left to sleep in my own bed. She also put the moccasins there for you. She is trying hard to make up for what her sons did to your daughter."

"She shouldn't feel angry at them for what they did, for I no longer do," Lavinia said softly. "Do you not know that it was Dorey's disappearance that finally gave us a reason to meet and become acquainted? I shall never blame those boys for wanting to talk to her, nor should anyone else. My daughter found her way here, where she belongs, just as you found me and brought me here."

"Yes, it was all in the Master of Breath's plan," Wolf Dancer said. He stepped back only far enough so he had room to slowly undress her.

"Master of Breath?" Lavinia repeated, hardly able to think now that he was sliding her dress over her head. He tossed the dress to the floor, leaving her as nude as he.

"Our people's Master of Breath is the same as your God," he said thickly. "Sometimes we call him the Great Spirit."

"I am grateful to your Master of Breath for making you the man that you are," Lavinia said.

She sucked in a breath of pure bliss when he leaned down and flicked his tongue across one of her breasts, and then the other.

It was something so wonderful, her knees almost buckled beneath her. But Wolf Dancer didn't allow that to happen.

He lifted her in his arms and carried her to his bed of pelts. Then he knelt down at her feet, taking the time to remove her moccasins.

When they were discarded, he lifted a foot to his lips, his tongue circling around her biggest toe. She inhaled a breath of wonder, and then she couldn't think at all. Just before he spread himself over her, she saw the true magnificence of his manhood at its full length, now that he was ready to pleasure her.

"Let me love you," Wolf Dancer whispered into her ear as he blanketed her with his body. She felt his fullness pressing in where she was wet and ready for him. She was swamped by a feeling of desire and joy she had never known possible.

She was feverish with desire.

Her body was yearning for him.

She felt an urgency building inside her that was new to her, yet she knew what it was. It was her body crying out for him and the wild, sensuous pleasure he would bring her.

"Please . . . please . . . do love me," she found herself whispering as she twined her arms around his neck. "Make love to me. I . . . shall . . . oh, so willingly return your love."

She moaned throatily when she felt him push himself inside her, causing pleasurable sensations that she had never felt before as he began his rhythmic thrusts.

His lips came down hard onto hers as he kissed her with a fierce, possessive heat.

She trembled and came further alive beneath his kisses and sweet caresses. He ran his hands over her body, lingering here and there when he discovered that touching and caressing her at a certain place gave her more pleasure than the last.

Wolf Dancer slid his mouth from her lips and moved it over one of her nipples.

He could hear her gasp of pleasure as he swept his tongue around the nipple, then softly nipped it with his teeth, just hard enough to arouse more pleasure in her.

With each of his thrusts in her, waves of liquid heat seemed to pulse through him, his body aching for completion since he had hungered so long for her.

But he held back, for he wanted her to know every pleasure possible. Already he could tell she was not familiar with sexual satisfaction.

She was wildly hungry for a man. It was obvious her husband had not offered her this kind of fulfilment. He could tell that she was new at this.

It was evident in the way she gasped with his each new approach to pleasing her.

Now, as his hands cupped her full breasts, his tongue moving from one nipple to the other, he could tell this was a new experience for her by the way she seemed to marvel silently over the pleasure it gave her.

The realization gave him double pleasure.

He kissed her again as his lean, sinewy buttocks moved, thrusting him into her. She locked her legs around him so that he could move more deeply within her.

And when he reached that sensitive place within a woman that he knew would bring her immense pleasure, he stroked it skillfully, and kissed her again as she gasped and moaned and clung to him.

He swept his arms around her and cradled her there, marveling that she was so deeply hungry for his loving.

He was so happy that he was the man who was giving her such pleasure for the first time, ever. He knew now what she wanted, and vowed he would give it to her.

He wanted her to be happy . . . to be fulfilled. He wanted her always to know that he was there for her, in every way.

His tongue brushed her lips lightly.

Then he whispered against them. "I want you now. Are you ready?" He knew she was. But he wanted to be certain.

"Yes, yes . . ." Lavinia groaned. "Please, now . . ."

Lavinia's mind seemed to splinter with sensation as she discovered the true meaning of passion . . . of intense loving . . . of giving!

She clung to him as he buried his face next to her neck and she knew that he was finding his own deepest pleasure. He thrust more deeply than before, over and over again, her moans proving that she was giving back to a man for the first time.

And she treasured this moment with him!

She would never forget it.

Afterward, they lay together, breathing hard.

It was so different with Wolf Dancer than with her husband.

If it had been Virgil who'd taken such pleasure,

he would already be gone, leaving her alone and unfulfilled. Instead, Wolf Dancer was holding her tightly as though he never wanted to let her go.

She brushed his lips lightly with kisses. She was flooded with emotions she could not even begin to thank him for.

She truly was a woman now, and she would continue to know a woman's pleasure as long as she had Wolf Dancer to love her.

"I would like to stay here the rest of the day," Lavinia said as Wolf Dancer rolled away from her and lay on his side, gazing at her with his mystical green eyes.

"I would as well, but there is something planned for today that I have not yet told you," Wolf Dancer said, sitting up as she propped herself up beside him.

"What is it?" Lavinia murmured, welcoming a blanket around her shoulders as she became aware of the coolness of the room.

"I have asked Shining Soul to cast a spell on Hiram Price," Wolf Dancer said. He saw shock in her expression. "We should be there, a part of it."

"A spell?" Lavinia gasped. "Of what sort?"

She didn't want to be afraid of this side of the Seminole's beliefs, yet she was, a little. But she knew that whatever Wolf Dancer had planned with his shaman, it could not be harmful to her.

"Are you hesitant to join me as Shining Soul casts his spell?" he asked, reaching up and gently pushing her long hair back from her shoulders.

"If I am with you, nothing will frighten me," she murmured.

"Something good for you and your daughter will come of this," Wolf Dancer said, putting his arms around her and drawing her into his embrace. "We must eat, get dressed, and go tell Shining Soul that we are ready to sit with him as he casts his spell."

"Should Dorey be there, too?" Lavinia asked, rising and feeling a quiet joy as Wolf Dancer slid the dress over her head, then knelt down and slipped her moccasins on her feet.

"The spell is meant to help Dorey, too, so, yes, she should sit with us during the spell casting," Wolf Dancer said.

He drew her against him. "Never be afraid of anything our people do, especially Shining Soul," he assured her. "He is a man of good heart. He works for the well-being of our people, including you and your daughter, as well as Twila and Joshua."

"Can Joshua and Twila join us?" she asked.

"It would be good to have them there, too," Wolf Dancer said. "But I will urge everyone else to stay in their homes until Shining Soul is finished."

The fact that he would have his people stay away made Lavinia wonder again about what was going to happen. Yet she cast her doubts aside, resolving to trust anything that Wolf Dancer had planned for her and her daughter.

She gave him a soft smile as he reached for full buckskin leggings instead of his breechclout. As he dressed, she marveled anew that she was there with him, loved by him.

It was like a dream come true for her!

Yet now she wondered what else besides spells she would witness while living with him. She hoped she was ready for whatever might come her way.

Chapter Twenty-eight

O! How this spring of love resembleth
The uncertain glory of an April day.
                            —William Shakespeare

The village was quiet. All but those who were participating in Shining Soul's spell were inside their homes.

Except for the birds' chatter in the trees, there were no other sounds as Shining Soul knelt in front of his hut, using his wand to draw a circle on the ground.

Lavinia sat close to Wolf Dancer, while Dorey, Twila, and Joshua sat a little further away.

All of their eyes were on Shining Soul as he sank down stiffly in the middle of the circle he had just drawn, his stuffed owl headdress on his head.

Gazing up, he lifted his hands heavenward and began to pray. Not a sound was made elsewhere as his voice rose into the cloudy sky. "Oh, Master of Breath, whose breath gives life to all the Seminole people, hear me as I come before you to seek your help," he cried. "I am one of your children, small and weak. Master of Breath, I need your strength to cast a spell on someone who has brought heartache to those who do not deserve it. Oh, Master of Breath, I seek not to be superior to my brothers, but I need power enough to cast a spell this day."

Lavinia gasped when she saw Shining Soul fall suddenly quiet, seemingly going into a trance, his eyes rolling back into his head.

Wolf Dancer had forewarned Lavinia of all that she would witness today, and she had then told her daughter and Joshua and Twila, so they would not be too afraid.

Wolf Dancer had told Lavinia that while Shining Soul was in a trance, his spirit would leave his body and soar to the heavens, where he would converse with the Sun God, asking this god to hear the same plea that he had spoken aloud to the Seminole's Master of Breath. It was then that Shining Soul would disclose his wishes to the Sun God.

Wolf Dancer had further said that the Sun God was the most important god to his Seminole people.

But now, in the midst of the ceremony, Wolf Dancer reached over and took Lavinia's hand as they waited for Shining Soul to return to himself.

Wolf Dancer looked over his shoulder and saw that Dorey and Twila were clinging tightly to one another, their eyes wide with a mixture of fear and wonder as Shining Soul's eyes remained rolled back in his head.

Wolf Dancer glanced over at Joshua, who seemed just as afraid, but who even now, as Wolf Dancer watched, placed an arm around both girls, drawing them closer to him.

Wolf Dancer sensed that perhaps enough time

had elapsed for Shining Soul to complete his conversation with the Sun God. Just as he turned to look at Shining Soul, the elderly man's eyes opened and blinked several times.

"It is done," Shining Soul said, looking from one to the other of his audience. "Visible only to me, the Sun God did not await my ascent into his sky home, but instead came to me and hovered just above my head as I spoke of my wishes. The Sun God replied, assuring me that he would play a major role in what happens to the evil white man."

"How will it be done?" Lavinia asked, even though she found it peculiar to act as though she believed in this strange sort of magic. But while she was with Wolf Dancer, she had begun to believe that anything was possible.

"He did not divulge to me how, but only said that it would be done," Shining Soul explained. "He told me to wait one sleep and then go to the huge white house when the moon is full. That will be the time when the evil man's end will begin."

Shining Soul rose slowly to his feet.

He teetered as though he might fall, then steadied himself just as Wolf Dancer went quickly to help him.

"When I enter trances, the magic takes away much of my strength," Shining Soul said, his voice drawn. "I must go and rest now. Just know that what I have told you today is truth."

"We know," Wolf Dancer said. He took Shining Soul gently by an elbow and helped him into his home.

"My owl headdress," Shining Soul said, leaning his head down for Wolf Dancer to remove it. "Please take it from my head and place it in its special case until it is time to wear it again."

Wolf Dancer gently lifted the headdress from the shaman's head and placed it in its magic case, then went back to Shining Soul and helped him down onto his thick pallet of furs.

After Shining Soul stretched out, his eyes already closed, Wolf Dancer gently placed a blanket over him. He knelt there beside his shaman for a while longer, and only when he saw that Shining Soul was asleep did he leave.

When he stepped outside the lodge, Lavinia ran up to him. "Is he alright?" she asked, having seen how the trance had weakened Shining Soul.

"He is elderly, but as I have told you before, he is a strong man, and will be among us for many more moons to come," Wolf Dancer said. He placed his hands gently on her shoulders. "He will witness not only the first child born of our love for one another, but also the second."

"You are looking ahead to children?" Lavinia asked, smiling into his eyes. "That is wonderful, Wolf Dancer. I dearly wish to give Dorey a sister and a brother. Except for Twila, Dorey has been lonesome for other children."

"She will have a true family again once we have spoken our vows," he assured her.

He looked over at Twila and Dorey, then at Joshua. "Joshua, care for the children today, will you? Lavinia and I have much to discuss concerning our future."

"I will do that for you and Lavinia," Joshua said, smiling at her. "Lavinia, you take your time with Wolf Dancer. De girls always have enough to do to keep dem busy."

"Before we can return to my home, which will soon be yours also, Lavinia, I must alert my people that they may leave their lodges and resume their normal day's activities," Wolf Dancer said. "You can wait for me, or go on to my lodge."

"I will wait here," she said, then stood alone as she watched Joshua and the girls go to Joshua's home, while Wolf Dancer asked one of his warriors to spread the word that their shaman had performed his spell.

Then Wolf Dancer returned to her. "Come with me," he urged, taking her by the hand. "There is something else I want you to see."

"What is it?" Lavinia asked curiously. Each day now she was being shown something new and exciting.

"You will see," he said, then led her through the thick vegetation until they came to the river.

He suddenly stopped. He bent to his knees and lifted a rock that was not too heavy for Lavinia to carry, then gave it to her. "You will need this," he said. "You have much to learn about my people, now, before we are married, and later, after we have shared our vows. From now on, we will share everything until we are no longer of this earth."

Lavinia hefted the rock and followed Wolf Dancer, then stopped and gazed in awe at what lay ahead of them.

There were many rocks, stacked upon one another in the form of a wide circle.

She gazed questioningly at Wolf Dancer. "Is this what you wanted to show me?" she asked, turning and gazing at the carefully stacked rocks.

"Yes, it is important for you to know about this," he said. "We should go close enough for you to place your rock with the others."

"Why am I going to do this?" Lavinia asked, following him until they came to the circle of rocks. Up close, she realized the rocks formed a wall higher than her head.

"This is a sacred circle of rocks," Wolf Dancer said. He stepped closer and placed his hand on one of them. "It has been built by people who bring stones here in memory of a loved one who has journeyed on ahead of them."

"I have brought only one stone, but I want it to represent my mother and father, as well as my husband," Lavinia murmured, wanting to embrace this Seminole belief.

"Lay it with the others," Wolf Dancer encouraged, stepping back. "Speak with all of the stones that are there and tell them what is in your heart."

Lavinia stepped up to the stones and very carefully placed the one she had brought with the others, making certain it was secure so that it would not tumble free after she was gone.

She gave Wolf Dancer a questioning glance.

"Tell them your feelings, but not aloud," he said. "It is between only you and the sacred rocks. They will hear your thoughts."

Lavinia began thinking to herself how she missed her parents and her husband, and thought of everything else that had made her feel so alone these past months, even when her husband was alive.

But she then thought with gratitude of what she had found with Wolf Dancer, feeling blessed in every way since their acquaintance.

Having thought everything that she felt needed to be expressed, Lavinia turned to Wolf Dancer and smiled. "Thank you for bringing me here," she murmured. "I felt the presence of my parents and my husband as I stood thinking about them."

"They were there," Wolf Dancer said, drawing her into his embrace and holding her gently against him. "They always will be, now that you have placed your stone there to represent them. Come here when you need them. They will be here for you."

"It's wonderful that you understand about my husband," Lavinia said, gazing up into his eyes. "Most men would be jealous, even of a dead husband."

"Jealousy is a wasted emotion," Wolf Dancer said, placing a gentle hand beneath her chin.

He brought her lips to his and kissed her, then whispered, "Let us go home, woman. I believe you have learned enough today about my people and their magic."

"I shall never tire of learning about your people," she said.

Holding hands, they walked back toward the village, Lavinia truly feeling blessed that she had found this wonderful man who cared for her so much.

Then she thought of Hiram. Although a spell had been cast to ensure that he would finally get his comeuppance, she knew how shrewd a man he was.

She prayed to herself that he would not find a way to escape what was planned for him.

While he was out there somewhere, possibly plotting how to get her, she knew she could not rest easy!

Chapter Twenty-nine

If you remember'st not the slightest
Folly that ever love did make thee run into,
Thou hast not lov'd.

— *William Shakespeare*

"It was so wonderful to awaken in your arms," Lavinia said as she sat with Wolf Dancer beside the fire, eating their morning meal. "And soon I shall do that every morning. It is so hard to believe that we are actually going to be married. The first time I saw you, I thought you were a figment of my imagination as you sat there looking so handsome in the tree. It is strange how seeing you didn't frighten me. I think deep down inside I knew even then that you were my destiny."

"And that you are mine," Wolf Dancer said.

His gaze roamed slowly over Lavinia, finding her beautiful in another new dress that Moon Beam had brought for her.

There were no beaded designs on it. It was just the brightest white doeskin he had ever seen.

It seemed to have been meant for a woman of such beautiful pale skin. The color of the dress blended with her skin tone, creating a vision of loveliness.

Lavinia gazed at the food spread before her on a

wooden platter. Everything looked delicious. Moon Beam had brought not only the lovely dress that Lavinia wore today so proudly but also a tray of assorted meats and orange slices.

Since she had moved to Florida, Lavinia had grown to love the fact that she could just reach up and pluck an orange from a tree. It was so special to enjoy the sweet fruit that way.

"There is enough food here for an army," Lavinia said, laughing softly when she saw how that comment made Wolf Dancer's eyebrows lift. "That's what my father often said about what my mother put on our breakfast table. Although we had servants and cooks, my mother always insisted on making our breakfast. And what a breakfast it was! I shall never forget her pancakes."

"My father called them flapjacks," she went on, giggling.

"I am not familiar with those words . . . pancakes and flapjacks," Wolf Dancer said, taking a bite of turtle meat and chewing it.

"I shall make you some one day soon," Lavinia replied, glad that she had learned how to make pancakes from her mother.

"How do you eat this . . . pancake?" Wolf Dancer asked, shoving his empty plate aside.

He leaned back on an elbow, stretching his bare, muscled legs out before him. Today he was again wearing only a breechclout.

"With maple syrup or also with honey," Lavinia murmured, reminded how Dorey had always enjoyed that particular breakfast.

Her daughter had come early this morning just as Lavinia was getting dressed, and asked to spend another day with Twila and the "boys," as she now referred to the two brothers. Dorey had also asked permission to go on a search for a honey tree with her three friends.

Lavinia had hesitated, uneasy at the idea of Dorey leaving the village. She would never forget her own close call with the snake, and also knew how quickly an alligator could appear out of nowhere.

Also she could never forget about the white panther that people said guarded the island. She hadn't seen the white panther for quite a while now.

Perhaps she never would again.

Something told her that neither she nor the children had anything to worry about as far as that panther was concerned.

But Hiram was another matter. He was a true concern, one that wouldn't go away, at least not until the Sun God's prophecy was fulfilled. Until then, she could not help being uneasy at the possibility that he was searching for her.

She wondered if he would have the courage to come this far into the Everglades to find her. Or had he given up on having her?

She prayed each morning and night for the latter.

"My people depend on honey as a quick source of energy," Wolf Dancer said as Lavinia pushed her empty wooden plate aside. "I am certain the two young braves know exactly where a honey tree can be found."

"Didn't I hear you say earlier that some warriors

have gone out this morning on a hunt?" Lavinia asked, suddenly concerned. What if the children got in the way of an arrow?

"Both young braves know where the hunters usually go, so they will not venture anywhere near," Wolf Dancer said. He gazed into the flames of the fire, and then into Lavinia's eyes. "In our village, the men bring to me all the game they catch. I will then divide it among the families according to their needs. Moon Beam will be one of those who gets the most, for she no longer has a husband to hunt for her and her children."

He smiled. "The chief is privileged to keep all hides, unless he wishes to give them to someone needy," he said. "I have enough hides, so I shall give them to those who do not."

"You prove over and over again how kind and generous you are," Lavinia murmured. She moved over to Wolf Dancer and slowly ran her hands across his bare, muscled chest. "Can you be as generous with me this morning?"

"And what can I give to you?" Wolf Dancer asked, reaching out for Lavinia and bringing her down atop him as he stretched out on his back on the rich pelts beside the fire. "This?"

He framed her face between his hands and brought her lips down onto his. He gave her a heated kiss, then put his hands at her waist and moved her beneath him.

He did not bother undressing her. He just smoothed his hands up under the skirt of her dress and began caressing her where she was already wet with want.

"Your breechclout," she whispered against his lips as he moved his mouth to her cheek. She was breathless with the passion building inside her as he moved his fingers skillfully over her love mound. "My dress."

He said nothing. Only sat up and pulled her dress up and over her, then tossed it aside.

He stood up long enough to remove his breechclout, revealing how ready he was to make love with her. His manhood was at its fullest.

Lavinia reached out a hand and filled it with his flesh, moving her fingers on him. She was soon very aware of how she was making him feel.

He was breathing hard. His head was thrown back in ecstasy, his long black hair hanging down to his waist behind him.

She saw his jaw tighten as the pleasure built within him, and then suddenly he took her hand away and surprised her by placing her hand on herself, where his fingers had been only moments ago.

He moved her hand over her mound.

She blushed with the wantonness of what she was doing, for she felt a pleasure from her own caresses that usually only came with Wolf Dancer's touch.

"How . . . ?" she said, searching his eyes.

"It is just one other way to receive pleasure," Wolf Dancer said, easing her hand away, then stretching himself over her and gently shoving his manhood into her.

"While the children are gathering sweetness in the forest, we shall gather our own in the privacy of my home," Wolf Dancer whispered into her ear. Lavinia's breath caught with rapture as he delved even deeper inside her. "I love you. How did I ever live without you?"

"I wasn't truly alive until that day I first saw you," Lavinia whispered back to him. "It was as though a magic wand had been waved between us, causing us to love one another at once."

"And it is forever," Wolf Dancer said huskily.

He gave her another meltingly hot kiss as his body continued moving within her. He was very aware of how she was writhing in response.

Her soft moans came rapidly, making him sure that this time it would not take long for both of them to reach that place of pleasure that only those who were truly in love ever found.

"Oh, how I need you," Lavinia said as his lips fell upon one of her breasts, even as he continued to stroke within her.

She gasped when he nipped at the tip of her breast, then swirled his tongue around it.

She drew a ragged breath. "My love, oh, my love," she cried as the heat of passion spread within her, her body growing even more feverish with this passion.

He paused for only a moment, so that he could look into her eyes. "My woman, you are so beautiful," he said huskily. "Your body was made for loving."

"And you are a master at loving," Lavinia said in

a flood of emotion. "You have awakened many pleasure points on my body that I never knew existed."

"There are many, many more, but I will awaken only a few at a time," he said, chuckling teasingly.

He kissed her again, his arms wrapped around her to draw her even more snugly into his embrace.

And then he reached the peak of his pleasure. The euphoria that filled his entire being was almost more than he could bear.

He thrust into her one more time and she clung harder to him, moaning as she found her own paradise in her lover's arms.

She watched him roll away from her, his body so beautiful she wanted to kiss him all over.

But she knew they should not stay undressed for long, for he had chieftain duties to tend to, and the children could arrive at any moment with their prize. And his warriors could arrive home with their own catch of the day!

"Will it always be like this?" Lavinia asked, pulling the lovely dress over her head.

She reached for a brush that Moon Beam had given to her. It was nothing like any she had ever seen before. It was made from the stiff bristles of some animal. She didn't want to know which, or she might not want to use it.

As it was, she didn't have her own brush, or anything else, for that matter. She hoped to get a few of her belongings when she went with Wolf Dancer to the mansion tonight.

This was the time that the Sun God had told them about.

Tonight they would go and see that Hiram got his comeuppance.

How?

She didn't want to know. She just wanted it over with, and quickly.

She watched Wolf Dancer pull his breechclout on, covering that part of him that awakened so many luscious feelings within her.

She felt shameful for thinking such things, yet this was a new life, with new awakenings each day, it seemed!

"I'm a bit uneasy about what we are going to do tonight," Lavinia said, her hair hanging neatly down her back.

"You do not have to go if you would feel better staying at home while I see to things," Wolf Dancer said. He took her hands and gently pulled her up before him. He wrapped his arms around her waist and gazed into her eyes. "Would you rather stay here?"

"No, I'd better go with you. I need to see what happens with my own eyes, and also I would like to get some things from the house," she said. "Dorey loves storybooks. I want to get some for her. She will enjoy reading to your people's children. She can even teach them how to read. She taught Twila. Now Twila enjoys the books the same as Dorey."

She paused, lowered her eyes, then gazed back up at Wolf Dancer. "And then there is my mother's Bible," she said, her voice breaking with emotion. "I brought it with me after my parents died. I feel she is with me when I hold it in my hands."

"We shall get everything you want," Wolf Dancer said, then stepped away from her and stood over the fire, gazing into its flames. "And then we will burn everything."

Lavinia gasped. "Burn . . . everything . . . ?" she asked, the sound of her voice bringing Wolf Dancer around to look into her eyes.

"That is what must be done to fulfill the command of the Sun God," he said. "I talked with Shining Soul after you went to bed last night. He told me things that he did not share with you, for fear that you would not want to see it done."

"But . . . to burn . . . ?" she said, searching his eyes.

"Yes, burn," he said thickly.

"The house is so big," she said, swallowing hard. "There will be . . . . such savage flames."

He nodded.

"What about the slaves?" she asked.

"Those who wish to come with us, can, and those who wish to go elsewhere, can also do that," Wolf Dancer said. He went to her and framed her face between his hands. "Will all of this be acceptable to you?"

"You will not tell me what you plan to do with Hiram," she said hesitantly.

Her husband had loved the mansion. She had

never felt the same. To her, it was just a home, a place for her to raise Dorey with much love.

"It is up to Hiram," Wolf Dancer said. Then he looked toward the closed door as he heard the laughter of the children approaching.

"They are home," Wolf Dancer said. He again looked into her eyes. "Are you going to be alright with everything?"

"I will be fine," Lavinia said. She smiled weakly at him. "It is . . . just so much . . . to accept so quickly."

"Once we are back home, after doing what must be done you will forget all that happened at the place where you never found true happiness," he said. He touched her cheek. "You were never happy there, were you?"

"No," she said, smiling slowly at him.

"Then let us go outside and see what the children have brought home from their venture this morning," he said, taking her hand.

They walked outside together, hand in hand.

"Mama, see?" Dorey cried excitedly, running up to her. "We have brought home a deerskin full of honey." She giggled. "And there was only one bee sting." She nodded over at Twila. "Twila, show them your bee sting."

Twila held out her hand.

"I removed the stinger myself," Dorey said, smiling proudly.

"Does it hurt, Twila?" Lavinia asked. She stepped away from Wolf Dancer and took the child's hand in hers. There was only a small bump.

"Running Bear found medicine in the forest,"

Twila said, glancing over at him. "It was some sort of plant. He rubbed the sting with it, and suddenly the hurt was gone."

"How kind," Lavinia said, glancing at Running Bear, and then at Dorey, who was standing near him.

Lavinia felt it was good that the children had become friends, and that Dorey had forgiven the young braves so quickly. But she was aware that her daughter and Running Bear seemed to have formed a special bond. She knew that her daughter was infatuated with this young boy.

Lavinia's eyes met Running Bear's. She smiled at him gently, hoping that he wouldn't take advantage of her daughter, then reminded herself that he, too, was only a child.

"Now let us see that honey," Wolf Dancer said, sensing Lavinia's uneasiness at her daughter and Running Bear's interest in one another.

He knew that it was natural for a young boy and girl to have these sorts of infatuations, and knew that it would probably be short-lived, as had his own infatuations with young girls in years past.

He took the deerskin and opened it, gasping at how much honey had been collected.

And then a bee buzzed out from the bag, making a quick escape.

They all laughed, but even though Lavinia was laughing, her mind went back to what she and Wolf Dancer had been discussing.

She was almost afraid for night to fall; with it would come a test of her true feelings for Wolf

Dancer and the life he was offering her. If she could stand by and watch the mansion burn, and accept its destruction without feeling much about it, then she would know that those savage fires had burned away the past, leaving her life clear for a new future.

Chapter Thirty

A great flame follows
A little spark.

—*Dante Alighieri*

Lavinia felt many things when she arrived at the
Price Plantation, mostly sadness over the loss of her
husband.

The moon was high above her as she stepped
from the canoe, with Wolf Dancer's help. As she
stood beside him on the riverbank, she stared at the
huge mansion, while Joshua and the warriors that
had accompanied them on their mission stepped
from their canoes.

Wearing a heavier buckskin dress than she usually wore, Lavinia trembled, not so much from the
cold as from knowing what would soon transpire.
The plans were to burn the mansion to the ground,
after finding Hiram and removing him from it.

She had not been told what was planned for
him, but she knew that tonight all of his cruelty
would end.

The slaves were going to be given their freedom
and allowed to go either to the Seminole village or
elsewhere.

She was glad that their days of fear and hurt
would be behind them. They would be freed of all
the pain and humiliation they had found under
Hiram Price's rule since he had taken charge of
their destiny.

After tonight, their destiny would be their own!

Once all of the warriors had left their canoes and
gathered around Lavinia, Joshua, and Wolf Dancer,
they set out. Nothing was said. They had already
been instructed as to what to do.

First they would go to the slaves' quarters and tell
them the good news.

Then they would enter the mansion, find Hiram,
and take him from it. Lavinia was to go inside to
get what she wanted of her possessions, then leave
and let the torches be lit to burn down the mansion.

Lavinia's gaze went to the windows of the study,
and then slid upward to Hiram's bedroom windows. She saw no lamplight anywhere.

Her spine stiffened. What if he wasn't there? And
why hadn't the servants lit the lamps in his absence,
even if he was gone?

Perhaps they had all gone to bed early. Maybe that
was why there were no lights on in the mansion.

She saw Wolf Dancer nod silently to his warriors.
She knew it was the sign to move onward and take
their places around the building.

Then Wolf Dancer nodded at Lavinia and Joshua.
Lavinia lifted the skirt of her dress from the dew-
dampened grass and ran between Joshua and Wolf
Dancer until they reached the slaves' quarters.

Soft light shine from the cabin windows. Voices

could be heard, and the smell of beans cooking wafted out to them.

Joshua ran on ahead of Wolf Dancer and Lavinia.

Tears came to Lavinia's eyes as Joshua hurried from one cabin to another, quickly explaining what was about to transpire.

Sudden laughter could be heard, and shouting. "Praise de Lord!" She could hear some people thanking Joshua and knew hugs were being exchanged.

One family after another left the slave cabins and soon were huddled together, their eyes wide and bright as they looked at Wolf Dancer. They could see the many warriors stationed at various places around the plantation grounds.

But when they saw Lavinia, they broke into large smiles, for Joshua had taken the time to tell each of them what she and Wolf Dancer were offering them.

Total freedom, whether they went with Wolf Dancer and Lavinia back to the Seminole village or elsewhere.

Several women and children broke away and ran to Lavinia. They hugged her, their tears mingling with hers as she brushed soft kisses across their brows.

Wolf Dancer stepped closer to Lavinia, swept an arm around her waist, and as the women and children returned to stand with the men, he began telling them that they would be welcome in his village, but it was up to each of them to make his or her own decision.

When they finally realized what they were being offered, they clamored around Lavinia and Wolf Dancer, giving them fierce hugs.

Finally Lavinia held up a hand for silence. "It is truly up to you where your freedom will take you," she said, her voice breaking with emotion. "As Chief Wolf Dancer has said, you can either go with us to the Seminole village and live where I am planning to live as the wife of this wonderful Seminole chief, or you can go and try to find a decent life elsewhere. The most important thing is that you are free now to make your own decisions. I am so sorry for the hell that Hiram Price has put you through since my husband's death. I wrongly neglected you while I kept to my room after my husband's burial, trying to avoid Hiram. I was wrong. I apologize."

Joshua stepped forward. "You have heard Lavinia and Chief Wolf Dancer," he said, looking from one to the other. "We can't wait long for your decision. We have Hiram Price to deal with, and then it is Lavinia's and Wolf Dancer's plan to burn de mansion."

That brought gasps of wonder from the crowd.

"Yes, I will even help set fire to it myself," Lavinia said with determination. "It has stood for all of the wrong things. It won't ever again stand like an overseer, looking down on the slaves' cabins and the fields where you have worked your flesh to the bone. It must go."

They all gave a loud cheer.

Lavinia grew pale and looked up at the mansion. She expected Hiram to lean out of his bedroom window to see what was happening.

"You don't have to worry 'bout Massa Hiram hearin' our excitement," said Caleb, stepping away from his wife Nada. "He ain't been here fo' two days. Aftah he threw your clothes from de window, he took off on his white mare and hasn't returned. We finished collectin' the tobacco and placed it in the tobacco barn. Since then, we have just waited in our cabins to see what de crazy man might do next. We were tempted to leave, like dose who ran away, but we were too afraid that he'd come and fin' us and shoot us. Dat's why we're still here, Missie Lavinia. Dat's de only reason except hopin' to see you again. We've missed you, Missie Lavinia. Lots."

Lavinia now noticed that many slaves were missing; they must have escaped since her departure. She could only imagine how furious Hiram must have been to discover not only her but also half his workers missing. She knew that the slaves who were still at the plantation were very fortunate not to have been shot after Hiram learned she was gone.

"We gathered your clothes and saved dem fo' you," Nada said, smiling sweetly at Lavinia. Then her smile faded. "But dey ain't worth nothin', Missie Lavinia. Massa Hiram tore and cut dem all with de scissors until no one could evah wear dem again. But since dey were yours, we saved dem for you anyways."

Stunned at this turn of events, Lavinia gazed up at Wolf Dancer, then looked at Caleb.

"You said he's been gone for two days," she said. "Do you know where he went?"

"He done told us to finish de harvest and dat he'd be home again soon, but he ain't come home yet. So's like I already said, we put de harvested tobacco into de tobacco barn and just stayed in our homes and waited," he said. "Where have you been, Missie Lavinia?" He gazed at Wolf Dancer, then at Lavinia. "You've been at de Seminole village? Is dat where Dorey is? And Twila?"

"Yes, they are both safe in the Seminole village, and that's where I am going once . . . once . . . I see to the burning of the mansion," she said. "We brought enough canoes so that you can journey back to the village with us if you like."

"But de white panther . . . de alligators . . . de snakes," Nada said, her eyes wide. "Is it safe?"

"When you are with Chief Wolf Dancer and his warriors, you are absolutely safe," Lavinia assured her. "We're going inside the mansion now . . . Wolf Dancer, myself, and Joshua. By the time we leave, you must have made your decision, for we will leave quickly once we've set fire to the mansion."

They all nodded.

Lavinia felt a weakness in her knees as she walked with Wolf Dancer and Joshua inside the house. It was dark and strangely ghostly inside. There was no lamplight or fire's glow from the massive fireplace in the parlor.

"I'll find a lamp and light it," Lavinia said, knowing exactly where to look. She soon found a lamp and touched a flame to its wick.

With the lamp supplying enough light to see by, Lavinia looked around each room, and was stunned speechless by the destruction everywhere.

Hiram had left nothing of value untouched.

Beautiful crystal vases lay in splinters across the lush carpet.

Expensive paintings had been taken from the walls and slashed with a knife.

Lavinia was horrified by the damage that Hiram had done.

"My room," she gasped out, looking up the winding staircase. "My clothes; my bedroom."

Although Nada had said that many of her clothes had been cut and torn by Hiram, she wanted to see if anything was left.

Clutching the lamp, and with Joshua and Wolf Dancer following her, she went up the stairs and down the hall to her bedroom.

When she entered it, she saw the full extent of Hiram's hatred for her. She realized now that she had been wrong to think he would want her as his woman after all that had happened.

No man who expected to bring a woman back to her own room would destroy everything he could, as Hiram had done to her personal belongings.

What clothes he hadn't thrown out the window lay in shreds across the floor, and even her mattress had been slashed, until the cotton batting fell away from it and was scattered all across the floor.

"My Lord . . ." Lavinia gasped, feeling faint.

Wolf Dancer moved to one side of her while Joshua went to the other, both holding her until she was steady on her feet.

"And I thought he was looking for me," Lavinia said, finding grim humor in all of this. "I had been so afraid that he would do anything to find me, and all along, he hated me so much he would never want me near him."

"He will return," Joshua said in a growl. "Remember the harvest and the amount of money he will get from it. And . . . he probably plans to come back and kill de slaves if he has no interest in stayin' here any longer. Dat's sure how it looks, since he destroyed all dat he could get his hands on in de house."

"We will finish what he started and make certain he has no place to return to," Wolf Dancer said sternly.

"What 'bout de tobacco plants de slaves worked so hard to harvest?" Joshua asked, searching Wolf Dancer's eyes.

"We will take the tobacco to my village and find use for it," Wolf Dancer said, smiling.

"I just want to get out of here and put all of this unhappiness behind me," Lavinia said as she once again looked at what remained of her clothes and precious belongings.

She went to the table beside her bed where she had kept her mother's Bible.

Opening the drawer, she gasped with horror when she found it ripped to shreds.

"Even this?" she cried, reaching down and touching what was left of the Bible. "He knew I would come back for my mother's Bible. He wanted to make certain I would never have it."

She gazed at Wolf Dancer. "All of this is the work of a madman," she said.

She hurriedly left the room, and Joshua and Wolf Dancer followed her.

They thought she was going downstairs, but instead she made a turn in the corridor and went to another room.

They stood just inside the door as Lavinia moved slowly around Hiram's room, which had not been touched at all. She opened the chifforobe and discovered that all of his clothes were there.

It did look like he would be returning.

Then she saw something sticking out from beneath the bed. It was a blanket wrapped around something long and bulky. She bent to her knees, set the lamp on the floor, and reached beneath the bed. She pulled out the blanket.

When she unfolded the blanket and saw what was there, she gasped and felt the color drain from her face. "Oh, my Lord," she said as Wolf Dancer knelt quickly at her side.

She looked over and saw the anger in Wolf Dancer's eyes. "A bow . . . and . . . arrows," she said. "This is what he used to kill Virgil."

"And to shoot me," Joshua added.

Wolf Dancer picked up one of the arrows and ran his hand slowly over the shaft. "Where did he get arrows like the ones used by my people?" he asked. "I know he wasn't ever on my island, or anywhere near it."

"Then he had to have gotten them from someone who has the same type of arrow as yours," Lavinia said.

She swallowed hard, remembering the full horror

of the moment when she had seen Hiram carrying Virgil with the arrow in Virgil's chest.

"These arrows and Joshua's testimony should convince Colonel Cox of what Hiram has done," she said angrily. "Surely he will arrest Hiram!"

Then she looked intently into Wolf Dancer's eyes. "But that isn't enough to satisfy my need for vengeance," she hissed. "What we have planned is what will truly tear at Hiram's sanity. We will leave absolutely nothing for him when he returns. We will burn not only the mansion but also every building that stands on this plantation, including the slaves' quarters. Everything he did will be for nothing! And when he does return and sees the destruction, he will experience the true feeling of loss."

"This is only the beginning of his comeuppance," Wolf Dancer said, laying the arrows back with the bow and getting to his feet.

He looked into Lavinia's eyes and gently placed his hands on her shoulders. "I will send Joshua to bring my warriors to set fire to the mansion," he said. He searched her eyes. "Are you certain this is what you want? This home is yours. Everything on this land is yours."

"That is why I want to destroy it all," Lavinia answered, swallowing hard. "It stands for all the wrong things. An empty piece of land is better than this huge mansion which has brought nothing but heartache into my life."

"Then, Joshua, go for several of my warriors," Wolf Dancer said. "By the time you return, lanterns will be lit. Those will be used to set fire to the house interior."

Joshua nodded and ran from the room.

There was a strange sort of quietness as Lavinia and Wolf Dancer moved through the house, finding and lighting the wicks of various lanterns and lamps.

After the warriors arrived, each took a lamp or lantern, and soon the drapes were aflame, as were many pieces of furniture. The flames took hold quickly, necessitating a quick escape.

Lavinia stood beneath the moonlight as the house went up in flames. The sky was now lit orange by the savage flames of the burning house.

And as it continued to burn, the tobacco, which had been tied up in bundles by the slaves, was taken to the canoes and placed in them. Then the horses were led out of the stable and set free.

As they galloped away from the chaos of the Price Plantation, even Lavinia's favorite mare, she felt a strange sort of emptiness. She truly loved her mare and had loved riding it.

But she knew that someone would claim it, as well as the others, and give them good homes.

The Seminole had no use for horses. Everywhere they traveled was by canoe, or on foot.

Some few of the slaves took off on foot, heading north, while the others boarded the canoes, among them Nada, Caleb, and their two children.

Lavinia took one last look around her at everything that was burning, and for a moment seemed to see Virgil standing there watching. The expression she saw on his face was not at all what she would have expected were he alive to witness the destruction of his plantation; it was a look of serene peace.

It was then that she recalled how he had so often said he would one day free his slaves. She knew that somewhere in the heavens he was looking down and approving of what she had done.

"Let us go now," Wolf Dancer said, sliding an arm around Lavinia's waist and leading her away from the heat of the many fires.

"It does seem so savage," Lavinia said, trembling as she took one last look over her shoulder before boarding a canoe. "Those flames are destroying . . . my . . . husband's dream, a dream that turned into a nightmare."

She eagerly boarded the canoe, and Joshua climbed in behind her. He and Wolf Dancer manned the paddles as they turned the canoe downriver.

Lavinia was thinking about Hiram's reaction when he saw that his world had been destroyed. Wolf Dancer had told her that he would come back and wait for Hiram's return.

Lavinia looked over her shoulder and gazed at the mansion, which was still aflame. She was glad that Hiram's reign of terror was over, and that he would be captured and taken to the Seminole village.

Lavinia knew that it was not the Seminole practice to murder anyone in cold blood, so she could only imagine that Hiram would be held prisoner, at least until Wolf Dancer decided what his final fate would be.

One thing was certain: She would be married to Wolf Dancer while Hiram was forced to watch.

That made Lavinia smile. Her only regret was that she wouldn't be there when Hiram returned home and saw what had happened, and that everything he had worked for lay in gray ashes! With the destruction of the Price Plantation went Hiram's dreams of being a man of power and wealth.

Chapter Thirty-one

A little still she strove,
And much repented.
And whispering,
"I will ne'er consent"—

—*Lord Byron*

The sun was tinting the sky a soft orange as morning came with the sounds of birds awakening, filling the air with their beautiful songs. A gentle breeze scattered the smoke that rose from the burned mansion and outbuildings.

As Hiram rode up the long gravel drive toward the plantation, he watched the smoke with growing anxiety. He felt a pain deep in his gut as he realized that the smoke had to be coming from his plantation, and that something large had to have burned.

"The mansion?" he whispered hoarsely. The pain felt like a hot poker in his stomach, for he knew that while he was gone, disaster of some sort must have fallen on his plantation.

Had the slaves rebelled and burned everything before making their escape to freedom? Or had natural disaster struck?

Afraid to find out, yet knowing he must, he sank

his heels into the flanks of his white mare and sent it galloping toward home.

The cool morning air stung his whiskered cheeks and burned his lone eye, causing it to run. He wiped his eye with the back of a hand.

He had not bathed or shaved for three days now. He could smell his own stench, a combination of whiskey, perspiration, and cheap perfume. When no decent women responded to his posters, he had gone to all the saloons and cribs in the two towns that he had visited.

When none of those women consented to be his wife, he knew what a horrible sight he must be. He had offered those wenches the world if they would consent to be his wife. And none of them had wanted any part of it.

"The one eye," he growled to himself. "It has to be the one eye. Or . . . perhaps the perspiration?" Or was it the rumors of his cruelty and whippings that had scared them off?

All he knew was that he was totally alone in the world. He now regretted having killed his brother. His brother had been the only person who had accepted him, no matter how distasteful his appearance, or how much he sweated.

His brother had loved him so much that he had made him part of his life. Until Virgil had died, the Price Plantation had seemed the perfect place to live, even though Hiram knew that his brother's wife had spoken against his living under the same roof with them.

It was the first time he'd overheard her object to his presence that Hiram had started plotting to make her his wife, no matter what he had to do to achieve this goal. Her dislike of him had made him want her all the more!

He now knew why. He had not wanted her out of love, but out of spite.

He smiled crookedly. He had wanted to make her uncomfortable every day she had to share a bed with him. That would pay her back for what she had said about him behind his back.

He had planned to force marriage on her, whether or not she consented. He had planned to threaten her if she declined to marry him.

"And then she up and disappeared on me," he growled out loud.

Well, it no longer mattered to him where she was, or who she was with, or what she was doing. He had grown sorely tired of plotting to have her. He now wanted no part of her.

She would only have made his life more miserable than it already was. She would have scorned him each day she was with him.

His thoughts were brought to a halt as he came close enough to the plantation to see that his two-storied home no longer loomed up into the sky like a sentinel. Instead, he saw clouds of smoke rising upward, black and ugly.

He shifted his gaze and noticed puffs of smoke coming from other places on the plantation grounds. He knew they had to be the outbuildings.

A thought came to him that made him feel as though he was going to vomit. The tobacco plants!

If they had been burned, his profits for this season were a part of that smoke rising into the sky.

The loss of his wealth was much worse than losing his home. He had grown to despise every inch of the mansion because it represented all that had gone wrong in his life since he'd come to Florida with his brother and wife.

Losing his tobacco and whatever profit he could have gotten from its sale meant that he had no money to take him far, far from this godforsaken place that had brought him nothing but heartache!

He wondered again what had caused the fire. The most probable answer made him so angry, he could hardly stand what he was thinking.

The slaves! They had surely not only fled to their freedom but also set fire to everything they thought was precious to Hiram!

"Including the tobacco," he shouted to the sky.

He had been stupid, leaving them to themselves for so long. Why, he should have known they would see his absence as a rare opportunity to do as they pleased.

"I'll search to the ends of the earth for you," he cried to the heavens, waving a fist.

He sank his heels into the flanks of his horse and rode harder toward the smoke. Each breath he took was now filled with smoke, and he could see the total devastation on all sides of him.

His heart sank as the worst of his fears was realized, for there was no sign of the tobacco crop.

He glanced over at where the slave quarters lay in ash. As he suspected, his workers had fled, but were they responsible for burning everything? Or had they fled after someone else did the dirty deed?

He doubted that he would ever know the true facts about the ruination of his planation. And for some reason, it suddenly no longer mattered!

His eyes lowered as he drew rein and stopped his mare. "The entire world is against me," he sobbed.

Then he lifted his chin and again looked around at all that had been taken from him.

Surely he was wrong to cast the blame on the slaves. He just could not envision them being audacious enough to do this.

Could it have been Colonel Fred Cox? Fred had sent Hiram away, refusing to help him.

Could Colonel Cox have done this out of pure spite? He had spoken more than once against slavery, knowing that Hiram's whole world centered around it.

Or had Lavinia returned and seen all of her belongings destroyed, then set the place afire out of revenge?

Or . . . had Indians come on his property, set it ablaze, and enjoyed watching everything burn? Had they taken the tobacco with them, to use themselves? It was no secret that Indians loved tobacco.

No matter who, or why, the fact remained—it had been done and now Hiram owned nothing!

The land was worth nothing to him without a home, its crops, and someone to share it all with!

He dismounted, feeling cold and lifeless, then started to get back on his horse again. It suddenly dawned on him that there was no point in staying at a place that was no longer useful to him.

He didn't have the strength, or desire, to rebuild. And he most certainly couldn't do it alone. He knew no one who would care enough to help him.

Suddenly he felt a presence nearby.

He stepped away from his horse and turned, looking quickly at a huge live oak tree that had somehow escaped the flames.

He gasped and took a shaky step backward when he saw in its branches the white panther he had heard so much about. Its white color seemed to glow in the sun that had broken through the cloud of smoke. The rays of the sun seemed even more brilliant today than usual.

Hiram could scarcely breathe, his fear was so intense. He stared in horrified fascination at the panther as it continued to rest on a limb, its green eyes watching Hiram.

Hiram started to draw his pistol, but stopped, feeling faint at what he now saw.

The panther was no longer there. It had changed right before Hiram's eyes into a man. And not just any man, but a powerful Indian warrior. He, not the panther, leapt from the tree and started walking toward Hiram.

Hiram gasped aloud. He had actually seen the

transformation of the animal into the powerful Seminole chief.

And then, once again, before his very eyes, the chief turned back into the panther, stalking now as it continued toward Hiram.

When it let out a loud screech, filling the air with the threat of the panther's cry, Hiram cried out in stark fear. He grabbed at his chest when sudden pain shot through his heart.

As he crumpled down onto his knees, the panther turned back once again into a man, who now stood directly in front of Hiram, so close that Hiram could reach out and touch him. Hiram cried out with pain as he collapsed to the ground, gasping for breath. His already weakened heart could not withstand the shock of what he had witnessed.

Wolf Dancer stood tall over the dead body.

He stared at Hiram for a brief moment, then smiled up at the sun and thanked the Sun God for helping to mete out justice.

He gazed at Hiram again, feeling nothing but loathing for him and the evil he had done. Then he turned and ran toward the river.

He boarded his canoe and headed for home.

He had slipped away from his village in the morning fog as Lavinia and his people slept peacefully.

Lavinia had no idea that the man she would soon marry was even more mysteriously magical than their people's shaman.

Wolf Dancer recalled the one time he had mentioned the panther to her. He had changed the subject so quickly, he didn't think she suspected the truth. He knew she had seen the panther several times, then seen him in its place, but he sensed that she did not know whether to believe her eyes.

As he continued drawing his paddle through the water, Wolf Dancer thought more about what his woman might think if she knew his secret. Should he ever share it with the woman he loved?

He shrugged and decided there and then that he would not tell her or anyone else.

With Hiram's death, the secret remained Wolf Dancer's and his shaman's.

He heard the cry of a black panther in the distance and was tempted to answer its call, but knew he had best leave it be.

He needed no panther searching him out in the night to mate. That made him smile, for there was only one mate for Wolf Dancer, and that was beautiful, sweet Lavinia!

Chapter Thirty-two

As happy a man as any in the world,
For the whole world seems to smile upon me.
—Samuel Pepys

Still somewhat unnerved by all that had happened the night before, Lavinia had not slept well.

She had realized that Wolf Dancer had had his own trouble sleeping when she had awakened during the night and found him gone. She had been tempted to go outside and sit with him under the stars, for that was where she thought he had gone. But she had decided not to.

She felt that he had much to sort out in his mind.

He had brought a woman, her daughter, and her two special friends into his life and village, and now he had many former slaves who had come to the village as well.

When Lavinia had awakened this morning as the sun crept through her window, she had discovered that Wolf Dancer was still gone.

But this time she thought he must be instructing his warriors about how many new huts should be built for the freed slaves and their families.

Also today the harvest would be finalized.

Yes, it was a busy time in this village, and should be a happy one for Lavinia. But as she sat beside the fire now, in deep thought, she just couldn't find the feeling of peace she wanted so badly.

Dorey had left a short while ago after sharing her morning meal with Lavinia to play with Twila and the other children.

Lavinia wanted to believe that everyone was safe on the island. But as long as Hiram was still out there somewhere, able to wreak havoc on them anytime he wished, how could she relax and enjoy life?

Soon she would be married to the most wonderful man in the world. She even hoped to discover that she was with child, for both she and Wolf Dancer wanted children born of their special love. But she could not help shivering at the memory of the mansion burning, and with it so many precious things that she had wanted to bring back with her to the village.

Hiram had even destroyed the books she would have brought home for the children to enjoy. Her mother's Bible was ruined and even now lying in ashes, as were so many other things she would have brought into her life as a Seminole bride.

What she regretted most were those destroyed books.

Yes, Lavinia had planned to use them to teach the Seminole children, as well as the black children, who had never had the opportunity to learn to read, as Dorey had secretly taught Twila.

Lavinia's jaw tightened with determination. She would not let those children remain uneducated. As soon as she felt it was safe, she hoped to go into the nearest town and purchase at least a few books, which she could use to teach the children.

She turned her head abruptly when she heard footsteps behind her.

When she found Wolf Dancer entering, she greeted him with a smile, then leapt up and went to him.

He took her in his arms and gave her a slow, sweet kiss, then put his hands at her waist and held her at arm's length.

She saw from his expression that he had something to tell her that was not pleasant.

"What's wrong?" Lavinia asked, searching his beautiful green eyes.

"It is Hiram Price," Wolf Dancer said thickly. "When my warriors went to watch and wait for him, they found him dead on the grounds of the property. There were no visible wounds on his person, so perhaps he died from grief after seeing everything he owned in ashes."

"And after realizing that the slaves . . . and his precious tobacco, were gone," Lavinia added softly.

She could not help feeling a little sorry for Hiram, yet not so much that she regretted his death. The fact was . . . she and her daughter no longer had to fear his interrupting their lives by coming and causing trouble at the Seminole village.

Nor did the slaves have to worry about their safety, especially beloved Joshua and Twila, who meant so much to Lavinia and Dorey.

"How do you feel about his death, now that it has happened?" Wolf Dancer asked softly.

"Do you really have to ask?" Lavinia said, sighing heavily. "You know that neither I nor Dorey would ever be completely safe if that man had lived. We would constantly have to worry about what he might be planning against us. It is sad, I must admit, that his life turned out to be so horrible, but I cannot regret the fact that he is gone. The future looks so bright now, darling Wolf Dancer. Thank you so much for taking me and Dorey in, as well as all the others. Without you, all of our lives would still be built around fear."

"I have told you before that you do not have to thank me for the things I do for you, or for those you love," Wolf Dancer said. He reached a hand up and slowly drew his fingers through her golden tresses. "My violet-eyed, golden-haired woman, you will soon be my wife. I would do anything for you. Now that you are free of that man, and everything connected with him, we can have a marriage that will shine with happiness and love. You are my happiness. You are my love."

"Oh, how I love you," Lavinia murmured. She twined her arms around his neck as he drew her up against him. "My love, I want to disappear into you. I . . . want . . . to be you."

"We are each other," Wolf Dancer said huskily, then gave her a meltingly hot kiss.

Lavinia returned the kiss for long moments. They parted from one another at the same moment, their eyes searching each other's.

"I wish we could stay here all day, alone," Lavinia murmured, her heart pounding with the need that had been born inside her the very first time Wolf Dancer had kissed her. "But . . . but . . . we have good news to share with others, don't we?"

"Yes, and it will give me joy to tell it," Wolf Dancer said, smiling.

He took her by the hand, and together they walked outside into the morning sunshine.

It seemed that the warriors who had returned to the village had already spread the news of Hiram's death among the people of the village. The man so many feared was no longer alive.

The former slaves' eyes were the brightest of all as they came and stood together before Lavinia and Wolf Dancer.

Wolf Dancer's people stopped their chores and joined the crowd, their eyes also on their chief.

"I am certain you already know what news has been brought to our island today," he said, smiling from one to the other, his eyes lingering longest on Joshua. "The man who harmed so many with his evil ways is no longer alive. We no longer have to fear that he might bring white soldiers to search for our island. We are safe, and peace is to be celebrated."

"And the harvest is finished," Joshua chimed in, beaming as all eyes were drawn to him. He was proud to have been a part of these people's harvest, for he wanted them to see him as a worthy member of their village.

"And we have much tobacco to share," he said proudly. "It no longer belongs to Massah, I mean *Hiram* Price."

He focused on those who had slaved in the fields with him under the hot sun at the Price Plantation. "When you think of dat man, do not think of him as your master," he said thickly. He pointed at Wolf Dancer. "Because of dat man—" he paused to turn to Lavinia—"and dat woman, we are free. If'n you want to take a day to just sit by de river and fish, you can do dat. If you want to take a leisurely walk among de trees, you can."

He laughed mischievously. "If'n you even want to make love any time of day or night, you can," he said, causing soft giggles and blushes among the women. "I mainly mean to say dat you are free now to do anything you wish to do, but you must spend a lot of your time helpin' in dis village, doin' whatevah you can do to thank Chief Wolf Dancer for what he has done for all of us."

Lavinia stepped up to Joshua's side. "Everything he says is true," she said, smiling from one former slave to the next. "With your freedom comes the freedom to do as you wish when you wish. There are many things to learn about the Seminole's way of doing things. I have found it delightful learning, and I am sure you will, too."

"Now go on and enjoy this beautiful day," Wolf Dancer said, stepping up to Lavinia's side. "You are all welcome here among my people."

The Seminole children had come and mingled among the newly freed slave children.

After Wolf Dancer said to go on, they all ran off together, laughing and ready to learn each other's various games.

Joshua turned to Lavinia and gave her a big hug, then embraced Wolf Dancer. Knowing now that he did not have to say "thank you" every time he thought he should, he only smiled and walked away.

Wolf Dancer swept an arm around Lavinia's waist as the last of the harvest was brought into the village, ready to be prepared for storage.

"It is a good day," Lavinia said, smiling up at Wolf Dancer.

"It is a good life," Wolf Dancer said, returning her smile.

Chapter Thirty-three

She shares the dawns with him in sacred
silence,
Love, who is most beautiful among
The immortal gods, the melter of limps,
Overwhelms in their hearts, the intelligence
And wise counsel of all gods and all men.
                                        —Hesiod

Several Years Later

𝒦neeling beside her crackling cookfire, Lavinia was grinding corn for her family's bread. She was using a stone mortar and pestle, just as all the other women did.

She used all of her weight to grind the corn, pouring the cornmeal into a wooden bowl when it was ground fine enough.

She was deep in thought as she labored. It was work she loved, for it was for her family, which now included two more children.

Dorey was so proud of her younger sister, Running Laughter, who was now five summers of age, and of her younger brother, Little Rock, who was four.

Lavinia beamed with happiness that she had two more children besides Dorey. And she was even now heavy with another child, who should arrive in two months.

Never had she imagined being this happy, especially away from the world of privilege she had known before meeting Wolf Dancer.

She would not give up her new world for anything. Every day brought her such contentment as she watched her children grow and her husband wisely lead his Seminole people.

It continued to be a good time for the Seminole under Wolf Dancer's leadership. They prospered on their island and were never bothered by anyone. The tale of the mysterious white panther that stalked the Everglades seemed to keep strangers away.

Her back tired from the grinding, Lavinia stood and walked to the door, gazing outside where her children were enjoying the beautiful sunny day.

She caught Dorey gazing at Running Bear with a look of utter adoration. It was no secret that Dorey had a crush on Running Bear, who returned her admiration. They were almost inseparable, as were Twila and Deer Shadow.

Never would anyone guess how these four young people had met. Lavinia would not be at all surprised if they ended up being married one day in the future.

She gazed elsewhere and saw Joshua. He was walking his wife to the stream, where he would help her collect water, for she was near the time when their second child would be born.

Joshua had married his wife's best friend, who had given Twila a brother. The little boy was one summer old now, and adorable.

Pretty Butterfly, his wife, had worked side by side with Joshua and his former wife Lorna in the fields at the Price Plantation. They each had lost a mate and had grown to love one another after they came to Mystic Island.

All in all, things could not be any finer on the island, nor could Lavinia be any happier.

She rested her hands on her hips, smiling to herself when she felt a soft nudge from what she imagined might be a knee inside her big belly.

That was a moment she always cherished, when a child inside her womb let her know just how alive it was, and ready to let out its first cry once it was born.

"A son," she whispered to herself, knowing that Wolf Dancer wanted another son, and then another. He was the sort of man who loved children, and the more, the merrier!

"I love him so much," she whispered to herself, her heart doing a sort of flip-flop as she caught sight of him entering the village on foot with a deer carcass casually thrown across his shoulder. He had been out hunting with his men, and she noticed that several other warriors had caught game as well.

"We shall have plenty of venison for the next several days," she whispered, again smiling.

Wanting to get her bread finished in time for the evening meal, so it would be ready to eat with that delicious venison, she went back to her grinding. She was so happy, she felt as though she were swimming in joy!

Dear Reader,

I hope you enjoyed reading *Savage Flames*. The next book in my Savage series, which I write exclusively for Leisure Books, is *Savage Abandon*, about the Winnebago tribe. This book is filled with romance, authentic history of the Winnebago people, and majestic Indian pride.

Those of you who are collecting my Indian romance novels and want to hear more about the series and my entire backlist of Indian books can send for my latest newsletter, autographed bookmark, and fan club information by writing to:

Cassie Edwards
6709 North Country Club Road
Mattoon, IL 61938

For a response, please include a stamped, self-addressed legal-size envelope with your letter. And if you wish, you can visit me at these Web sites:

My personal Web site: www.cassieedwards.com
MySpace: http://www.myspace.com/cassieedwardsromance

Thank you for your support of my Indian series. I love researching and writing about our nation's beloved Native Americans, our country's true first people!

Always,
Cassie Edwards

In his darkest hour, Gabriel found Solace. She was full of life, energy and daring. And it was up to Gabe to defend her when all society shunned her for the very individuality Gabe loved. But this time he had the strength and know-how to protect his woman; this time he would have faith that, "Surely goodness and mercy will follow me all the days of my life."

Read ahead for a sneak preview of
Gabriel's Lady by **Charlotte Hubbard**.

"Gabe! Gabe, it's so dang good to see ya! But I'm so—"

When Billy grabbed his hand, the grip stunned Gabe—because it was so strong from his years of working with horses, but also because it swung him into an unexpected hug. A choking sound made Gabe's eyes go wet: for the first time, someone *felt* his pain instead of just giving it lip service. Billy Bristol's arms clamped around his body like steel bands, yet he sensed that his friend—this blood brother of his childhood—would be the one to free him from his misery.

When the redhead stepped back, his blue eyes sparkled with unshed tears. "It's so good to see ya," he repeated, "I don't want to get to that other part. But it tore me up pretty bad to hear about Letitia. I'm real sorry for your loss."

Billy glanced toward the train then, where porters scurried to unload Grace's belongings at the encouragement of her pretty smile. The platform was stacked with an impressive number of trunks and boxes. "Good thing I drove my biggest buckboard," he remarked with a chuckle. "Can't thank you enough for escortin' Gracie, since any man with eyes'll try to sweet-talk her. And she so obviously hates that!"

Gabe laughed. "Yes, she could charm the socks off any fellow alive."

"Yeah, well it's what those fellas'll charm off her that scares me."

He stood back then, a rugged man in denim and homespun,

clean but well-worn. *Comfortable* had always been Billy Bristol's way, in clothing and behavior. His hair had turned a darker shade of auburn and he wore it a little longer now. Gabe tried to imagine him as a desperado, like his twin brother had been, yet the direct gaze of those blue eyes bespoke a man of utmost integrity. A man who'd earned his place in the world by the sweat of his brow and the strength of those broad, calloused hands.

"It was a small favor, considering your generous invitation to—"

"Well, how *else* could I get ya here? Been way too long," Billy insisted. "It's a shame it took a situation like yours to get us together again."

He sighed. "Yes, well...situations happen, don't they?"

"And we'll hash all that out after we get you home and outta these fancy city clothes. Gotta say I like that derby, though. Never owned one myself." Billy plucked at the sleeve of his brown plaid suit. "Looks like you've done right well for yourself practicin' the law, Mr. Getty."

"It's what's beneath the suit that's taken the beating," he replied with a sigh. "Appearances can be deceiving, my friend."

"And I want to hear whatever you gotta get off your mind— but meanwhile it appears our new tutor is ready to load up." Billy grinned. "You were the perfect escort, Gabe. Professional, well-heeled air about ya—to discourage anybody else who might be givin' her the eye. And lots of practice at totin' a woman's trunks, I bet!"

"It's amazing how much luggage one tiny female requires. Where would any of them be without men for pack animals?"

For a fleeting moment he wondered how Cranks, the butler, spent his time now that he no longer accompanied Letitia on her shopping excursions. It was a good sign that such a thought didn't depress him today; a better sign that he could laugh at himself for ever depending on domestic help.

It felt good to shoulder those trunks with Billy; they'd worked together as boys, and it was only his bent for book learning that had sent him away from such a salt-of-the-earth existence. As he heaved Gracie's trunks up to the buckboard, his muscles told him he hadn't pulled his weight lately. Maybe this trip to rural Missouri would balance him...show him what he was made of, without stylish clothing and someone else's mansion to live in.

When they pulled into the Bristol driveway, lined with maple trees in their shiny spring leaves, Gabe's heart fluttered. It was still the homeplace he'd envied when he came here for Billy's wedding: the house glowed with fresh white paint and its pillars suggested Southern grandeur of a bygone era. Lilacs scented the breeze, and beyond the large red barn stretched miles of white plank fence. Beautiful grazing horses dotted the lush pastureland.

He couldn't have painted a prettier picture if he'd been Michelangelo.

A dog raced toward them then, white with distinctive markings around his eyes and ears. Some of his fondest childhood memories returned: Billy letting him pick out a border collie puppy born in the Monroes' barn...their four dogs herding Texas longhorns that had cut across their Kansas farms. Those black and white collies were long gone, but Gabe still glowed, thinking about them. Everything about this family took him back to better days, and Gabe felt happier than he had in weeks. Maybe years.

"Rex!" a loud voice called. "Rex, you ornery mutt! We're not finished practicing!"

Billy halted the horses while Grace sat taller on the seat between them. "Don't tell me that's Solace, riding without—"

"Haven't you ever seen your sister practicin' her act?" Billy cut in. "She's trainin' her new dog, and he's a handful."

"Mama would be having a—time and again she's told Solace not to—"

"Which is why Solace loves to come here." Billy leaned his elbows on his knees to include Gabe in his grin. "You and Lily were cut from silk and satin, honey, and Aunt Agatha's academy was the place you needed to be. But while you were away, how do you s'pose Solace entertained herself? She *sure* wasn't perfectin' her needlework."

Gabe chuckled. He gazed at the approaching figure in rapt fascination, for she was standing barefoot on the back of a bay gelding that cantered alongside the driveway. Solace Monroe wore old denim pants and a red plaid shirt, and with her dark brown hair flying behind her—and a daredevil grin!—she seemed like something from a dream. She balanced so confidently on the horse's back that she appeared to be floating. Or flying.

And then, a few feet before she reached the buckboard, Solace dropped down to straddle her mount as though these acrobatics were second nature to her. Such effortless grace bespoke hours of practice, and Gabe wondered how many times she'd tumbled off—how many bones she'd broken—to reach this level of performance perfection.

"Gabe! Gabe Getty, it's been way too long!"

Her hands shot out and he grabbed them. A warm tingle of energy raced through his body when he felt the strength in Solace's sturdy hands. Her face was flushed from riding and her breath came in exuberant bursts as she grinned at him. The little girl he'd danced with at his wedding was anything but a child now.

"I was so happy to hear you'd be—" Her face clouded over then, but her brown-eyed gaze never wavered. "We were all so sad to learn about Letitia, Gabe. How horrible it must've been for you to—but you're here now! Family again, like when we were kids!"

His heart turned a cartwheel. When had anyone ever greeted him with such enthusiasm? Such all-embracing sincerity? He opened his mouth but it took a moment for the words to come out.

"It's good to be back," he murmured. Grace and Billy watched him closely, so he gave them the best smile he could muster. "The past few weeks have been sheer hell. The Bancrofts blame me for Letitia's untimely—"

"How absurd!" Solace had no need for more details. She believed without question in the Gabriel Getty she'd known all her life.

He swallowed hard. Her compassion nearly overwhelmed him. He wasn't sure he deserved such outright confidence in his innocence. Those bold brown eyes unnerved him, too, yet the glow on Solace's face drew him in and warmed his very soul. And she did all this as effortlessly as she'd ridden her horse standing up.

"Don't mind my sister, Gabriel," Gracie murmured. "She wants the best for you—as we all do. But she needs to rein herself in."

Anguish froze Solace's face, and then Gabe watched a play of familiar emotions: despair and betrayal...the sense of being an outcast in her own family. And in that brief moment, he heard the cry of a kindred spirit. How often had he himself felt despised and belittled these past six years?

"Now Gracie," Billy began, "you shouldn't doubt your sister's intentions about—"

"No, Billy, she hasn't a *clue* about what anyone else might think or feel," Solace huffed. "So nice to see you again, Saint Grace. How have we gotten along without you?"

Before Gabe could offer Solace encouragement, she whistled. Her dog leaped onto the horse, in front of her, and Miss Monroe wheeled her mount in a tight circle. Then she charged full-tilt toward the pasture—but the gate wasn't open! He held his breath, wondering if—

As though the horse were a part of her, flying on her will alone, it leaped up and over the white plank fence to land proudly on the other side. The dog was still seated, and so was Solace, who urged the bay into a breakneck gallop. Had he not seen it with his own eyes, he wouldn't have believed it.

LEIGH GREENWOOD

The freedom of the range, the bawling of the longhorns, the lonesome night watch beneath a vast, starry sky—they got into a woman's blood until she knew there was nothing better than the life of a cowgirl . . . except the love of a good man.

Born and raised on the Broken Circle Ranch, Eden never expected to fall head over heels for the heir to a British earldom. As the youngest of the Maxwell clan, she was used to riding her mustang across the plains, not a carriage through Hyde Park, and she'd sooner have coffee from a chuck wagon than tea in a society drawing room. But there was one thing London offered that was not to be found in all the Lone Star State: A man who captured her heart and thrilled her senses. Now the only challenge was convincing him to try love, Texas style.

Texas Loving

ISBN 13: 978-0-8439-5686-3